PRAISE FOR *EVERY LAST SECRET*

"A glamorous and   you
sideways. I love this story   on they
generated in me. I devoured every word. Exceptional."

   —Tarryn Fisher, *New York Times* bestselling author

"Raw and riveting. A clever ride that will make you question everyone
and everything."

   —Meredith Wild, #1 *New York Times* bestselling author

EVERY LAST SECRET

OTHER TITLES BY A. R. TORRE

The Girl in 6E

Do Not Disturb

If You Dare

EVERY LAST SECRET

A. R. TORRE

THOMAS & MERCER

Text copyright © 2020 by Select Publishing LLC
All rights reserved.

Published by Thomas & Mercer, Seattle

www.apub.com

Amazon, the Amazon logo, and Thomas & Mercer are trademarks of Amazon.com, Inc., or its affiliates.

ISBN-13: 9781542020190
ISBN-10: 1542020190

Cover design by Shasti O'Leary Soudant

Printed in the United States of America

To the wives

PROLOGUE

NEENA

Now

The detective was beanpole tall, with a gap in between her middle teeth that I could push a pretzel stick through. Last night she had been unattractive. Now, under the harsh overhead light, she was downright ugly.

She stayed quiet, flipping through her case folder with the speed of a tadpole. I sighed and brought the flimsy foam cup to my lips, forcing the bitter coffee down and wondering where my attorney was. It was fine, for now. I would find out as much as I could, skirt the obvious traps, and keep my mouth shut. Keeping my mouth shut was a skill I'd perfected a long time ago. It was the gossipers who got in trouble. The braggers. People like Cat Winthorpe, who couldn't just have the perfect life. She had to throw it in your face with her casual comments, her drip of wealth. Which is why she needed to be punished. You can't blame me for what happened. I was simply putting her in her place.

"I listened to the call you placed to 9-1-1." The detective studied me. "It was interesting. At one point, you yawned."

I shifted in my seat, and the handcuffs clinked together. Twisting my wrist, I tried to find a more comfortable position. I had been hoping the phone hadn't caught that yawn. It was one of those inescapable ones that sneak up on you right in the middle of a sentence.

"Do you realize the damage that a gunshot through the mouth creates?" She flipped over a glossy image and pushed it forward with a slow and calculated hand. "The bullet passes through an enormous number of blood vessels before piercing the brain and exiting out through the back of the skull."

I leaned over and looked at the photo without comment, unsurprised to see a large exit hole in the top of the head. Nasty stuff, but I had seen worse. A face bloated, the lips splitting open as the features swelled past recognition. The alarmed look on the face of a man you had once loved, just before he dies. The sound of his begging that still echoes in the dark recesses of my mind.

I set down the cheap coffee. "Do you have a question, or is this just your show-and-tell time?"

The woman paused, the simple gold band on her left hand stilling as she studied my face. "Mrs. Ryder, you don't seem to understand the gravity of this situation. You are under suspicion of attempted murder."

I understood the gravity of *her* situation. That cheap wedding band? Those bags under her eyes? She'd chosen the wrong path. With braces early on and a strict fitness-and-diet routine, she could have done something with her life. Been someone. Put herself in a position to enjoy the finer things in life. I focused in on her face. "*Dr.* Ryder," I corrected her.

She smiled, and there was something in that gesture that raised my hackles. I looked toward the wide mirror and studied my reflection, verifying that everything was in place.

My hair, freshly cut and dyed.

My skin, glowing and Botox smooth, despite the horrific lighting in this place.

My body, trim and thin underneath the designer workout gear.

My wedding ring, still in place, the large diamond glittering from my hand like a spotlight.

I had clawed my way to the top of this world, and they couldn't take me down now. Not with the mountain of lies I'd worked so hard to construct.

"You moved to Palo Alto two years ago, is that correct?" At my silent agreement, she cleared her throat. "So, let's start there."

PART 1

MAY

FOUR MONTHS EARLIER

CHAPTER 1

CAT

The first week of May, we held a party. It wasn't our biggest. There were no aerialists hanging from the great-room beams. We didn't hire the valets or put up the tents. It was a low-key party, a fundraiser for local performing arts, and one that would double as a going-away party for the flyers.

That's what I called them: flyers. Every summer, like migrating birds, the members of our community scattered south to apply sunscreen like tourists on boutique cruise ships and private islands. I had just a month and then they'd be leaving me, the group of women currently clustered around me, too concerned with children and cultural experiences to suffer through "another frigid summer" in Atherton.

"When you have kids, you'll understand," Perla had once whispered, her hand tapping a metronome beat on my shoulder. "Your life becomes about them, and they want to be in swimsuits, like normal kids."

When you have kids. Such a cruel thing to say to a fertility-challenged woman. Besides, it was pure crap. No child in Atherton wanted to be normal. Children in Atherton wanted Instagram videos jumping off yachts in taggable locations like the Greek isles. Our heated pools and chilly San Francisco gloom didn't impress their classmates when they stepped from chauffeured sedans and returned to Menlo School in the fall.

I had smiled at Perla and wondered if she knew that her seventeen-year-old son was screwing our maid. "I know," I'd said. "When we have kids, maybe we'll join you."

William and I would be "suffering" through the chilly summer with our heated tile floors, indoor and outdoor saunas, hot tubs, and six fireplaces. We'd be fighting off the gloom with day trips to Beverly Hills and weekends in our Hawaii home. And honestly, it was kind of nice to have a break from my friends and their always-present collection of children.

"I'm telling you," Johanna drawled, eyeing a passing waiter with a look of longing. "Puerto Rico is where we're buying next. A four percent tax rate? Think of how much we'd save."

"Have you been to Puerto Rico?" I asked, following my husband's path as he moved through the entrance hall, his head bent toward the older man beside him. "For an island, the views suck. If I'm moving that far away, I need a beach and a view."

She shrugged. "We could buy an island off one year's tax savings. That's worth dealing with a subpar view. Plus, think of the cultural impact on Stewie and Jane. They could learn the language. Interact with the locals. See how struggling families live."

Jane had received a boob job for her sixteenth birthday. The last time I saw her, she was sagging under the weight of a dozen shopping bags with a cell phone stuck to her ear, climbing into the passenger seat of an exotic car. I hadn't seen Stewie in over a year but had heard of his expulsion from Menlo and rumors of an exclusive drug-rehab center that Johanna was touting as a study abroad.

"Forget Puerto Rico," Mallory chimed in, one of her diamond chandelier earrings caught in her hair. "The home next to us in Cabo is going up for sale. One of you needs to buy it." Her chin swung to me, and she raised a delicate, dark brow. "Cat? Come on. You could use a summer away."

There was a general murmur of agreement among the women, and I laughed, carefully reaching forward and untangling her earring. "Not going to happen. I love my pasty-white skin. Plus, William can't leave the office for a week, much less three months."

Kelly tossed her arm around my neck. "You guys forget. Cat's got Eskimo blood. Anyway, do you blame the woman? William's keeping her warm."

The conversation turned to my husband, their tones quieting as they criticized his work ethic while groaning over his good looks.

I leaned my head against Kelly's shoulder and sighed. "You know you're the only one I'll miss," I whispered, and it was true. Kelly—though she had the requisite +2 children Atherton admired—was the only one who displayed any sensitivity to my fertility woes. As an added bonus, she had been the only wife to welcome me to Atherton, sans snobby judgment. It had been a kindness I had never forgotten.

"I bet you say that to all the girls," she said out of the corner of her bright-red mouth.

I smiled and straightened, half-heartedly participating in the conversation as I looked out over the party. It was the normal mix of familiar faces atop glittery gowns, the men's tuxedos evenly mixed in with the colors. While I hadn't personally met every guest, it was a small town, and we women had formed our own exclusive circle, one that centered around the Menlo country club and branched out.

A waiter bent to deliver a drink, and I watched as a monogrammed napkin fluttered from his tray to the dark wood floor. Excusing myself from the group, I moved toward the fallen item, checking on details as I went. Caviar buffet, stocked. The band was halfway through their set, the soft blues pairing well with the clink of champagne flutes and laughter. I was pleased to see that the great room wasn't crowded, guests evenly dispersed between our home's indoor and outdoor spaces.

"Cat!" A statuesque older woman approached, her gold gown brushing the floor as she reached out with both hands and fiercely gripped my shoulders. "I never had a chance to thank you for the donation to our new rehab clinic."

I smiled at Madeline Sharp, one of the largest donors to tonight's event and the chairwoman of a New York City charity for drug addicts. "I'll pass on the thanks to William. It was his doing, not mine."

"Oh!" She shushed me. "We all know who's really holding the purse strings, dear. Men wouldn't know where their shoes went if we weren't there to point to their feet."

I laughed, the visual so false in regard to my highly capable husband, one who had led covert operations in Afghanistan, managed his firm with cutthroat efficiency, and would go barefoot out of spite rather than take instructions on his footwear. Still, she was right about the purse strings. William *hadn't* been aware of the six-figure donation. While my husband had many distractions on his time, our money—and how I spent it—wasn't one of those.

"You'll have to come to the clinic once it's done," she urged me. "We're heading there for the summer. It'll be set up by fall!"

Another bird, this one flying east. I felt a moment of presummer blues, our full life always a little lonely once our jeweled town vacated. Just as quickly, I reminded myself of the positives. Peace and quiet. Time for just William and me to focus on our marriage and refortify our bond. We always left each summer stronger. Closer.

We are a team, he once said to me. *Summer is our season.*

"Maybe we can make it to the opening."

"Absolutely, you must. Now, I've got to go find my husband." Madeline leaned forward and placed a baby powder–soft kiss on my cheek. I smiled, clasping her in a hug, then watched her leave.

"Crab cake, Mrs. Winthorpe?"

I glanced to my right and nodded at the waiter, taking a miniature creation off the silver tray and placing the petite stack on my tongue. I crushed the delicate layers of crab and crust in my mouth, the key-lime sauce playing nicely with the flavors, and watched as a couple moved through the arched opening of the east balcony.

At first glance, they fit in well. An attractive blonde, paired with a balding and stocky husband. Late thirties, though the blonde was trying hard to hide the fourth decade. As I watched them weave through the crowd, the minor details emerged. Her dress, an off-the-rack number that could be found at a discount retailer, if an aspiring woman hunted hard enough. His cheap watch, the rubber band sticking out from the sleeves of a tuxedo that looked rented. I returned my attention to her, watching as she wound through my party, her eyes scanning over the room, her husband trailing obediently behind.

I moved through the crowd, keeping her in my sights, and mentally clicked through the guests I had invited. Everyone on the exclusive list was a well-known Winthorpe Foundation donor or board member. I stopped next to one of the butlers and gave a subtle nod toward the couple, who had stopped beside our Picasso and were admiring the painting. "Franklin, who is that couple by the staircase? The woman in the blue dress?"

He nodded with a pleasant smile, his eyes never roving over to the area, his professionalism impeccable. "That's Matthew and Neena Ryder, Mrs. Winthorpe."

My gaze sharpened. "They weren't on the list."

"I believe they are guests of your husband."

Well, *that* was interesting. I nodded with a grateful smile. "Wonderful. Thank you for the information."

"Absolutely, Mrs. Winthorpe. It's my pleasure. May I get you a glass of champagne? Or perhaps something from the cellar?"

"No." I stepped away, anxious to find William.

"Mr. Winthorpe is on the veranda."

I paused and met his gaze. "Thank you, Franklin." I made a mental note to pad his tip appropriately.

I was a few steps onto the veranda when a hand curled around my waist, pulling me back. I turned and melted into William's side.

"Hey," he said softly, a grin tugging at his lips as he looked down at me.

Devastatingly handsome. That was how my mother first described him, and it was apt. I held him at bay for a moment, examining his strong arrangement of features, then pressed my lips against his, enjoying the protective way his hand tightened on the small of my bare back.

"The silent auction is going well." He nodded to the balcony, where long glass tables displayed two dozen different items. As I watched, a woman in a beaded gown and a massive emerald ring bent forward and picked up a pen. I had spent the past month soliciting items for the auction, which ranged from an Alaskan spa getaway to a Menlo country club initiation fee.

"Franklin said you added a couple to the guest list." I ran my hand through his short dark hair, then tugged gently on a thick tuft of it.

He nodded. "Our new hire at the company. Dr. Ryder and her husband."

How incredibly sexist of me to assume that Dr. Ryder had been a man. I remembered William's mention of a new employee, some sort of motivational coach for his staff. We'd been at dinner, and I'd been distracted by an odd taste to the pâté and had barely paid attention to his enthusiastic mention of the doctor who he believed would solve the morale issue at Winthorpe Technologies.

Money would solve the morale issue. The team had spent four years on a new medical device that could replace pacemakers; pass through metal detectors; and reduce allergic reactions, infections, and surgery complications by more than half. The team's profit sharing and bonus structures were tied into the successful launch of the product, which had already dragged eighteen months past expectations. Everyone was tired and frustrated. We'd lost our top technician last month, and there was a general feeling of dissension among the ranks.

William was über-intelligent, decisive, and charming. He was also a cutthroat workaholic who valued money over personnel and demanded perfectionism without excuses. Leading a team had never been his forte, and I feared that Winthorpe Tech's staff was close to mutiny.

"Here she is now. Neena," he said warmly, and in that smile, you'd never think that he had kept the team working on Christmas or cut bonuses as punishment for a failed FDA trial. "This is my wife, Catherine."

"Cat," I said, extending my hand. Her grip could have cracked an egg, and I fought back a wince.

"Matt Ryder." The husband beamed as he shook my hand. "Beautiful home you have here. This thing would survive an earthquake, if need be."

"I hope it doesn't have to." I laughed and didn't miss the way her arm curled protectively through his. An amusing act, given how much my husband overshadowed hers. "Thank you both for coming. The party is in support of a great cause."

"It's for the Center for the Performing Arts, right?" the man asked, his fair eyebrows linking together intently. On the right breast of his tuxedo shirt, there was a pale-golden stain. Chardonnay? Tequila?

I checked William's shirt, unsurprised to see that it was spotless, my husband as ready for a photo shoot as he was a party. "That's right. Are you familiar with Atherton? The center is on Middlefield Road."

"We're growing more familiar with it. In fact, we've put a home under contract just next door," the woman supplied with an unnaturally white smile.

I stalled, surprised by the response. "You mean *right* next door? The Bakers' old home?" *Home* was a nice term for it. It was the neighborhood's resident teardown, a foreclosure that had spent the last five years dragging through the courts. If it ever came up for sale, I had plans to knock down the entire structure and replace it with an expansion to our pool area and gardens.

"Yep." Dr. Neena Ryder's beam grew even wider. "Matt had an inside track with the bank. He's in real estate development."

"Demolition," her husband corrected with a self-deprecating smile that crinkled the edges of his eyes. I immediately warmed to him.

"So, you'll be tearing down the house?"

"Oh no." He shook his head quickly. "We can't afford to rebuild, not to the neighboring standards. We'll renovate, then decide what to do."

Sinking a single dollar into that heap would be a waste. It needed to be bulldozed, the pool yanked out, and a fresh foundation poured. I smiled. "Well, if you ever want to make a quick buck, we'll take it off your hands. I've had my eye on that lot for years. I'd love to expand our pool deck all the way to the edge of the view."

"I appreciate the offer," he said, running a hand through the sparse hair crowning his head. "But Neena and I are pretty set on the house, especially with Atherton's proximity to her new job."

"I can't tell you how *excited* I am to work with Winthorpe Tech's team." Neena glanced at William, and I didn't miss the appreciative linger in her eyes. Then again, there wasn't a woman in town who hadn't given my husband a second look at some point or another. His looks and charm were one draw, the dollar signs that kept multiplying beside his name, another.

"And what is your position exactly?" I glanced at William, trying to remember how he had referred to the hire. Something odd.

"I'm the director of motivation," Neena supplied.

"I'd never actually heard of that before." I kept my tone mild, not wanting to ruffle her feathers. "Is it in the personal-coaching sphere?"

Her lips thinned, an almost imperceptible adjustment that pulled at the skin around her mouth. "It's not exactly coaching. I'm responsible for keeping the energy and motivation of the team high. I'll work with the team to help them achieve their goals, overcome obstacles, and eliminate workplace issues that may hamper productivity. It's amazing how small changes and shifts in a person's life can lead to huge results."

"Dr. Ryder comes highly recommended, from Plymouth Industries. We were lucky to steal her away." William lifted his drink in the doctor's direction, then took a sip.

"And you should have seen her parting bonus!" her husband said heartily, his head swiveling to follow a platter of crab cake bites that passed by. "Excuse me," he said quickly, then darted after the waiter, leaving us alone with his wife.

A parting bonus? Did those even exist? I watched as Matt hustled through the crowd, calling out to the crab-toting waiter. "What are you a doctor of?"

"Mental health and psychological studies. I'm a PhD, not a medical doctor." She brushed over the designation with a shrug, her wine almost sloshing over the lip of her glass and onto the white sheepskin rug—a 1940s piece we'd gotten in New Zealand.

"Well, it's wonderful to have you on the team." I smiled, and her eyes sharpened.

"Do you work for the company, Cat?" She glanced at William. "I thought you stayed at home and handled the, ah . . . foundation? Is that what it's called?"

I laughed, and if she looked at my husband like that one more time, I was going to stab my crab-cake fork through her jugular vein. "You're right," I admitted sheepishly. "I don't work for the company. But I do own half of the preferred stock of Winthorpe Technologies, same as William. So I'm heavily invested in its success and our employees." *Employees like you.* I pinched my brows together in a regretful frown. "William, it looks like the Decaters are leaving. I promised her an introduction to you. Would you mind me stealing you away for a bit?" I turned back to Neena without waiting on William's reply. "It was such a pleasure to meet you and Matt. Best of luck with the property next door."

"I'll see you on Monday," William interjected, lifting his glass in parting. "Tell your husband it was a pleasure."

Her eyes darted from William to me, and I could almost see the gears turning behind her blue eyes. Taking a step back, she gave a tight nod. "Thank you again for inviting us."

I placed a possessive kiss on William's cheek as we walked away, my arm tucked into his. We passed Matt, who was scurrying back in Neena's direction, a fresh drink in hand. He beamed merrily, and I struggled to connect his friendly demeanor with her ice.

"Was it just me," William said carefully, "or did that feel a tad territorial? I thought leading with your stock options was a bit on the aggressive side."

"It was a *wee* bit territorial," I admitted, coming to a stop along the railing, out of the cover of the veranda, under the brilliant night sky. Before us, the pools and lit gardens extended out like a glittery array of jewels. "I don't like her."

He groaned, pulling me closer. "Don't say that. I'm drowning right now in grouchy doctors and engineers. I need someone to babysit them or I'm going to go postal and fire everyone."

"Okay, *don't* do that," I instructed firmly, then smiled at the pained look he gave me. "I'll try to like her, okay? I'll be nicer."

"Pull out that prom-queen smile," he urged, lowering his voice. "Only no poison this time."

"Ha." I scowled at him. "Don't even joke about that." I'd spent years running from the Mission Valley High rumor that I'd spiked my prom-queen competitors' drinks with laxatives. The rumor had hit William's ear at my tenth high school reunion, spilling out of the drunk mouth of Dana Rodriguez, one of the diarrhea-ridden candidates who had peaked in high school and now clipped grocery coupons when she wasn't driving three kids around in a Chrysler minivan. I had laughed and wrapped Dana in a hug, hoping that William would forget and dismiss the rumors. He hadn't, and Dana had paid for her loose lips with an accidental electrical fire in her she shed, followed by a well-timed *Great to see you again, hope all is well* note on embossed Winthorpe stationery.

"Do I actually need to speak to the Decaters, or was that just a ploy to escape the conversation?" He placed his tumbler on the wide stone railing, and I watched as the night air ruffled his salt-and-pepper hair.

"It was a ploy, but let's do it anyway, for appearances' sake." I started to head back into the party, and his hand wrapped around my wrist, tugging me toward him.

"Stay out here." He cupped my face in his hands and stared down at me, studying my features. "I'm with the most beautiful woman in the world. Let me enjoy her for a moment."

I looked up into his eyes and smiled. "I'm here for as long as you want. In fact . . ." I lowered my voice and glanced back at the party. "Let's ditch this place. If we hurry, we can get to that diner by Stanford that has the apple crisp you like. And if you're lucky . . ." I bit my bottom lip. "I'll let you feel me up in the car."

He chuckled, and that bad-boy glint lit in his eyes. "What about all the guests?"

"The butlers will watch them. And Andi will emcee the silent auction." I stepped toward the dark end of the balcony, where the steps led down to the gardens. "Come on . . . ," I teased. "I know where they keep the keys to the Ferrari."

He caught me just before I sneaked down the stairs and pulled me into his chest, kissing me deeply. I sank into the contact, my hand fisting the front of his tuxedo as I stole a deeper kiss.

There were men you owned.

There were men you borrowed.

And then there were men you took.

I would never let anyone take him from me.

CHAPTER 2

NEENA

There were four- and five-letter words for women like Cat Winthorpe. I stood in our bathroom and stared into the mirror as I plucked a bottle of moisturizer out of the cardboard box beside our sink. My crow's-feet were deepening, despite the reassurances of my surgeon. I turned my head to one side and examined the lines in my neck, grateful when the skin rolled smoothly and naturally against my throat. No paunching. No pulling. I thought of Cat Winthorpe's throat, the delicate bob of her chin, the perfect complexion. She had to be thirty-five, tops. Thirty-five and probably still got carded at the grocery store. Not that Cat Winthorpe went to the grocery store.

"What a night." Matt stood behind me and fumbled with the bow on his tuxedo. His jacket and vest had been abandoned at the door, the items already hung back in their rental bags. "Some place, right?" He wheezed out a breath that smelled of alcohol, and I flinched at the visceral reminder it brought of my father. Matt's clammy hands pawed at my waist, and I stepped aside.

"Careful with that bow tie," I said sharply. "You already spilled something on the shirt." They'd fine us for that stain, probably keep the rental deposit. Unlike him, I'd been careful. My designer dress still had its tags on. I'd be able to return it tomorrow morning for a full refund.

I had seen the way Cat Winthorpe's eyes had swept over the dress, critiquing and comparing it to the others. I had planned ahead to ensure that the brand was appropriate, the price range exorbitant enough. This evening had needed to go smoothly, and it had.

"I can't get this damn . . ." He tried to look down at the knot, then swayed a little from the effort.

"Here," I said, softening. "I'll get it." I turned to him, not missing the pull of his eyes to my cleavage, the push-up bra offering up my perky and perfect breasts, a recent enhancement courtesy of my last boss. I had been surprised by Cat's small breasts—a lazy oversight in the maintenance category. In a few years, she'd probably ignore the slight bags that would appear under her eyes. The deepened wrinkles along her forehead. The sag of her skin beneath those underworked arms.

Her husband had certainly noticed my breasts. His gaze had lingered, even as his hand had curled around her waist.

Matt's eyes glazed over, and he fumbled a limp hand across the top of my cleavage, his thick sausage finger dipping between my breasts as if he were checking the oil on a car. I quickly unknotted his tie and pulled the material apart, working open his shirt buttons with quick efficiency.

I reached back and undid the strap of my bra, letting my new breasts tumble free before him. Turning my head away from his bourbon-heavy scent, I twisted his cummerbund around and undid the cheap buckle. His breath grew shorter as he cupped and massaged the generous D cups, his touch rudimentary but acceptable.

"Tonight?" he gasped hopefully.

I considered the request. It had been weeks since we'd last had sex, the quick event occurring after Matt had, from out of nowhere, put an offer on the Atherton house. Granted, it was a horrible home. Ugly and with a choppy floor plan that was badly out of style, but *still*. For my cheap husband, it was a huge and unexpected step in the right direction for our social standing and my happiness.

"Yes." I moved closer, as if in enjoyment of his touch. Matt had been a sexual disappointment early on, one that required me to take care of my own needs. Most recently, I had done so with the explosive but short-lived Ned Plymouth dalliance. I'd had high hopes for that pairing, and I frowned as I placed the cummerbund on the counter, thinking of the lost potential with my former boss.

Matt grunted, his mouth now sucking at my nipples with loud and frantic wet smacks of his lips. I undid his pants and pulled down on the zipper. "Let's go to the bed." I injected some husk into my voice, as if I were eager, and not just to get it over with.

On my back, with him above me, I thought of William Winthorpe. There was something dark and delicious about him, a temptation that had existed as soon as he'd introduced himself at my interview. *William.* There had been a tug in his tone, a tightening of the cord between us. *It's a pleasure to meet you.* Gruff and sexual. He was a walking chunk of masculinity and instantly more alluring than any of my prior affairs.

William was, among the rich and successful men of Silicon Valley, the best. Top tier. The sort of man I should have gone after, had I not tied myself down to Matt right out of high school. Back then I had been so desperate to escape my father that I hadn't understood my true potential. I'd thought I was winning the jackpot. A life with Matt had seemed so decadent at first. A new Mustang convertible. Our own home, gifted by his parents as our wedding present. A credit card with my name on the front and a three-thousand-dollar limit, the balance paid off each month, no questions asked.

I had needed security and attention, and he had given both to me. But as we'd moved up in the world, I'd slowly realized everything I didn't have. Frankly put, the dream my husband had delivered wasn't good enough. My needs had increased, and I was starting to become desperate for the life I didn't have.

"Right there?" Matt panted, and I moaned appropriately, wrapping my legs around his waist and thinking of the heat of William Winthorpe's stare.

CHAPTER 3

CAT

Eight days after the party, our new neighbors closed on the Baker house. I stood on our front balcony with a glass of chardonnay and watched as a single cleaning van traveled down their long drive, bumping over the cracks. In any other neighborhood, there would be knee-high grass covering the large yard, weeds clawing over the abandoned flower beds, vines inching up the brick. But we hadn't paid fourteen million dollars to live next to an eyesore. I'd spent the last six years paying for weekly lawn maintenance on the abandoned home. I'd had Ted replace the front gate lamps when they had burned out. I'd wandered the property at the end of my morning walks and kept an eye out for rodent holes and standing water where mosquitoes would breed.

I'd also, unbeknownst to my husband, spent a great deal of time inside the home. It used to be interesting. Four years ago, before the IRS's liquidation team swooped in and took everything, it had been a house full of memories and secrets. A life suddenly abandoned. Dresser drawers still open, a negligee set hanging half-out. The safe door open, the combination stuck to a Post-it on the inside wall, its shelves almost empty, a photo album cockeyed in the back corner. The Bakers had fled in the middle of the night, their Mercedes still sitting in the garage, their cell phones left on the kitchen counter. Tax evasion was the rumor in the neighborhood, though I found the more likely culprit behind neatly folded pillowcases in Claudia Baker's linen closet.

Cocaine. Five wrapped bundles that weighed in at two pounds each, according to their bathroom scale. I found another ten in an upper cabinet in their kitchen, behind boxes of Frosted Flakes and Honey Nut Cheerios. I found another bundle ripped open in their office, two lines tapped out on the cover of a *Rolling Stone* magazine.

For months after the Bakers disappeared, I would duck between the line of bushes that separated our lots and roam their house. I pocketed a ring of keys that I found in their junk drawer and skipped over the window I had initially used, coming and going as I wished. I spent afternoons in the big leather chair behind John Baker's desk, flipping through their files. I combed bank and credit card statements, fascinated by the personal glimpse into their life. I stood in Claudia's bathroom, before her big, wide mirror, and carefully applied her lipstick and shadows.

She'd been an interesting housewife. In the drawers of their master closet, I'd found ball gags and blindfolds, furry handcuffs and phallic-shaped toys. I spent an afternoon sifting through her lingerie and naughty costumes. I claimed a mink stole and Vuitton clutch, along with several pieces of abandoned jewelry. I spent one morning stretched out on their bed, dressed in her clothes, listening to their playlist crackling through the overhead speakers. And one day, just a few weeks before the IRS came and took everything—I found the second safe.

This one didn't have a lock. It was a fireproof box in a hidden floor compartment, underneath the faux Persian rug in their master bedroom. I'd been on my stomach, reaching underneath their bed, when my knee dug against a bump in the rug. I'd shimmied back from the bed and peeled back the rug, thrilled to discover the trapdoor. Excitement had hummed through me, my fingers slipping on the inset pull, and it had taken three tugs to get the door open. Inside, the iron cavity held a variety of empty money wrappers and a collection of crude porn. I had examined the construction of the secret compartment and considered installing a similar feature in our house. It might be a good place to put the thirty pounds of cocaine that I now had tucked in our attic, the parcels high and dry behind three rows of Christmas decorations, in a box labeled *Dollhouse*. There were, after all, things you never knew you might need. My mother had taught me that. Granted, she'd been referring to a heating pad that had been marked down at a yard sale two blocks from our home, but I had taken the advice to heart in more ways than one, and it had come in handy in a number of moments.

Now, I sipped a chilled glass of juice and wondered how one cleaning van could possibly tackle the layers of dust and grime inside that house. It would take them weeks. Not that I minded a delay before Matt and Neena Ryder moved in. I hadn't quite warmed to the idea of a new woman moving into both Winthorpe Tech and our street. Especially *this* woman.

I settled into one of the balcony's chaise lounges, trying to pinpoint the cause of my trepidation. She wouldn't be the first attractive woman inside WT's sleek corridors. William had hired more than a dozen female doctors and engineers, seeking the best of the best, regardless of their gender or appearance. Typically, the brighter the mind, the more unattractive the appearance, but every once in a while, there was a unicorn like Allyson Cho, our stunningly beautiful lead researcher. Or Nicole Finnegan, our public relations powerhouse. Both Nicole and Allyson were arguably more attractive than this blonde director of motivation—and what a stupid title that was. So, why were my hackles raised?

There was more movement at the front gate, and I sat up, surprised to see a moving semi attempt the tight turn through the Bakers' front gate. Unless the moving truck contained a pile of cleaners, it was wasting its time. The truck stopped and reversed, and a beep echoed over the barren lawn. From the pocket of my cardigan sweater, my phone rang.

"Are you watching this?" Kelly's voice hissed through the receiver, and I smiled, certain she was up on her widow's walk, in earshot of the Bakers' gate.

"I don't think it's going to make the turn," I remarked.

"I thought you said the place was in ruins. How could they be bringing in furniture already?" There was a crackle of wind against her mouthpiece. "Oh my God, Cat. There's a U-Haul coming down Greenoaks. We should call security. Tell them not to let any more in. They're going to clog up the entire street."

I didn't respond, watching as the semi's front wheels narrowly missed the cherub fountain.

"This is a disaster," Kelly clipped on. "What if it's still blocking the road when church gets out? Paul hasn't left yet to pick the kids up. Paul?" The wind diminished as she made her way inside her home in search of their manny. "Paul!"

"William is calling me," I lied. "Let me run."

"Okay. But tennis tomorrow morning, right? Nine o'clock?"

"I'll be there." I ended the call and winced as the side of the shipping container scraped along the gate, then broke free, the truck lumbering down the drive. The sun moved behind a cloud, and I shivered at the sudden drop in temperature. Wrapping the cashmere tighter, I decided to abandon the view and move inside.

I found William on his phone in the kitchen and interrupted his call long enough to steal a kiss. I opened the fridge and removed a parcel of wrapped steaks, holding them up so that he could see the butcher's writing on the front. He nodded, and I placed the package on the counter.

"Look, if you need a break, come up here. You can audit our books."

I untied the knot on the package and took out the filets, tuning in to the conversation.

"Bring her with you. We've got the guesthouse you can stay in. Plus, Cat hasn't seen Beth since last summer. They'll enjoy hanging out."

The clues aligned. Beth. A break. It had to be Mac. I slid the plate toward my husband and grabbed a spatula from the rack, setting it beside the blue china.

"It's not charity," William growled. "You're my brother. And I could use you. I need someone I can trust with these numbers."

Someone he could trust. I wasn't sure that Mac fit that bill. I turned away from William and returned to the fridge, opening both sides of the Sub-Zero and staring at the contents. Unless we had specific plans, the chef had the weekends off, and I looked through the shelf of labeled salads. I pulled out a container of avocado and spring mix.

Over the last decade, I'd lost count of the things we'd done for William's brother. It was like giving leftovers to a stray dog—the half rack of lamb didn't solve its problems but still gave you the sense that you were doing something to help.

I wasn't sure that we'd helped him at all. It was hard to help an alcoholic who didn't want to stop drinking. We'd paid for six rehab stints. Moved him three times. Paid off a gambling debt with some ugly Vegas characters. Pulled strings to get him jobs that he had tanked on. And now William wanted to bring him to Winthorpe Tech? A terrible idea, but I loved the fierce dedication he had to Mac, and I was desperate to grow his limited family to include children of our own.

William moved out onto the veranda, and I popped open a beer, certain that he'd need a drink after he finished with Mac.

The beeping of a truck's reverse faintly sounded, and I moved to the sink, glancing out the window.

"Mac's on tilt." William strode through the opening, pushing his shirtsleeves up to his elbows. "Won't leave the house. Drunk."

"Oh God." I ripped open the salad's bag and evenly divided the contents onto two plates. "Has he been fired yet?"

He grimaced. "I was afraid to bring it up. Can you call the bank and have them make a deposit into their account? And check with their landlord—"

"Rent's paid through next year," I interrupted. "I did that a few months ago." I slid the beer toward him.

"Good." He downed half of it in one long gulp. "He doesn't want to come here."

I fought to keep the relief from my face. "I'll talk to Beth and see if there's a good day for me to drive down for a visit. I'd love to see the baby."

"Yeah, I'd like it if you could put eyes on him." He moved forward and kissed me.

I tried to be disappointed in his refusal to come, but Mac was always a volatile guest. I once came home to find him in our master bedroom, naked and facedown on the bed, vomit spewed over the expensive duvet.

The beep sounded again, and William glanced toward the noise. "They already moving in next door?"

"Yep." I pulled two sets of silverware out of the drawer and stacked each on the plate. "I can't believe they're bringing furniture in with it in that condition."

"It's not uninhabitable. It's neglected." He cracked a grin, and maybe the conversation with Mac wouldn't ruin his day. "Don't tell me you've already forgotten that cramped apartment I pulled you from. Your shower handle was held together with a rubber band."

I picked up both plates and headed around the marble island. "You *pulled* me from? I was an unpaid college intern. I was doing just fine on student loans and fast food. You're lucky I gave all that up to move in with you."

"Oh, sure." He blocked my way, taking the plates, and leaned forward, asking for a kiss. "You were an angel to sacrifice all that just for me."

"Better." I accepted his kiss. "And hey—my tiny apartment had charm."

"Well, compared to it, they're moving into a palace." He turned. "We eating outside or in?"

"Outside." I returned to the kitchen's window and could see Neena, standing in the driveway in cutoff shorts and a long-sleeve shirt, directing traffic. I let my eyes drift over the home's brick exterior, the wide porches and double fireplaces. William was right—it wasn't uninhabitable, just dated and dirty. Fifteen years ago, I would have considered it a castle, but a decade as Mrs. Winthorpe had made me a snob, one who now thought of heated towels and ironed sheets as a necessity.

Neena yelled something at the driver, and I thought of the day I'd moved into this house. The wedding-ring set was still unexpectedly heavy on my finger. All my belongings would take up a laughably small portion of the massive closet. I had stooped to lift a box of personal items from the trunk of my brand-new Maserati, and William had stopped me with one gentle shake of his head. "Do you see this?" He'd pulled at my hand, bringing the diamond up between us. "This means that you don't move your own things. You're Mrs. Winthorpe now, and everyone bows and caters to you."

"Even you?" I had said saucily, even as the thrill of power had swept giddily through me.

He had laughed and never answered the question. I hadn't cared. I had stepped into this house and devoured every opulent inch of it. I had settled, immediately and comfortably, on my throne and never lifted a box again.

In contrast, Neena staggered around the back of the truck, her arms wrapped around a heavy cardboard box. She squatted, setting the box carefully on the ground, then stood and brushed off her palms. Turning to the side, she examined our house. From this distance, across the manicured gardens and behind a row of Italian cypress trees, I felt protected, even as her stare lengthened. I didn't blame her. There was a reason that cars lined the street to see our Christmas decorations, and *Architectural Digest* had devoted a center spread to our home. It was stare-worthy. Gawk-worthy. I watched as her gaze cataloged the stone framework, the modern lines, the copper roof and glass railings.

William moved beside me, following my line of vision. "Should we go over? Welcome them to the neighborhood?"

"Not yet." I watched her, waiting for her to turn, but she kept in place, her gaze locked on our house. "She's just staring over here."

He shrugged and began to wash his hands.

"It's a little creepy."

"It's a big house, babe. Lots to look at."

"How was she this week? Does the team like her?"

He frowned. "I'm not sure. She hasn't met with all of them yet. I've gotten a few hostile comments and a few supportive ones. Some think she's a little too rah-rah." Using the back of his wrist, he turned off the water.

I grinned. "Let me guess: Harris?" The Nigerian scientist was the sort to scowl when words like *teamwork* or *cohesion* were used. His annual evaluations always garnered the lowest scores from fellow team members on communication skills but the highest on aptitude.

"Yep. I think his exact quote was, 'We don't need the Kumbaya stuff to save lives.' Which"—he pulled a hand towel off the rack—"I agree with. I told Neena to steer clear of him."

Neena. No longer Dr. Ryder. I notated it, then dismissed it, aware that everyone at Winthorpe was on a first-name basis. Even the janitorial staff referred to William by name.

He tossed the towel beside the sink. "Come on. Steaks are almost ready."

I remained a moment longer, waiting until she turned away from our house and back to hers. Her husband appeared in the open garage door, and she pointed to the box. I folded the hand towel into thirds and placed it back in its position. Pulling a Pellegrino from the cooler, I glanced out the window. She was gone, swallowed by the house. At a second-story window, I watched a maid spray cleaner on the glass and wipe a cloth across the surface.

I didn't understand anyone moving into a dirty house. It was like skipping past blank pages in a notebook and then starting your story on one that was already half-full. It was bad karma.

CHAPTER 4

Neena

I was on a ladder beside our bedroom wall, a pencil in hand, when the power went out, the abrupt event punctuated by a clap of thunder that shook the home.

"Neena?" Matt's voice came out of the black, somewhere to my right. "Are you okay?"

"I'm on the ladder," I snapped. "Can you help me get down?" The darkness was disorienting, and I clutched the top rung, forcing my panic down.

"Just a second . . ." Matt's phone's flashlight illuminated, sweeping over the interior of the room and blinding me as he moved closer. I chanced a descent, making it down one rung before the light bounced, then swung wildly as he tripped over something. He cursed and I paused, my foot hovering in space.

"You okay?"

"Yeah." He grunted, and the flashlight refocused on me. "Here. I'll help you down."

We worked in silence, and my tension eased once I was back on firm footing. Making our way downstairs, we stared at the fuse box in ignorance, then discussed our options. Outside, sheets of rain peppered the roof and poured loudly from uncleaned gutters.

"It's got to be the storm. Probably blew a transformer. I bet the whole neighborhood's out." Matt swung the fuse-box door shut and latched it.

I shook my head. "I saw the lights on next door when we came down the stairs."

"They probably have a generator." He moved past me and headed to the dining room. Peering through the glass panes of the window, he jumped when a bolt of lightning lit up the sky. "I vote we wait it out, unless you want to drive around and see what areas have power. I've got a small generator at the shop. It could get us through the night, if you don't mind being a little hot."

I kept close to him, uncomfortable in the dark house. "I could go next door and speak to William. And Cat." I hadn't intended to separate their names, but it happened, the gap hanging in the sentence like an out-of-place comma.

"What?" Matt pressed a button on the side of his watch, lighting up the digital dial. "It's almost nine."

"No one's in bed this early. We can ask them how long these outages normally last or—if it's just us—if there's an electrician they recommend." I warmed to the idea. I'd spent most of the day wondering if I should head over to say hi—and being a little surprised they hadn't shown up here. Wasn't it a common courtesy to welcome someone to the neighborhood? Or maybe that sort of thing was done only in our old neighborhood, where the homes didn't have private gates, uniformed staff, or police officers who patrolled the streets on horseback.

"I don't know," Matt said slowly, and this was why he'd never really amounted to anything. As I had just told that Asian doctor at Winthorpe—Allyson Cho—you had to act decisively and take the consequences. Grab life by the balls. My husband liked to tickle them with a feather and then wander away.

I rerouted my path and navigated to the back door, my decision made. This was a blessing, actually. The perfect excuse to pop in. Maybe

Cat would be in pajamas, her makeup off, and I could replace my Instagram-perfect images of her with something more attainable. I thought of William and wondered what he'd look like. I'd seen him only in a tuxedo—at the party—and in suits at the office. Would he be in workout shorts and a T-shirt? Jeans and a polo? Underwear and no shirt?

I swung open the door to the garage, my sneakers making the transition from wood floors to the spongy welcome mat, and I heard Matt follow me into the dank interior, his phone extended like a sword, the flashlight beam cutting past me and reflecting off the hood of my car.

It wasn't a surprise. Matt would follow me anywhere.

~

We rang the bell twice before Cat answered, her cheeks flushed, eyes warm. They'd either been in bed together or she was drunk, and I hesitated on their front porch, rethinking the hour.

"Matt, Neena, hey!" She swung the door open farther, and the three-story foyer glowed with light. "Is everything okay?"

"Our power's out," I said, suddenly aware that I should have done as Matt suggested and waited out the storm. Instead, we looked like dripping-wet cling-ons, begging for scraps and favors. I pulled on the top of my leggings, making sure the wide band was holding in my stomach. "We didn't want to bother you, just wanted to see if it's a neighborhood-wide thing or just our house. Obviously you have power, but—"

"We have a generator," she said quickly. "It just started up a little while ago." She swung her arm, gesturing us in. "Get in before you catch a chill. William's in the shower, but he'll be out any minute."

We ended up in their kitchen, perched on stools at a massive marble island, shot glasses lined up before us as Cat poured an African liquor into each one. I watched her slide the first glass toward Matt.

Her thick, dark hair was up in a messy bun, wisps of it hanging loose. My wish had come true—she was makeup-free, in silk pajama pants and a long-sleeve Mission Valley High soccer T-shirt—but the effect was the opposite of what I'd hoped for. Maybe it was the high school logo across her small chest, but she looked young and beautiful. I watched Matt carefully to see if he noticed. He didn't seem to, and I stretched my face forward, hoping my neck scars weren't showing.

"What's this?" William approached, his stride lazy, his smile wide, and my insecurities grew deeper. He had jeans on, his feet bare, a white T-shirt sticking to a torso that was still damp from his shower. "Are we celebrating?"

Cat lifted a shot glass and held it out to him. "We are celebrating and commiserating. To new neighbors and the headaches of California storms. Cheers."

Glasses clinked, and over the rim of his glass, William's eyes met mine for a brief moment. I held the look and tilted back my glass.

~

Three drinks later, we were lounging around the fireplace, Cat and William on one sofa, Matt and me on the other. I relaxed back on the soft leather, settling into Matt's side, and put my bare feet up on the ottoman, careful not to disrupt the mirrored tray of lit candles in its center.

"I swear, Neena could give Tiger a run for his money," Matt protested. "She's a freak of nature with a putter in her hand. It was the worst place I could have possibly tried to impress her."

I smiled at his recollection of our first date. "You should have known better, given that my father was a course superintendent." I lifted the glass, needing a drink at just the mention of my father.

"You grew up playing?" William ran his hand over Cat's knee, his fingers caressing the joint through the thin fabric.

I pulled my eyes away from the motion. "Yeah. My father wanted a son, so he tortured me with the burden." I laughed in an attempt to hide the bitterness that crept into the response. *Tortured* had been an apt description. Hundreds of hours in the sun, sweat dripping down the back of my legs, the sound of his voice raised in frustration at each inaccurate drive. The yelling had been rough, but when he'd picked up the switch, things had turned bad. I'd worn jeans my entire freshman year to hide the welts on the backs of my calves. I still couldn't sit in a foldable chair without thinking of him settled back in his, boots crossed on the grass, the switch waving through the air in anticipation of my failure.

"She's really great," Matt said proudly. "Almost won state her senior year."

"Further proof that putt-putt was the worst idea of a first date," I pointed out.

He shrugged. "It worked out for me in the end."

"So . . . high school sweethearts," Cat cooed. "I love that."

"Where did you two meet?" I asked, anxious to move off the topic.

"I was an intern at an investment firm that William led. This was before Winthorpe Tech."

"Or Winthorpe Capital," William added proudly. "She fell for me back when I was a pauper."

"Well," Cat chided, "not *exactly* a pauper." She laughed. "I was the pauper. I was impressed by anything fancier than a TV dinner or ramen noodles." She kissed his cheek. William beamed at her, then glanced at me.

"Do you still play golf?" he asked.

I fought the urge not to respond too eagerly. "Absolutely. Once a week, if I can. Not that I've found a course since we moved here."

"You should teach Cat. I'd love to be able to play with her."

My enthusiasm waned at the suggestion.

"Oh, please." Cat waved off the possibility before I had to respond. "I've tried. I can't even connect with the ball. It's embarrassing."

I liked the idea of an inept Cat Winthorpe but didn't believe it. "I bet you're not that bad. Maybe you just need a few pointers."

"No." She set down her glass on the flat arm of the couch and shook her head. "Honestly, I'm terrible. I don't have the patience and temperament for it."

William grinned. "It's true. And it doesn't help that she's competitive. She once threatened to divorce me over a foosball game."

She shrugged. "I don't like to lose. Which"—she turned to me—"is why I won't try golf. It's setting myself up for failure."

Her psychology was interesting. She was overly confident but also just vulnerable enough to be likable. What I had yet to figure out was if the vulnerability was calculated or authentic. It was certainly annoying. Everything about her was annoying, though I was self-aware enough to understand that my jealousy played a part in my irritation.

The lights dimmed, then relit. Cat straightened up, off William's chest. "Oh! That's the power coming back on."

"Well, that wasn't too long." Matt clapped his hands together and pushed to his feet. "Neena? Should we let them get back to their night?"

He was too polite for his own good. I followed him reluctantly, searching for something, anything, to prolong the conversation. I drew a blank and exchanged a stiff hug with Cat at the door.

"So, dinner on Thursday, right?" Cat held open the door, all but pushing us through it.

"Sure." I stared at William until I caught his eye. "See you on Monday."

He nodded with an easy smile, and I tried to understand where the intense dislike from his employees came from.

∼

"There's something off about Cat." I dabbed on eye cream as I leaned over our master-bathroom vanity, struggling to see in the dim light. I glanced up at the light fixture above me; only one bulb of the eight was working.

"Off?" Matt sat on the toilet, his pants around his ankles, and peered at me through the open door. "She seems nice."

I snorted. "Nice? Matt, you can't take everyone at face value. You don't know women like that. They have nothing to do all day but cause trouble." Which was one of the reasons I had always worked. Some women enjoyed sitting at home, but I didn't. I needed interaction. Friendships. Relationships. My own identity. Otherwise, there was no security blanket. No fallback plan. I refused to be held hostage in a marriage without knowing and exploring my other options. My mother had taught me that. She'd realized that a better life existed for her, and she'd put a plan into place and then taken it, leaving her alcoholic husband and daughter behind and driving three states over to live in a McMansion with an attorney she'd met through a classified ad. I would have liked her to bring me, but she did a full upgrade and now posts photos on Facebook under her new name, with her stepdaughter, Aspen vacations, and quotes about Jesus. I friended her under a fake account and now follow the entire family. I've considered seducing her husband but haven't had the energy or enough ill motivation. I've kept the possibility as a delicious late-night snack I might one day consume.

"Well, I like them." Matt nudged the door closed with his toe, not waiting for a response.

Of course he did. He liked everyone, which was one of the reasons he needed me in his life—to point out shortcomings where they existed. Not that the Winthorpes had many. I put toothpaste on my brush and started on my teeth, thinking over the evening. I'd spent most of it looking for flaws in Cat, which had been an annoyingly arduous task. Quite frankly, she was prettier than I was. Younger. More delicate. But my body was better than hers. She had almost no muscle tone and probably skipped weight training altogether.

I ran my toothbrush under the water and remembered the beautiful moment this week when I'd bent over to grab my purse on the way out of William's office. I'd glanced up, catching his gaze on my butt, and his mouth had curved into a smile, his cheeks pinking as he had glanced away. Tonight, I'd given him multiple opportunities to look, but he'd remained focused on Cat.

The toilet flushed, and I pulled the toothbrush out of my mouth and leaned forward, spitting into the sink.

Five minutes later, I lay next to Matt and stared up at the coffered ceilings, the light from the television dancing across their details. A late-night comedian delivered a punch line about the royal family, and Matt laughed.

Moving into this neighborhood could be monumental. The women who lived inside these gates all partied together, shopped together, vacationed together. And already, things were clicking into place. I had a job with one of the most promising tech companies in Silicon Valley. An office adjacent to William Winthorpe's. Thanks to the power outage, we'd just spent two hours bonding with them. We'd made dinner plans for next week. The proximity that our houses would grant and the potential social introductions from Cat could be the keys to the kingdom I deserved to live in.

Except that now, sinking into our soft bed, I was overwhelmed by the discrepancies between us. Cat and me. William and Matt. Their gorgeous showcase mansion and our ugly foreclosure.

Matt coughed, and I reminded myself of all his good traits. He bought me this house. He made me look less risky to a wife like Cat, who might otherwise see me as a threat. And if he managed to build a friendship with William Winthorpe, there would be many additional possibilities.

I turned toward Matt and moved closer, fitting my body into the side of his, my arm stealing around his chest. He patted my hand, his eyes already beginning to sag with sleep, and I felt a wave of deep affection for the man who loved me so much.

I'd upgrade from him at some point, but not yet.

CHAPTER 5

Cat

The neighbors had left, and William's legs were tangled with mine, my head in the crook of his shoulder. I ran my hand along his stomach, enjoying the warmth of his skin. "What did you think of them?"

"They were fine," he said, the words elongated by a yawn. "Better than the Bakers."

Better than the Bakers. I flicked back through the events of the night. My distrust of Neena had mellowed as the night had gone on, the transition heavily aided by alcohol. She'd been entertaining to watch and had a crass humor that was funny, if not a little bitchy at times. She'd gotten sharper with her husband as the night had progressed, growing more bossy with each drink. But that was how some couples communicated. Not everyone was like us. I was reminded of that each time I visited my parents, their forty-year marriage no weaker despite their constant fights.

"Is that what she's like at work? Coy and snarky?" I ran my hand over his upper abs and mimicked the pursed-lip pout that Neena had adopted at several moments during the night.

He chuckled and ran his hand over the top of my head, smoothing his fingers through my hair. "More like a stiff and efficient cheerleader. Rah, rah, rah, fill out this questionnaire about your feelings, rah, rah, rah."

I snorted and scooted farther up his chest until our faces were aligned. "If I recall correctly, you have a thing for cheerleaders." I brushed my lips teasingly over his. "Should I be worried?"

His hands tightened on my waist, and a thrill of pleasure lit through me at the glow of arousal that hit his eyes. "Still got that uniform from high school?"

I kissed along his jaw, then whispered in his ear, "And the pom-poms."

He groaned, the brand of his arousal hot and hard against my hip. "God, I love you."

I met his kiss, my heartbeat quickening. In the warmth of his hands and the loss of our clothes, I forgot all about our new neighbors.

~

Eight hours later, after a leisurely breakfast in the gardens and coffee, I drove to the country club and met Kelly on one of the tennis courts. Rolling my neck slowly to the left, then right, I watched as she tossed up and then delivered a serve that could have decapitated a mouse. I lunged right for the ball, missed it by inches, and shot her an impressed look.

"Thanks," she called out breezily. "I've been logging extra lessons with Virgil."

"It shows." I scooped up the ball and tossed it over the net toward her, then motioned her to come up closer to practice short shots. "How's he compared to Justin?"

"Twenty years older, thirty pounds fatter, but Josh doesn't complain nearly as much, so it's worth the lack of eye candy." She tossed up the ball but hit it a moment too early, lobbing an easy target over the net toward me. I met the ball early and quick, snapping it to the far left side of her court. Kelly's husband was notoriously jealous, the sort who combed over her cell-phone log and popped into our lunch dates to make sure they were legitimate. I wasn't surprised to hear he'd found fault with Justin O'Shea, the club's best-looking tennis pro, but Justin was flamingly gay. Virgil could be a toad and he'd still be more of a risk.

"How's the new neighbor?" She wiped her white-sweatbanded wrist across her forehead.

"Not sure yet." I bounced a fresh ball against the clay court. "We're having dinner with them on Thursday. She's hard to read. A little . . ." I caught the ball and held it for a moment, trying to find the right word. "Reserved. She seems to be studying us very closely." On our brief stroll through the house, she had seemed to mentally catalog our possessions, as if she were adding up their valuations in her head.

"No offense, but you're very studyable." Kelly grinned, her freckles almost bleached by the sun. "Honestly, I don't even like tennis—I just like seeing what car you're going to pull up to the club in."

I made a face and knocked the ball toward her. She hit it back and we volleyed for a good dozen times before she missed a shot. Kelly was good, but I had trained for six months before joining the club, taking daily private lessons in San Francisco and weeklong camps at Stanford. My "natural aptitude" had needed to look effortless, and from the first day at Menlo, it had. I had intentionally lost a few early matches, blushing and stammering through the friendly ribbing, then quietly and almost immediately became the strongest player in the club.

That was the secret to success in this town. Presenting a picture of effortless perfection with behind-the-scenes ruthless hard work. Everyone thought I woke up as Cat Winthorpe one day, but I had clawed and scraped for every piece of this life. Still did.

We played a quick game, then headed for our bags. Kelly turned to face me, her racket swinging loosely from her hand. "Does it bother you, the new neighbor working for William?"

"No." I dipped, picking up a ball and leaving the others for the collection crew. As I watched, they jogged onto the court, their baskets in hand, all-white uniforms darting to pick up the bright-yellow balls. "Why would it?"

"I don't know. You and him were a workplace romance . . . she's in his workplace now." She shrugged. "There's a reason I don't let Josh hire any single women at the office."

"She's not single," I reminded her, coming to stand beside her at the bench. Unzipping the side pocket of my bag, I pulled out a monogrammed hand towel and dabbed at the sweat along my forehead.

"Oh, right. The chubby husband. He's in construction, right?"

"Demolition." Which, from my uneducated perspective, seemed to be the easiest of the trades. Smash things down, haul them away. I'd pulled up his company and glanced over their website. It seemed like a small operation, one that couldn't support the Atherton lifestyle. Which . . . would make for an interesting sideshow. Even if they did get the Baker house for a steal, trying to keep up in this town would burn through their money quickly. And Neena Ryder *wanted* this lifestyle. I had seen it in her eyes, had heard it in the offhand comments she threw out in an attempt to fit in. She wanted it—the only question was what she would do to attain it. I made a mental note to check with Human Resources and see what we were paying her.

"Well, that's good that she's married. Maybe he and Josh could connect. He's always complaining about the stuffed shirts I make him hang out with." Kelly tilted back her head and squirted a stream of lemon-infused water into her mouth. "Not William, of course."

I didn't respond, well aware she wasn't talking about my husband. Unzipping the small coin pouch I kept in my bag, I worked my wedding-ring set back onto my finger.

"I'll plan something," she continued on, her eyes following a muscular ball boy as he dipped over the net. "Something to get her husband and Josh together. Maybe a going-away party. You know we leave for Colombia on the eighth?"

"I know." I pulled at her arm. "Come on. Loser buys me breakfast in the club."

CHAPTER 6

NEENA

I learned to play chess on a broken board at the Boys and Girls Club. My teacher was Scott, a guy three years older than I was, who stared down my tank top at my thirteen-year-old chest and offered me cigarettes behind the dumpster while I waited to be picked up. My dad was often late, and one time, night falling in the questionable neighborhood, I took my first quick puff. The next week, a deep drag. A few months later, his fingers were down my pants, and my lit cigarette fell to the soggy ground. I watched it burn out against a wet red leaf and wondered how far away my dad was.

Chess is easy if you think ahead, the further out the better. You have to weigh the strengths you have. Decide what pieces can be sacrificed. Choose what pieces need to be protected. But the key, Scott preached, if playing against any skilled opponent, was the fake. You had to convince them that you were moving down one path—maybe a dumb path, an innocent path—while you skillfully tiptoed through your true plan, the one that would lead them straight to checkmate.

"Neena." William smiled at me from the doorway to my office. "Got a moment?"

"Of course." I gestured to the seat across from my desk. He ignored it and stood before me, his hands in the pockets of his dress pants, his legs slightly spread, his shoulders back. The pose of a man secure enough to put the weapons of his fists away. "How can I help you?"

The grin dropped from his face with unsettling ease. "Marilyn just spoke to Courtney in HR. She's putting in her two-week notice."

I frowned, irritated that I hadn't picked up on any signs in my initial meeting with her. "That's interesting."

He moved forward and gripped the back of the chair I had intended him to sit in. His fingers drummed against the cloth, and he leaned forward, putting weight on it. I watched his clean and short-cropped fingernails bite into the gray upholstery as he cleared his throat, then spoke softly and precisely. "It's not *interesting*."

I settled back and fought the urge to cross my arms defensively over my chest. Picking up my silver pen from beside my calendar, I tapped the tip of it against the paper and stayed silent, holding his gaze calmly.

"I may have been unclear in why I hired you, so let me make it perfectly obvious. I hired you so that I would know whatever Marilyn is thinking *before* she puts in her notice. I hired you so that I don't have to deal with *interesting* situations. I hired you to spy on this team and manipulate them into building the best damn medical conduction system that any heart has ever seen and to make me a billionaire. Do you understand that objective?" The last sentence was spaced out as if there were periods behind each word.

"Yes, sir." I lifted my chin enough for him to realize I wasn't intimidated.

He straightened, and when his hands fell from the chair, the imprints remained, like little teeth marks in an eraser head. "Convince her to stay or you're fired. You have two weeks."

Or you're fired. Two weeks. He picked up his tie and smoothed it down the front of his shirt. On another man, it'd be a nervous tic. On him, it was merely a return of everything to order. I'd bet he was controlling in the bedroom. Precise. Authoritative. *Dominant.*

My lips parted slightly at the thought. "I'll convince her to stay."

He turned and ambled out of my office, his broad shoulders pinned back into their natural position.

I let out a slow breath, my heart racing, and turned to the computer, pulling up the calendar software and locating Marilyn's schedule. So *there* was the real William Winthorpe. Not the charismatic husband who had pulled Cat to his side on the couch. Not the affable businessman who had offered me the job. Not the polished intellectual I'd watched videos of, speaking at medical conferences and corporate events.

The real William Winthorpe was an asshole, and I was fascinated by him.

CHAPTER 7

CAT

It was interesting to see the dynamics of another relationship. William and I were together against everything. His competitors. Judgments against our childless state. Our families. We were a bond.

Neena and Matt were the opposite. A break. If I hadn't seen it in our power-outage visit, the truth reared its head at our first dinner together.

"Don't eat that," she warned Matt, tapping his hand with the top of her fork. "It's not grass-fed." He reluctantly put down the Wagyu rib eye skewer, which was a shame, because it was one of the best items on Protégé's menu.

I lifted an amused eyebrow in William's direction. "Does it matter if it's grass-fed?"

"It does if you don't want to get cancer," she snapped, her voice a little loud for the intimate restaurant. I glanced at the closest table and was relieved to see no reaction from the couple there. Leaning forward, I stole the abandoned skewer, which was absolutely delectable, regardless of its source's dietary history. Her eyes narrowed.

"We're strictly keto," she announced, and I wasn't well informed on the diet, but I'd be surprised if the wine she was guzzling down was part of it. "Matt's down fourteen pounds."

"Wow." I nodded as if fourteen pounds would make any difference on her husband's stocky frame. "Matt, that's great."

He nodded warily, she glared at me, and I stifled a smile at the long list of things that appeared to piss Neena off. For one, not including the doctor title before her name. We'd introduced them to the club manager, as well as some friends of ours, and in both instances, she interjected the designation after I made the introduction. She also seemed to intensely dislike anything that tasted good. And she was insecure to the point of being unbearably possessive with her husband, yet overly friendly with mine.

In contrast, Matt was wonderful. Gracious throughout all her snide remarks. Funny and endearing, with a catalog of stories that kept us laughing during the entire meal. He was obviously head over heels for Neena, despite her neurotic behaviors, which only made me like him more. He and William had hit it off immediately, talking politics and sports, their conversations often leaving Neena and me to our own discussions.

Now, she leaned forward and gently touched my arm. "That couple you introduced us to? The Whitlocks? You said that you sit on a board with them?"

I nodded. "The charity wine auction. It's an annual event that raises money for local and national charities. It's the largest fundraiser in the county. Last year, it raised over ten million dollars."

"I'd love to be a part of that." She scooted her chair closer to mine.

"We're always looking for volunteers." I beamed. "I can add you to the list."

"Well, sure, sure." She waved off the mention with a flip of her skinny wrist. "But I was thinking more of the board. Helping with the administration of the event."

I struggled not to laugh. She wanted to be on the charity wine auction board? It was the most prestigious event in town. I'd spent the last decade building the relationships and climbing the complicated maze of social ladders required to lead that board. I lifted my wineglass and took a moment to respond.

"The board applications are accepted in July." I shrugged. "I'll be sure to let you know when they open and can give you a recommendation."

"That would be great." She smiled, and the gesture pulled unnaturally at the tight skin by her ear, a telltale sign of a facelift—and a poor one at that. During the meal, I'd kept a careful catalog of her surgeries. A neck job, definitely. Eye work, if I had to guess. Breast job—without a doubt. Her thin lips would be the next item on the surgeon's block, if I were a betting woman. And it was sad. Beneath all that, she had probably been a natural beauty.

Under the table, William's hand settled on my knee, and he gave it a tender squeeze. I placed my hand over his and met his eyes. He smiled, and I knew what he was thinking. He wanted to be alone. Our last date here had stretched until almost midnight, as we had taken our time with the tasting menu, polishing off two bottles of wine during the five-course meal. He leaned forward, and I met him over a piece of kataifi-wrapped langoustine.

"You look good enough to eat," he whispered in my ear.

I pressed a kiss against his cheek, then straightened, unsurprised to find Neena watching, her gaze darting between William and me as if paranoid that we were talking about her. I turned to Matt. "How's the house? Any unexpected issues?"

"No issues," Neena said quickly. "It's wonderful. Really needs very little at all."

"It's not anything compared to your house," Matt began.

"But it's great." Neena's grin grew strained. "Matt, eat the rest of the sablefish."

"We've always loved that lot," I offered. "It's so private. And the neighborhood is so safe."

"I've got to be honest." Matt wiped at his mouth, oblivious to the daggers his wife was sending his way. "I expected, with it sitting vacant for so long, that it'd be ransacked. Normally you'll see the appliances stolen, light fixtures gone—even the copper wiring stripped out."

"This isn't Bayview," Neena said sharply. "It's Atherton. Things like that don't happen here."

"It's true." William settled back in his seat as the delicate sounds of a harp began in the background. "Plus, everyone's so nosy. You got a hundred housewives spying on each other through diamond-studded binoculars. Add in the private police force, security cameras, and guard gate, and no one even tries to do anything. That house could have sat wide-open for the last five years and no one would have taken a thing from it."

I nodded in agreement, thinking of the sweet irony that the tennis bracelet on my wrist had come from Claudia Baker's personal collection. "It's true. Honestly, we don't even lock our doors most of the time." I sectioned off a bite of the poularde. "In the daytime, there's no point, especially in the backyard. I'd rather come in to the fresh breeze, especially when the gardens are in bloom."

William frowned at me. "You should keep the doors locked."

I shrugged off the instruction. "You focus on WT and I'll watch the house." He chuckled, and I pierced a wedge of Wagyu and held it out to him, smiling as he ate it off my fork.

"I always lock the house," Neena said firmly. "They say anyone would steal if given enough opportunities and lack of consequences."

"I agree." William nodded, and I didn't miss the way Neena straightened with pride at his support. "It's like leaving keys in a Lamborghini. At some point, even if not to steal it, someone is going to borrow it for a test drive."

"Exactly." She picked up her almost-empty glass of wine, and I wondered if she had changed the locks since they'd moved in. If so, had they gone to the trouble with every door? I thought of my key ring at home, a duplicate of the one I had returned to Claudia Baker's junk drawer.

"Neena, how is Winthorpe Tech?" I smiled at her. "Everyone treating you well?"

I may have imagined it, but it seemed as if her shoulders stiffened with the question. "It's going well." She set down the glass and focused on her own plate, her knife scraping across the china as she cut into her piece of lamb. "The team has been very receptive to my presence."

William, as expected, shifted immediately into work mode. "Any progress with Marilyn?"

"Some." She pierced a piece of meat. "I'm meeting with her again tomorrow."

"Marilyn Staubach?" I said, confused by what the capable surgeon would need help with. "What progress does she need?"

"I'll tell you about it later." William smiled, but his voice was tight and irritated. "Neena has another week to work with her." He glanced over his shoulder, catching the attention of the waiter and signaling for the check.

I brought the wineglass up to my mouth and didn't miss the tension that crossed Neena's face.

Another week. I knew every tone in my husband's arsenal, and that had sounded like an ultimatum.

CHAPTER 8

NEENA

If my job had been solely in Marilyn Staubach's hands, it would have been doomed for failure. I studied the petite woman carefully, looking for some tell that could unlock her motivations, and was grateful for the grenade I'd found, one currently tucked into the side pocket of my jacket.

She stared back at me, then opened her mouth in a yawn. From the back of her mouth, I saw the silver glint of a filling.

"Why did you originally start working for Winthorpe?"

"Money," she said flatly. "And I've decided I've had enough of it." She lifted a delicate dark wrist and examined the face of a chunky plastic timepiece, one I'd considered buying myself—the built-in GPS an interesting but fairly useless feature.

"Well, surgeons make good money." I drew a tiny dollar sign in the first bullet point of my notepad. "You could certainly go back to working in the field."

She looked at me as if I were an idiot. "Thank you, Neena. Excellent career advice."

"The stress rate of cardiac surgeons is one of the highest out of all the surgical specialists," I pointed out, my cheeks burning at her sharp remark. *Stupid Neena,* my father used to say. *Shut up, Neena.* It'd been twenty years. Would I ever stop hearing his opinions? "Would you gauge your stress level to be higher or lower during your time at WT?"

"It feels like these questions could all be answered through an exit survey." She changed the cross of her leg, and I watched the pale-blue scrub lift to reveal a functional white tennis shoe and ankle socks. I had to remember what she was. A lamb/owl, if I went off Charles Clarke's personality profiles. Caring. Exacting. Detail and numbers oriented. She wouldn't have put in her notice without researching other options and doing an extensive pro/con list.

"They could be." I aimed for a demure smile. "But an exit survey can't negotiate."

She let out a harsh laugh. "Negotiate with what?"

"FDA approval is almost here," I pointed out. "You're talking about a seven-figure bonus that you're walking away from. Help me understand what is so terrible about staying here for another three or four months."

"You're new." She sniffed. "You don't know what it's like. The men are pricks. The women are catty, and William—" She arched a brow in my direction. "That man has spoken to me as if I was a piece of toilet tissue on the terminal floor at LAX. Granted, he's an asshole across the board, so at least it's not a racial thing. But I'm too old for that. I'm getting seven-figure offers shoved in my face every time I turn around. My life is too short and my 401(k) is too padded to accept working for William."

She was right. I was new, but two weeks here had been enough for me to understand exactly what she was dealing with. The affable gentleman by Cat's side had a temper. During this morning's team meetings, he'd destroyed any warm emotions I'd nurtured in our opening meditative affirmations when he'd ripped the newest testing report into pieces and addressed the group as "a bunch of overpaid morons."

"What if I kept William away from you?" I suggested. "You can skip the team meetings. Complete your final action items on your own. Work from home two days a week."

She cocked an eyebrow. "You're going to keep William from speaking to me? Impossible."

She was probably right, but I plowed ahead, ready to use the thin envelope in my jacket pocket if necessary.

Maybe it wouldn't be. Maybe this alone would be the key to getting Marilyn to stay. I hoped it would.

She was already shaking her head, as if she could hear my inner monologue. "My decision is made. I'm leaving in a week. He's lucky I'm sticking out my two weeks." She pushed to her feet. "I have to get back to my work."

I reached in my pocket and pulled out the envelope. "I have one more thing to discuss."

"Like I said, my decision's made."

"Marilyn." I met her eyes. "Trust me, you'll want to hear this."

"Spit it out, Neena."

"I know about Jeff." Four short words that tasted so good on my tongue. I had practiced different ways to deliver the blow and heard the ring of victory in my response despite my best attempt to keep it out.

She didn't move. Didn't slump with defeat or stagger back to her chair. She didn't blink or quake or react in any way at all. Her gaze swung toward me with the slow and practiced control of a woman who had been through it all. "Jeff's dead," she said.

I met her eyes squarely. "I can attest from my visit with him yesterday, he's not."

~

Forty-five minutes later, I watched as Marilyn revoked her resignation via email, the "Send" button clicked with a hostile amount of contempt. I didn't care. I had secured my job, and her four kids and husband would continue thinking that her fifth son had died in early labor and wasn't living in a convalescent home, blowing out the candles on his thirteenth birthday cake without a single family member in sight.

I brought the paperwork to William, quietly entering the sleek and sophisticated space that showed a sliver of the ocean. Everything was glass—the door I pushed to come inside, the walls between us and the adjacent office, the floor-to-ceiling windows that separated the room from a fifty-foot drop. There would be no quickies on the desk in this office, not unless he wanted the entire team to watch.

He glanced at the paperwork without lifting his hands from his computer keyboard, then nodded. "Fine. Close the door on your way out."

The dismissal would have made a regular woman bristle with irritation, but I only wanted more. A psychologist would have blamed the unhealthy pull to rejection on my father, but I knew what a ticket into this world would cost me. Dirty, underhanded deals. Slow and relentless seduction. A twisted contortion that might break my spine in two but would roll me higher and higher on the rungs of society until I was where I belonged, looking down on women like my mother and Cat Winthorpe and in complete puppet-master control over men like my father and William.

It would come. Already, I was closer.

CHAPTER 9

CAT

William quietly worked the Aston Martin's stick shift, his hair ruffling in the breeze as he took the curve leading up to the small cliffside restaurant. The night was silent, the wind soft.

I turned in the seat to face him, admiring his profile in the dusk, the blue glow from the dash faintly lighting his distinguished features. I fell in love with those features my junior year in college as I peeked at him over the top of my computer screen from the corner of the interns' room. We'd all been slightly terrified of him, his rare visits to our room punctuated by lots of cursing and—more often than not—the firing of whoever had screwed up. Our turnover rate was insane, and crying was common among the interns, everyone tense and dreading the moment that they'd invariably make a mistake.

My own misstep had come just before Christmas. Our fellow students had all flown home, their social media accounts full of Christmas trees, ice skating, and spiked eggnog. A dwindling group of five had stayed to meet the increased workload of a corporate takeover that William was masterminding. I'd spent six hours on a spreadsheet and, at some point in the process, sorted a column without including all the fields—an error that completely invalidated every other cell in the spreadsheet. Four hours later, relieved to finally be through with the task, I'd added the spreadsheet into the shared drive without noticing the error.

When William burst into our room, I snapped to attention, watching as he carried a printout over to our supervisor's desk and set it before her, stabbing the page with one finger. I heard my name and straightened, steeling myself as she pointed in my direction. His gaze swept over the room and stopped on me.

It was our first eye contact, and I felt empowered by it, rising to my feet as he strode toward me. His expensive dress shoes clicked along the tile, and his eyes were as dark as his suit. He'd stopped before my desk and held the spreadsheet up. "I suppose this piece of worthless shit came from you?"

I don't know why I smiled. It was something we'd dissected over champagne on our honeymoon and in late-night walks down memory lane. I should have been terrified. I should have stammered out an apology. But instead I met his eyes with a smile he later described as cocky and sexy as hell. I smiled and . . . stunningly enough, William Winthorpe, destroyer of companies and notorious prick . . . began to smile back at me.

I came to work the next morning and found a first-class ticket to Banff in my desk drawer. I lost my virginity to him in a mountainside cabin on that trip. When we returned to San Francisco, I packed up my apartment and moved into William's sleek downtown condo without a minute's hesitation.

He tapped the horn at a passing opossum, and I held on as he swerved.

"I heard about Marilyn." I captured a loose tendril of hair and cupped it against my neck. "She's definitely staying?"

"For now." He accelerated through the turn, his gaze on the road. "Neena talked to her. Brought her to her senses."

There was no doubt that we needed Marilyn. She'd spent months working on our FDA trials and had developed a key relationship with the testing contacts. Losing her would set us back six months, easily. "She's probably being heavily recruited." There weren't many scientists with her pedigree. Add in that she was black and female and she was probably getting a fresh job offer every day. It was impressive that Neena had changed Marilyn's mind, and without offering her more compensation or perks.

"She is." He glanced at me. "Neena thinks I need to work on my management style." He wasn't happy with the assessment. I could see it in the way his second hand joined his first on the steering wheel, the set of his mouth, the rigid line of his long body as he hunched forward in the seat. My husband, for all his confidence, was also impossibly hard on himself.

"I don't know about that," I said carefully. "You're a genius. Without you, there wouldn't even be a Winthorpe Tech, or a Winthorpe Capital to fund it."

"She said the team hates me."

I let out a slow breath. "Wow. Diving right in with the heavy punches." She'd been there only a few weeks. Couldn't she have eased in with the attack? "Hates? No. They don't *hate* you."

He slowed, the restaurant just ahead, and pulled over on the shoulder, putting the car into park and turning the ignition off. A cool breeze came, and a shiver of chill went through me. "I told her that I didn't care if they hate me. I'm not in the business of being liked."

But he did care. I knew that he cared. He just didn't care enough to fix it. "Does she have a solution?" If she didn't, he would have fired her. You don't bring problems to my husband. You bring a problem *and* a solution. Otherwise, you're useless.

"She wants to work with me on my style. And on my"—he paused and squinted, trying to think of the term—"personal development."

"Screw that." The words snapped out of me, and he glanced over, surprised. "You're William Winthorpe. You don't need an egocentric housewife from some San Francisco gutter telling you how to lead your company."

He chuckled and found my hand, squeezing it. "You've been a little vocal yourself, Cat, about the way I've handled some things in the past."

"That's because sometimes you're a jerk." I twisted in the seat to face him. "And you're blunt. But you're also the smartest man in every room. I don't want you to dilute yourself to try to salvage someone's feelings. This is business. They're all adults. They can take it." My hand tightened on his. "And don't compare me to her just because we both came from nothing. I know you—she doesn't. I built Winthorpe beside you. She didn't."

"Hey." He leaned forward and cupped the back of my neck, his hand stealing into my hair. "I'd never put you in a category with her. Nobody can hold a candle to you." He pulled me toward him, and our mouths met, our kiss gentle at first, then stronger. More violent. I kissed him as if I were desperate, and he clutched me to him as if I gave him strength.

He was horrible to everyone, but not with me. With me, he was vulnerable and kind. Generous and loving. He plucked the good things, like petals on a rose, and kept them in his pocket, then showered me with them at night. No one was going to change that about him. Especially not her.

~

"I'm confused . . . ," Kelly said slowly, her glossy purple nails picking through the Menlo prep school uniform catalog. She paused at one ensemble, and I shook my head. "I thought you were happy that she was there. I thought you said that William needed someone to keep morale up and improve the"—she lifted her gaze to the sky—"cohesion? Is that what you said?"

"I did, and I *do* see the value in her sticking Band-Aids on hurt feelings and putting inspiration posters up in the bathrooms, but I don't want her screwing with William." I spun the notebook in front of me around and tapped on a girl's white tuxedo shirt with three-quarter-length sleeves. "This is cute."

"Hmm." She peeled off a gold sticker and stuck it to the item. "Keep looking. You don't want her screwing with him or you don't want her screwing him?"

I grimaced. "Well, preferably both. But the latter isn't a possibility or I wouldn't have her working there at all."

She looked up from the catalog. "Spoken as a woman who hasn't yet discovered an affair. Trust me, Cat. There's always a possibility." She moved aside a few pages, collecting the stack together. "Think of Corinne Woodsen. Her husband slept with that aardvark of a woman with the wooden leg."

"It wasn't a wooden leg. She had knee-replacement surgery. The brace was temporary."

"Well, it wasn't sexy."

"Just because Corinne Woodsen's husband can't keep his hands to himself doesn't mean that I need to be paranoid over a new employee of William's. She's married," I pointed out. "I'm telling you. It's fine."

"Uh-huh." She moved two fabric swatches to the middle of the table. "I'm going with these patterns, but in the school colors."

I reviewed the options and gave a supportive nod. "Looks great."

She moved beside me and thumbed through the narrowed-down list of options for the uniform shirts. "How much digging did you do into her?"

"Neena?" I shrugged. "I checked to see if they had applied for membership to the club."

"And?"

"They toured it but didn't put in an application. I'm guessing the initiation fee scared them off."

"Hell, that almost scared *us* off." Kelly laughed, as if the six-figure initiation fee had ever been a concern for her or Josh. "And where did she work before?"

"Plymouth Industries. Apparently they loved her there. I read the recommendation letter from Mr. Plymouth. He couldn't say enough great things about her or how much they'd miss her."

"Well, Josh knows Ned. Says he's a total hard-ass, so she must have some sort of skill."

"Which is why we hired her." I picked up my bag, mentally done with the conversation. "Look, I love you, but I'm going to run."

"Okay." She kissed my cheek and gave me a warm hug. "We leave Thursday, so let's grab lunch before then. And wait a minute." Walking over to the bookshelf, she pulled out a thin binder and set it on the counter. Flipping through the pages of business cards, she paused, then worked a white card free of its plastic holder. "Here."

I examined the gold-embossed print on the card. Tom Beck. Beck Private Investigations. "Is this the guy who followed Josh?"

"Shhh . . ." She glanced into the hall to make sure her teenagers weren't around. "Yes. He's good. Really good."

"I'm not having anyone follow—"

"It's not for William. Lord knows that man is head over heels for you. But if I were you, I'd have Tom do some digging on Neena. She's your next-door neighbor and your employee. You should find out more about who you're bringing into your life."

"I don't know . . ." Even as I wavered, I dropped the card into the open neck of my purse.

She shrugged. "Just keep his info and think about it. And if you do call, tell him that I sent you. He'll take good care of you."

I gave her a hug and tried to dismiss the idea of hiring a private investigator to look into William's newest employee. He'd be furious. HR would have already done a criminal background check and drug test. William would accuse me of paranoia and snooping.

It was a crazy idea. But then again, what harm could it do? And how would he ever find out?

CHAPTER 10

Neena

With the phone pressed to my ear, I rounded the far end of the lake and glanced at the Winthorpe building, the reflection of water and sky glimmering against its all-glass facade. The first floor was retail, the second Winthorpe Capital. Tech occupied the third and fourth floors, and the top was under construction—rumored to be the future home of Winthorpe Development.

Matt was in the third minute of a long and drawn-out story about propane-tank relocations. I cut him off as I entered the north section of the trail, and the view of Winthorpe disappeared behind the row of cypress trees. "I have to run. I'll call you in a few hours. I love you."

He returned the sentiment, and I ended the call and worked the cell phone into the side pocket of my bag.

I did love Matt. No matter where our marriage and relationship would eventually go, I would always love him—if for no other reason than the fact that he was heartbreakingly in love with me. I could screw William Winthorpe on the middle of Matt's desk and he'd still take me back. Beg me to stay. Bring me flowers and believe that I deserved them. With that sort of unwavering loyalty and security, why wouldn't I stray?

My first affair was so innocent. Lust plus opportunity equals sex. It was quick, dirty, and pointless, the excitement fading as soon as the man returned to his twenty-two-year-old girlfriend.

The next lasted longer. A series of midday meetings, my enjoyment heightening as the affair grew deeper. When it ended, I immediately returned to the hunt, addicted to the tumultuous risk.

Matt's younger and better-looking brother was next, and the close proximity fueled my arousal to new levels. After our first time together, he cried, dismayed at what he'd done—and I'd never felt so empowered. After all, what better ego boost than to know that a man had risked his most crucial relationship to be with you?

I watched as William Winthorpe rounded the bend in the trail, his head dropped in thought. He was a man of habit, and I quickened my pace, wanting to meet him before he moved past the services center that housed, among other things, a restaurant.

William was a man with everything to lose. The perfect wife. The perfect life. The reputation of the community, of his businesses, and of his charity foundation. Would he risk any of it for me?

Mark had been a feather in my cap. Ned Plymouth, a million-dollar payday. An affair with William Winthorpe would overshadow them both by leaps and bounds. At just the thought, my thighs tightened, my breathing shallowed, and I struggled to walk slowly, casually, as the distance between us shortened.

"Neena." He came to a sudden stop. "What are you doing out here?"

"Needed to clear my head." I glanced around, pleased to see that the path was empty. "The fresh air helps."

He chuckled. "Yeah."

I nodded to the sleek glass building beside us, a smaller version of the Winthorpe tower, and one that contained a small bistro. "I was actually about to stop in and grab something to eat. Have you had lunch?" I knew he hadn't. His schedule, like everything else in his life, was precise.

A long walk at eleven thirty, followed by lunch. Afternoon meetings, then home by seven. Tick. Tock. Every day. Was the monotony killing him yet?

"Not yet." He glanced at the building, hesitating.

"They have a killer grilled-cheese sandwich," I offered. "You have to try it." I took a few steps backward toward the entrance and gave him a teasing smile. "Come on . . ."

"Grilled cheese?" He squinted at me. "I thought you were no carb."

"I like to cheat every once in a while." I winked at him and could tell the moment when his resolve wavered. The fun side always got to them. Dark and tempting was intriguing, but light and happy paired with breathless admiration was the strong cocktail that fed bad decisions. An unexpected combination of the two and I'd have him naked in my bed within the month.

He glanced at his watch, and I turned away, striding up the hill and toward the building, my best asset showcased to perfection in my three-inch heels. "Come on!" I called out, not giving him the chance to decline.

By the time I reached for the door handle, he was there, his hand on the small of my back, ushering me inside with the manners of a true gentleman. I bit the inside of my cheek and tried to hold back my grin.

~

My father once held a drinking contest with me. Death in the Afternoon was the drink. Getting to leave the bar was the prize. Winning was accomplished by continuing to drink until the other passed out or vomited. I was thirteen, and the bartender liked my tits. He told my father that on our third drink, and a meaty grope of them paid for our fourth. I vomited ten minutes later, my hair held back by that same bartender as his hands squeezed each tiny breast as if pumping them for milk.

Breast implants were one of the first things Matt paid for, my second augmentation and size upgrade footed by Ned. I had lost all sensation in my nipples from the surgeries, yet I could still remember the rough pinch of that bartender's hands.

"Did you want to sit in the bar?" William followed my gaze, which was stuck to the bar, the memories of the drinking contest still raw in my mind.

"Ah, no." I ripped my gaze away from the dark space and quickly nodded at a table by the window. "How about that one?"

"Works for me."

We settled in, an awkward silence falling, and I forced a self-deprecating wince. "I'm sorry. I'm nervous."

"Nervous?" He laughed, the rigid tension leaving his posture, and smoothed down the front of his tie. "Why?"

"I don't know. You're very powerful. And, quite frankly, brilliant. I didn't realize how much so until I had a chance to see you in action, at the office." I picked at the edge of my menu, then blushed. "It's intimidating."

"We've had meetings before. You never seemed intimidated then."

"Well, I don't know." I laughed. "It's different outside the office. No glass walls to hide behind."

He smiled. "The walls were actually Cat's idea. She liked the open feel that they created."

"The open feel?" I winced. "I'm not sure that's how the staff sees them."

He raised an eyebrow in question.

"There's just no privacy. It feels like they're under a microscope."

"They've told you that?"

"Yes," I lied. "Several have mentioned it. I'm sure Cat meant well, but it's hard to develop a feeling of intimacy and trust when everyone can see what you're doing, all the time." I met his eyes. "Don't you ever want to . . . I don't know . . . relax in your office? Kick off your shoes?

Loosen your tie?" I let my voice grow husky, and he dropped the eye contact, his focus moving to his menu as his jaw tightened.

The waiter approached, and I sat back in my seat, letting William off the hook as we placed our orders.

～

He liked the grilled cheese. I could see it in the way he relaxed into his seat, a grin widening across his handsome face as he ordered a beer. The sun streamed through the window, lighting up our table, and I felt, for the first time since we moved into the Atherton house, deeper possibilities. He could fall for me. This could be more than just a game. This could be real. This could be my future, the one I'd been dreaming of. For a moment, I let myself sink into the potential scenario.

Vacations in Tahiti.

Second homes in Aspen.

A full-time staff, dedicated to fluffing my pillows and fetching my coffee.

"I'm glad we did this. You were right. The grilled cheese . . ." He nodded in approval, and I fought not to wipe a crumb off the edge of his mouth. "It was amazing. Honestly, I don't think I've had a grilled cheese in a decade, maybe longer."

I stretched, sticking out my chest as I ran a hand along my flat stomach. "I know. It's the butter they use. It's lethal." The buttered bread was one of the reasons I'd be vomiting it up as soon as I returned to Winthorpe Tech. The number of calories in that sandwich would take three hours of intense cardio to burn off. But for now, I played the cool and carefree woman, grinning playfully at him over my own bottle of beer, as if twelve hundred calories weren't justifiable grounds for panic. "Sometime I'll have to make you my french toast. It's hard to say that it compares with that, but . . ." I tilted my head. "It kinda does."

"Well—" His phone rang, and he glanced at the display, then swore. "I've got to take this. Here." Sliding to his feet, he hurriedly pulled out his wallet and withdrew some cash and placed it on the table. "I'll see you back at the office."

"Sure, I—" I abandoned the sentence as he walked away through the tables, the phone to his ear, his voice too low to hear. Was it Cat? Irritation burned through me at the abrupt interruption to our meal, to the first real conversation we'd been able to have.

I stood and moved toward the bathroom, the grilled-cheese sandwich already fighting its way up my throat.

It didn't matter. I had plenty of time.

CHAPTER 11

N E E N A

Every wife in this neighborhood was the same. All spoiled girls who grew up with Daddy's money, then married Daddy's friends, then popped out future heirs like a Pez dispenser stuck to open. Rich all their lives and absolutely unspectacular.

I deserved all this so much more than any of them. I stepped onto the Vanguards' back porch and inhaled the scent of juniper and fresh-cut grass, scanning the backyard for a glimpse of William and Cat. I was getting close. Two years ago, we would have spent a Saturday afternoon staring at the television screen, but now we were at Josh and Kelly Vanguard's going-away party, the invite as easily tossed out as candy from a float. Further proof that proximity was half the battle in this world. I elbowed Matt in the soft part of his gut as he reached for a miniature cupcake display. He pulled his hand back.

"No sugar," I hissed. "And that's Josh Vanguard right there." I nodded toward the contractor, who was speaking to Perla Osterman's husband. "Go introduce yourself."

He went, wiping his hand on his thigh, and I flinched at the sweaty handprint it left. He hesitated on the outskirts of the two men, his thumb tapping nervously on the side of his slacks, and I fought the urge to shove him into their midst. While there were many things I loved about my husband, he was so socially timid. While I had pored over social media accounts and Menlo club membership rosters, learning the major players in Atherton, he had dragged his feet in even attending this party.

Josh Vanguard noticed him hovering and moved back, opening up their conversation, and stuck his hand out, introducing himself. I breathed a sigh of relief as Matt stepped forward and smiled, their grips connecting. I had coached him on Josh's current projects and the possibility of a joint venture between him and William. If Winthorpe Development fully materialized, they would need site work and clearing. There would be a continual stream of dollar signs that could head in Matt's—our—direction.

A boy in bright-blue swim trunks sprinted around me and launched himself into the pool, feet lifted high, arms outstretched. A future CEO or board member. He'd be a Stanford legacy, access his trust at age twenty-five, and probably marry one of the brats at this party. Inherit a turnkey lifestyle without ever understanding what true sacrifice was.

"It's Neena, right?"

I turned to see a wife, clad in all white, a red scarf tied around her neck. She had the pixie haircut adored by women who were on the verge of lesbianism or had given up on pleasing their husbands. I plastered my smile into place. "Yes. Dr. Neena Ryder. And you are?"

"Cynthia Cole. We're just down the street, on Greenoaks. Cat says you're in the old Baker place."

I wasn't sure if she meant old in terms of age or prior inhabitant, and my smile grew thin. "That's right."

"Well, I hope you join the club. We'd love to have you and Mike as members."

"Matt," I corrected her. "And we're looking at the club now."

"Oh, good." She leaned in, and I watched as her mojito tipped to one side, a bit of it sloshing out. "You know, it's hard to connect with people otherwise. We just moved into the neighborhood a few years ago, and I'm not going to lie, it was a little cold at first. I told Bradley—that's my husband, Bradley Cole." She pointed to a man by the back doors. "I told him that I wanted to move, to find another neighborhood, and he said, 'Cyn-thi-ah, just join the club.'" She lifted up her hands in a shrug. "And he was right!"

"That's wonderful." I nodded, unsure of where this sales spiel was headed but 100 percent certain that I would not be able to convince my cheap husband to drop the quarter of a million dollars for the initiation fee. Buying this house had already been out of his wheelhouse, and he was shooting down my renovation ideas the moment they were brought up.

"Anyway"—she patted my arm—"if you need a cup of sugar or anything, just call me. I'll have one of the staff run a bag down to you."

I hesitated, unsure if that was a joke, and when she laughed, I joined in, feeling like a caricature. I caught a glimpse of William, moving into the house, and stopped. "Cynthia, excuse me. I just saw someone I need to say hi to."

"Sure, sure." She lifted her mojito, and there was an edge of annoyance in her tone, as if I had beaten her to the punch of leaving. "Go ahead."

I moved through the house, ignoring the clusters of conversations that I stepped around. William wasn't in the front foyer, and I passed the coat check and pulled open the heavy front door, peeking out.

It was peaceful and quiet, and through the twitter of birds, I heard the faint sound of arguing. Stepping out, I eased the door closed, blocking out the sound of the party.

"You need to leave. You're embarrassing me and yourself." William's deep voice carried, and I walked down the front stairs of the home carefully, keeping my steps soft. I paused in the shade of the porch, surprised to see William toe to toe with Harris Adisa, his hand gripping the front of the scientist's baby-blue collared shirt. They were almost identical in height, though William was toned and athletic, his biceps developed, his shoulders strong. Harris sagged before him, his smile slipping as he stumbled to one side and said something too softly for me to catch.

William shook his head, and Harris shoved at his chest. The men broke apart, and William glanced over his shoulder toward the valet, then swung in my direction. I stepped back, hiding behind the pillar, and held my breath, hoping he hadn't seen me.

"Get in the car. The driver will take you home."

I moved deeper into the shadows, trying to get another glimpse at the men, and almost fell, my brand-new sandal catching the edge of the steps. I grabbed the column for stabilization and glanced up, my gaze connecting with William's. *Crap.* He grabbed Harris's shoulder and squeezed, then pushed him down into the open door of the Town Car.

I turned, suddenly anxious to be away from their private conversation and back in the party. While our grilled-cheese lunch early this week had certainly improved our dynamic, I was still wary of crossing him when he was on the warpath.

"Neena."

I climbed the steps toward the front door, hoping it wouldn't be obvious that I had heard his call.

"Neena!"

I stopped.

"Come here."

Come here. He was a man of few words, but they carried the weight of stones. I turned and retraced my path down the steps.

William's face was dark. "You make a habit of spying on people, Neena?"

"I wasn't. I—um—just stepped out for some fresh air." I looked back at the house, the doors closed, no one privy to our conversation.

The shiny sedan passed, and I imagined Harris watching us from inside. I glanced back at William, who settled against the side of a

Lamborghini as if he owned it. My tension eased as he sighed, his head dropping back, his strong profile looking to the sky.

"Harris is a little on edge," he said quietly. "Unfortunately, he chose to relieve that stress at this party."

"He seemed okay. A little tipsy, but"—I shrugged—"everyone in there is drinking."

"It's not that. He . . . ah . . ." He scratched the back of his neck, and if I didn't know better, I'd think he was embarrassed. "He's drunk and beelining straight for any blonde in sight. Waitstaff, wives . . ." His gaze settled on me. "Potentially fellow employees."

"Oh." I turned over the information, warming at the protective look in his eye. "I thought he was married."

"Come on, Neena. You've been around long enough to know that a ring on a man's finger doesn't mean much. Especially not in this world." He studied me. "I want you to be careful when working with him. Skip any one-on-one meetings."

I moved closer, crossing my arms over my chest in a gesture that would press my breasts together and up against the low neck of my wrap dress. "That's fine. To be honest, we haven't exactly hit it off."

His eyes found my enhanced cleavage, and there was a moment when the powerful William Winthorpe lost his train of thought. "Well, I—"

I waited, and he fell silent, visibly struggling to pull his gaze away from my breasts. I laughed, and he winced.

"I'm sorry. I blame it all on Kelly's mojitos. They're almost straight rum."

"Yeah, I've stuck to wine. And no worries. I'm honored." I blushed and fought to keep the victory from my features, my heartbeat increasing at the cat-and-mouse game. "They're a little, uh, neglected at times. The attention is nice."

He didn't respond, but I could see the processing of information. It would be stored. Cataloged. Referenced every time he got a glimpse of my cleavage. He'd start thinking of them in terms of being needy. Sensitive. Craving. I had studied personality profiles until I knew each by heart, and he wasn't the sort of man to go after the slut. He'd want a conquest. A discreet housewife who wasn't sexually satisfied. One who would worship him while keeping her mouth shut and her knees parted—but for him and him alone. If I decided to take this risk, I could play that role with the best of them.

"Look." He glanced toward the house. "I'd prefer you keep this to yourself. I'd like to keep the Winthorpe Tech reputation as clean as possible during—"

I placed my hand on his arm. "Don't worry about it. I'm good at keeping secrets." I held his gaze and hoped he saw the opening in the words.

"Are you?" His gaze dropped to my lips, then flipped back to my eyes.

My stomach tightened in anticipation. So close. Chess pieces, moving into place. But I had to be careful. Very, very, careful. "My loyalties are with you. If you want something to stay between us, it will."

"Good to know." He straightened, and I backed away before he had a chance to.

Halfway up the porch, I paused, turning to face him. "You know, I've been working with every employee of Winthorpe, except for you."

A lock of hair fell over his forehead, a break in the precise exterior he always presented. "There's a reason for that. I don't need any help."

"Well, just think about it." I held his gaze. "Some one-on-one sessions might do us both a lot of good."

The front door swung open behind me, and I turned, flinching when Cat Winthorpe stepped out on the porch.

"Oh, Neena." She brightened and gave me a sunny smile. "Have you seen William? Teddy Formont is looking for him."

I turned, but the Lamborghini was alone, her husband gone. I shrugged. "Haven't seen him."

"Damn." She turned back. "I'll head upstairs. If you see him, will you tell him to find Teddy?"

"Absolutely." I smiled as she turned, her dark hair bouncing as she breezed through the door, off to find her husband.

Compared to me, she was bland. A pretty face with nothing behind the facade. William saw it, just as I did.

It was why he was edging toward me, calculating the risks and weighing them against the temptation.

Her blandness was why I would win.

Neena

Now

The detective peered at me over the edge of her black notepad. "I must say, in the last two years, you've become one of our most interesting residents. Your husband and you started in a conservative three-bedroom in Palo Alto but eighteen months later made a sizable upgrade and moved into Atherton. Is that correct?"

I nodded.

"And you work at Winthorpe Tech—or rather, used to work at Winthorpe Tech."

"That's correct." I fought to keep my mouth from twisting into a snarl.

"And prior to Winthorpe, you were at Plymouth Industries." She paused, and I kept my mouth shut. "You started out as the executive assistant for Ned Plymouth, but were promoted to"—she flipped through her notes—"team business coach after a few months." She pronounced the title as if it were distasteful. "Is that correct?"

"Yes." If she thought I was going to elaborate on that, she was wrong.

"Did you receive a raise when you were promoted?"

"Yes." I pulled at the neck of my shirt, irritated with this line of questioning and well aware of what she was about to imply. The promotion had been quick, my raise substantial. Detective Cullen hadn't been the only person to draw jagged lines between the actions—she was just the first one uncouth enough to verbalize it.

"Neena, this is going to take a lot longer if you keep giving me single-syllable answers." The detective sighed, as if this investigation was taking up too much of her time.

She probably had a granola bar to finish eating, or a lesbian wife in cargo pants who was waiting for her at a coffee shop, expectantly tapping her Mickey Mouse watch.

"Elaborate. How much did your salary increase when you were promoted?"

"I don't know offhand." I shifted in the hard plastic seat. "I would say that my income doubled."

"More like tripled," she mused, scanning a document that looked like my tax return. "And you maintained that level of salary when you moved to Winthorpe, correct?"

"It's industry standard for motivational coaches. We're well paid because we deliver results."

"Yeah, I'm worried that wasn't the only thing you were delivering." She closed the folder on my financials. "Why did you leave Plymouth Industries?"

I warred over how to respond, unsure if she knew the full story or if she was fishing. "I wanted to move into the tech sector. Experience new things."

"Interesting . . . because we spoke to Ned Plymouth." She crossed her arms and set the scaly nubs of her elbows on top of the papers.

Of course they did. Beneath the table, I dug the toe of my sneaker into the floor.

"Ned says that you were fired."

"I have a recommendation letter from Ned that raves about my job performance." It was a weak attempt in a battle that was already lost, but I still stood my ground.

"Ned says that it's a lie. Ned, in fact, had a lot to say about you, Dr. Neena Ryder." She raised one bushy eyebrow with a confidence that I hated.

Yeah, I bet ol' Ned did.

PART 2

JUNE

THREE MONTHS EARLIER

CHAPTER 12

CAT

"I just don't understand where they're at." Neena craned her neck, trying to see around a sunscreen-covered family who had stopped right beside our cabana.

"Are you worried they'll get lost?" I kicked the towel loose, letting my feet get some sun. "Relax. William has a homing beacon to me. Plus, they're big boys. They can manage themselves at the pool." Though, if any pool was a danger zone for wealthy men, it was the Menlo country club's. William was easily recognizable and understood to be off-limits. Matt was a fresh face, and the single vultures scattered around this pool wouldn't care if he was balding and a little chubby. What they *would* be scared off by, and why Neena had absolutely no need for concern, was the guest wristband he had on. Neena was displaying hers proudly, unaware that it was a giant "Not Rich Enough to Be Here" red flag.

She rattled her drink, the ice clattering against the glass, and I tuned out the sound, focusing on the music that floated by on the cool breeze. I reached out and turned the flame of the tabletop heater higher.

"There!" Her chair banged against mine, and I cracked open one eye to see her at the edge of the cabana. "They're by the towel stand."

"Good for them," I mumbled. "Maybe they'll grab you another drink on the way back."

"What are they doing over there?" She cupped her hand over her eyes, shielding the sun. "Oh my God."

The dread in her voice spoke of plagues and famine, nothing that could possibly be happening inside the gates of the country club. I took a sip of my apple-and-spinach juice and considered the lunch options on today's pool menu.

"They're literally surrounded by women. Cat, *look*."

"So?" I made a half-hearted attempt to see our husbands, then adjusted the pillow under my head and exhaled. William and I should have come here alone. I could be reading the latest bestseller instead of listening to the insecure ramblings of a semidrunk wife who would go into jealous territory in three . . . two . . . one . . .

Silence fell, and I was pleasantly surprised at being wrong. I risked a glance up. Neena was standing ramrod straight, staring across the pool deck, with her giant breasts almost hanging out of her skimpy red bikini. Muttering under her breath, she crossed her arms, shivering a little in her spot away from the heater.

"Relaxxxx," I intoned, my patience running thin. The more time I spent with Neena, the more her insecurities were beginning to drive me crazy. Every move seemed to be a calculated attempt to thwart an opponent who didn't exist. It was exhausting to be around her, and I was planning a slow withdrawal from the friendship I had carelessly begun. Our first solo activity—brunch last weekend—had been a painful process that had reminded me of why I had stopped taking on new friends. I could only listen to someone brag about themselves for so long before I needed to see a genuine side. Neena had yet to show me one.

"Matt's coming back this way," she announced. "William's still talking to them." She glanced at me with a look of warning.

"I honestly couldn't care less." I fluffed the pillow of her chair, 100 percent confident in William's ability to thwart flirtation. "Sit down. You're giving me a headache."

She turned away from the view and cupped an insecure hand over her four-pack of a stomach as she sat down in the chair. "I don't understand how you aren't more concerned about William."

"He's not going anywhere," I drawled. "And you have nothing to worry about, either." I couldn't see why, but Matt *adored* her. Doted on her. Spoiled her. It was sweet, if not a little sad. All that love, and I had yet to see her reward or return any of his affections.

I studied her as she pulled out a compact mirror and painstakingly applied a dab of moisturizing SPF cream to the soft skin under her eyes. "You guys have been married, what? Twenty years?"

She nodded, then ran her finger over her lips.

"Two decades is a long time. He's obviously head over heels for you. What are you concerned about?" I kept my tone light, hoping not to offend her and genuinely interested in her response.

"I'm *not* worried about Matt. I was watching out for you. Are you telling me that William hasn't ever looked at another woman?" She shot a dirty look toward a blonde mother of four who turned onto her stomach two cabanas over.

I fought to ignore the bristle of irritation that ran up my spine. "William is loyal, always has been. You don't need to watch my husband for me."

She gave me a sharp look. "Cat, there's nothing wrong with having an awareness of potential risks. If you tempt fate long enough, something will happen. It's a biological fact that . . ."

I took a sip of my juice and tuned her out, biting off the urge to tell her what I thought of her opinions. She certainly had a lot of them. Maybe that's what a life coach was. Someone paid to dish out opinions about every part of your, well, life. And, according to the whispers I'd heard, that's what she really was. A life coach–slash–admin assistant who had somehow jumped the fence into corporate territory and greatly inflated her prices with the transition and title change.

I watched as Matt approached and wondered if she was as motivating with our Winthorpe Tech team as she was with him. Matt certainly seemed happy, his eyes glued to her large breasts as he skirted around the end of a chaise lounge and climbed the steps to our cabana. No side glances at Terri Ingel, who was slowly performing the backstroke through the heated water. No quick smile to the nineteen-year-old lifeguard.

He entered the cabana, and Neena snapped her fingers, then pointed to the empty lounger as if instructing a dog.

He sat.

I glanced at Neena to see her response, but her attention was on the other end of the pool. I followed it and found William, who was tugging off his shirt and wading into the pool, his abs well defined as he moved into the water.

"I think you're right," I said, setting my empty glass beside me on the table. "There's no point in tempting fate. Not if you can eliminate the potential risks."

CHAPTER 13

NEENA

A week later, I squeezed through the Winthorpes' bushes at their thinnest point, jogged across their beach-pebble border, around the perfect planters, and hit their driveway at a run. Sprinting up the side steps, I unlatched the courtyard door, moved into the small garden, and breezed past the hibiscus blooms and bench. My first time in the space, I had inwardly burned at the arched openings, the water feature that cascaded down the far wall, the white brick floor. Our side entrance had a broken screen door and a pot of geraniums that hid an extra key. I'd been meaning to change the locks to one like Cat's, a touch keypad that had a camera, held a hundred combinations, and could be remotely locked and unlocked from her phone. All useless, considering her remarks that she never locked her doors.

I'd tucked away that tidbit for later. One day. Someday. I pressed the doorbell and knocked urgently on the glass window of the door. Waiting, I looked down at the monogrammed "William & Cat" mat, then wiped my shoes on it, right on top of Cat's name.

I was growing closer to both William and her, my patience almost ragged from the tap-dance routine that it took to arrange casual get-togethers. Still, I was getting there. I'd finagled our double dinner date, last weekend's pool day, and yesterday, a private brunch with just Cat and me. It had gone well. She'd laughed at my jokes, empathized with my early struggles, and seemed interested in becoming friends. I had big plans to use that naivete to my advantage.

"Neena?" Cat opened the door. "Is everything okay?"

"Sort of." I wrung my hands together. "Can I borrow William really quickly? There's a bird in the house."

"A bird?" Cat gave me a blank look. "Can't you just shoo him out?"

William appeared in the doorway behind Cat. "Morning."

Damn, he sounded good. Husky. The kind of voice that could be on whiskey ads or staff a 900 number. I smiled at him, then quickly pinched my features into a worried frown. "Can you come over real quick? There's this bird—it's terrifying."

"Of course." He turned away. "Come on in. I'll put some shoes on."

Cat stepped back, opening the door. "William," she protested, "send over one of the staff. You've got that call."

I peeked past her, surprised to see their kitchen empty, no staff in sight. Maybe they let everyone off on the weekends. So kind of Queen Cat.

"I can be quick." William pulled on a sneaker and yanked at the laces, quickly tying a knot. "Where's Matt?"

"At a job site." I sniffed the air. "Is something burning?"

"No," Cat snipped, at the same time as William said, "It's toast."

"He likes it well done," she explained, then shot William a look that dared him to argue.

"I do." He grinned and bent over, giving her a quick kiss on the cheek. "The crispier, the better."

That was bullshit. At our joint dinner date, he'd gotten it lightly toasted. I'd watched as he had spread butter on it, noticing how he'd done it one-handed, the other arm hanging over Cat's chair, his fingers gently rubbing along her bare shoulders.

"If you give me a minute, I can get dressed." Cat looked down at her silk pajamas, the shorts and tank top set barely appropriate for this conversation, much less a jaunt across their property and over to ours. In contrast, I was dressed for a workout in skintight leggings that lifted my ass and a low-cut bra top that always attracted attention at the gym.

She'd probably just gotten up. Took her dear sweet time rolling around in bed before strolling downstairs and burning her hardworking husband's toast.

"I've got that call, remember?" His hand ran down her side, and I watched as he gently slapped her butt, the connection of palm against flesh loud. I flushed.

She glanced at me, then smiled up at him. "Okay, but be quick. You've only got fifteen minutes."

I fought the urge to loop my arm through William's and pull him toward my house. "We will," I promised.

～

I eased back through the bushes easily, William's journey a little rougher, given his size. He batted away branches and came loose, brushing off his T-shirt and jeans. I waited for him, bouncing softly on the toes of my shoes.

"What kind of bird is it?" He strode toward the house, all business, but I could see his excitement in the hunch of his posture. I could have smashed the bird against the wall with a broom but had seized the opportunity to get William alone and boost his self-esteem.

It was a Bicknell's thrush, but I shrugged, feigning ignorance. "I don't know. Something small? A pointy beak. Beady eyes."

He headed toward the side entrance, and I hoped he wouldn't compare it to his own. "Where is it?"

I pulled him to the right. "In my bedroom. Let's go in the front door."

Inside, we climbed the curved staircase in silence. At the top, he glanced toward the wall of closed windows. "How'd he get in?"

"I had the balcony doors off the living room open. He must have flown in and found his way upstairs."

I pulled the handles of the double doors, unveiling our master bedroom in its perfectly staged condition. Messy sheets. My perfume still in the air. A lacy bra hanging from the arm of the lounge. I reached for the bra and yanked it off as if I were embarrassed by it. "Sorry. I didn't have a chance to straighten up."

"It's fine." He closed the door behind him, and our eyes met. Time suspended. He cleared his throat and looked away, walking slowly around the room. His brows rose in surprise when he spotted the bird, perched on the top of a lamp. "Oh. He's a little guy. Looks like a thrush."

I shrugged in mock ignorance. "Is that what he is?"

He turned his back on the bird and worked the lock on the balcony doors, swinging them fully open. Ignoring the view, he used his foot to turn down the braces and locked the doors in place. "I'm surprised he flew all the way up here."

I wasn't. I'd spent twenty minutes chasing him up that staircase and into this room.

"Next time, just open these doors. If you had, he'd have flown away by now."

I nodded somberly. "It's just . . . birds terrify me. I have visions of them pecking my eyes out." I shuddered and moved to the farthest corner of the room, away from the bird. It twittered.

He chuckled and took a step toward it, raising his arms and creating enough motion to scare the thrush into flight. It immediately went up and out the door. Problem solved.

"Oh." I snorted. "Well, that was easy."

He stepped out on the balcony and loosened the first door, then the second, pulling them closed.

"Talk about embarrassing." I pulled at the ends of my ponytail, tightening it. "I should have just done it myself. It's just, he was way over there when I saw him, and . . ." I pointed to the far end of the room, then covered my face with my palms, hoping he would come over and comfort me. "I'm sorry."

Ned Plymouth would have had his pants unzipped by now. William Winthorpe only grunted. "It's fine." He touched my shoulder on the way to the bedroom door, which wasn't the warm embrace I was hoping for but was apparently all I would get.

He opened the bedroom door and glanced at his watch. "I've got to get to that call."

So much for my powers of seduction. Not a whiff of hesitation about heading back to Cat. I followed him as he jogged down the stairs. "Thanks for getting it out. I couldn't leave to work out with it up there. I'm heading to that gym they opened on Alma Street. Have you been there?"

He paused. "Uh, no. We have one at the house. Cat has a trainer who meets me there."

"Oh." I frowned. Of course. A private trainer, and here I was, schlepping to the public gym like white trash. "Does Cat ever run? I used to have a jogging partner in Mountain View, but ever since we've been here . . ." I shrugged.

"Cat?" He laughed. "Not unless she's being chased by something."

"Oh." I let the bait dangle and watched to see if he'd bite.

"But I do. There are some trails in the neighborhood, ones that lead up into the canyon. I can show you them sometime. It's a nice long path if you have the stamina for it."

I struggled to stay aloof, my body humming as our eyes met in the dim foyer. "That'd be great. Stamina isn't a problem. I can go for hours."

"Huh." His gaze fell from my eyes and slowly wound down my body before he snapped back into place. "Tell Matt I said hello."

"Will do." I held open the door. "And thanks again."

There was a final moment of eye contact, and then he was gone. *One pawn, taken.*

CHAPTER 14

CAT

The days passed, and my unease with Neena Ryder grew. Wednesday, I stood on our upper balcony and watched my husband and Neena sit by her pool, their chairs turned toward each other. I glanced at my watch, irritated. They both should be at the office, yet they were there as if settled in to stay.

To add to my unease, William never *sat* with employees. He paced. Threatened. Hovered over their workstations. Stood if in meetings. Years ago, his brother had pointed out that William only relaxed and let down his guard with me. He'd called me the William Whisperer, then asked if we could lend him some money.

"Mrs. Winthorpe?" I turned to see the newest maid standing in the doorway, the phone in her hand. "There is a call for you. Your sister."

"I'll have to call her back. Tell her I'm in a meeting."

The woman nodded, and I rested against the railing and watched as William leaned forward, his elbows settling on his knees. His back was to me, and I made a mental note to invest in a pair of binoculars.

Neena was beginning to creep into our lives in a way that made me uncomfortable. We'd had an agonizingly long brunch where she'd made doe eyes at me the entire time. She was dead set on being my friend and had no issues with popping by unannounced or proposing events in front of Matt and William, where I had no opportunity to make an excuse or decline. And as our husbands grew closer, she kept swarming tighter, like a fly you constantly heard but couldn't quite manage to smack.

I turned away from the view and forced myself to enter the house.

I moved down the stairs.

Sat down in my favorite chair in the reading room.

Picked up a magazine and flipped through the pages, struggling not to look back down at my watch.

Seriously, *what* were they talking about? I tossed the magazine onto the ottoman and stood. Pacing before the floor-to-ceiling windows, I cursed the wall of thick hedges between our lots. The privacy, while nice, was screwing with my sanity.

I eyed my purse, then dragged the side zipper open and withdrew the small white card Kelly had given me. I moved to the desk and picked up the phone from its base, punching in the number printed in gold on the front of the card.

Kelly was right. Neena was getting too close—both personally and professionally. It was only smart to know more about the woman who seemed to be systematically moving into our lives.

"Mr. Beck?" I paused. "This is Catherine Winthorpe. I have someone I would like you to investigate."

~

"What was that all about?" I met William at the side door, a cup of coffee in hand, prepared just the way he liked it.

His eyebrows raised in surprise as he took the cup. "You're done with yoga early."

"I didn't go." I followed him into the kitchen, waiting for an explanation. Stopping at the counter, he pulled the paper toward him and flipped to the financial section.

"Well?" I pressed.

"Well, what?" He glanced up at me.

"What was that all about? Why were you over there?"

"Oh, I was going over some issues with team members. Neena didn't want to do it in the office. Too public."

"Uh-huh." I studied him. "So why didn't you meet here?"

The corner of his mouth twitched in a grin. "Are you jealous?"

I rolled my eyes. "I'm annoyed. Since when do you scamper over to employees' homes? It's weird and rude."

"I was over there anyway, talking to Matt about the new neighborhood bylaws they're proposing. Neena asked if I had a minute to go over her feedback on the team, and I said yes." He crooked a playful eyebrow my way. "Satisfied?"

"Not really." I pulled a plate from the cabinet. "Want a biscuit?"

"Nah, I'm good." He studied the newspaper page before him, that sexy brow furrowing in concentration.

"How are things going with the team?"

He shrugged. "It's going well. Everyone seems happier. More relaxed. I'm hearing less complaining, or she's insulating me from it. Either way, it's what I needed."

"What Winthorpe Tech needed," I clarified.

He looked up from the paper. "Yes. But also me. I feel a lot less stress and more confidence in the company."

I didn't like that at all. Neena was *what my husband needed*? I felt an uncomfortable crawl of jealousy working its way through my chest and clawing at my heart. I gave him a warm smile. "Good. I'm glad to hear it."

I feel a lot less stress. More confidence.

It was official.

The newest member of Winthorpe Tech needed to be gone.

CHAPTER 15

NEENA

In the Winthorpes' kitchen, I made dinner, stir-frying shrimp with vegetables and cauliflower rice. Outside, our husbands talked over the grill, the lobster and steak already prepped and beside them. I glanced across the spacious kitchen, getting a glimpse of them through the far windows, pleased to see smiles on both of their faces.

"You didn't have to cook." Cat perched at the far end of the bar, a glass of wine in her hand. "Seriously. Relax. I can handle cooking the vegetables."

I swallowed my opinion of her culinary talents and crouched, opening her lower cabinets until I found the organized rack holding her Hestan frying pans. They looked brand new, and I flipped the first one over to make sure it didn't have the price sticker still on it.

"I just feel lazy, doing nothing," she called out. "Besides, we have staff for a reason. Let them do the work."

Oh yes, her staff. I couldn't pop in for a quick moment with William without running into one of her uniformed minions. It would make an affair more difficult, which was a shame, because there was a unique power surge when you had a husband inside his own home. Being naked in Cat's bed was a fantasy I was already entertaining, and

I ran my hand along her white marble countertop, making a silent vow to christen that surface, also.

I glanced over my shoulder and gave her a friendly smile. "Are you kidding me? Cooking in this kitchen is a dream. I'm making notes for our future remodel."

She made a face. "Kitchen remodels are horrible. We planned ours when we were on a cruise. If you can, get out of town when you do yours."

I flipped on the front burner and dripped a line of olive oil into the pan. "Duly noted. Assuming I can get the vacation time off." I gave her a coy smile.

"Assuming it's after FDA approval, done." Cat leaned against the counter, her silk pants shimmering in the light of the stove. "William seems happy with your work with the team. He told me everyone is working hard, that the prototype is close to acceptance."

I kept my features neutral. "There are a lot of issues to work through. I haven't done much more than ask the right questions. And everyone, including William, has been open to accepting the changes and feedback in their life."

"Right." She adjusted the diamond-studded Rolex on her wrist, then crossed her arms. "Though William doesn't exactly need changes. Or feedback, for that matter. Wouldn't you say that he's succeeded just fine without your coaching?"

I paused, the spatula poised over the skillet. "It's more than just coaching. It's putting him on an easier path with the team. Making him a better leader." Though honestly, I still hadn't had a chance for real one-on-one work with him. All our meetings had been spent with him viscerally critiquing his employees and me offering my best solutions on how to better address them. I'd been able to re-create our run-in and impromptu lunch once more—but any more surprise encounters would look suspicious. He had already raised one speculative brow upon spotting me again on the path around the pond.

"William has been a huge success without your help. Maybe it's time you focused more on the team and less on him."

"Do you think my methods haven't been effective so far?"

"I think your focus is a little lopsided." She delivered the criticism without cushioning, and I let out an awkward laugh.

"It would take time to explain the specifics of our motivational plan. But"—I shrugged and flipped on the faucet, pulling the heavy nozzle toward the bowl of cauliflower—"if you're curious, just ask William."

I could feel the irritation seep from her skin, even as her perfect white teeth flashed in a smile. "Of course," she said smoothly. She lifted her wine and took a long sip. "I must say, it feels odd, the two of you getting all chummy."

"Chummy?" I frowned, watching as the water lifted the clustered vegetables. "I wouldn't call us chummy. If anything, most of our sessions are fairly dictatorial—which is another thing I'm working on with him."

"Uh-huh." She didn't look convinced. I stole a longer glance at her, picking up on the contrast of her glossy dark hair with her sleeveless white sweater. She looked like a model, except for the steel in her gaze and the suspicion in her tone.

I flipped the tables on her before she gained the upper hand. "You're not jealous, are you? Because you don't have—"

"No." She straightened and set the wine down on the counter hard enough for the delicate glass to crack. "I'm concerned. He has a lot going on right now, and all we need to do is get the team to the FDA goal line in one piece."

This was interesting. Cat Winthorpe, the most confident woman in the world, was insecure. It was a power rush. Even if I hadn't made much progress in breaking through William Winthorpe's morals, I had nicked Cat's world. And that was almost as sweet of a victory.

I moved the spigot away from the pot, wondering if I should bring up the pending wine-charity application. I glanced toward Matt and William, confirming that they were still by the grill, beers in hand. "You've got nothing to worry about. William's excellent at multitasking, and I am going to help his ability to handle things, not weaken it. Plus, I need a project. I'm not sure if you heard, but I didn't make the cut for the wine-charity board." I let my voice drop, soaking each syllable in disappointment.

Cat straightened, and I could almost feel her awareness spike. "The board nominees haven't been announced yet."

I frowned. "I thought the letters for nominee interviews went out this week?" My faux confusion played well, the question rolling out perfectly innocent in nature.

"No." She shook her head. "We meet Thursday to discuss the applications."

"Oh." I brightened. "Well, then, I spoke too soon. I'm dying for a spot on that board, though it will drag my time and focus away from William. Not that I can't still help the team," I hastened to add. "I've just heard that the board is practically a part-time job."

She didn't respond, but I was sure she understood the proposed negotiation. Deliver the wine board and I would step back from her husband.

It was a fair trade, though I didn't plan on keeping it. The more time I spent with William, the more my interest in him grew. While most of the others were entertaining conquests, he was something more. Fascinatingly brilliant and with a sexual pull that was impossible to ignore.

Still, if she got me on the wine board, my social standing in Atherton would take a gigantic leap forward. I would, for one of the first times in my life, be regarded with respect. Looked at as an equal. I would rightfully belong in this diamond-studded world. That would be worth taking a step back from William. Let that affair mature at a slower pace. Draw out the cat-and-mouse game until he was begging for my touch.

I picked up the paring knife and met her eyes, giving her my own sparkly smile.

The wives of this town were all identical. Cat Winthorpe, whether she liked it or not, would eventually lose this game.

CHAPTER 16

Cat

The phone buzzed next to William's plate, the display bright in the dim restaurant. I sighed, and he chuckled, sliding it off the table and into his pocket.

"You promised me. One meal without work," I reminded him.

"I know, I know."

The waiter produced the bottle of wine, and he waved off the presentation of it.

I held my hand over my glass as the tuxedoed man began to tilt it forward. "None for me, thanks." After he left, I nodded to the bottle. "That's one of our vendors for the wine-charity festival. Let me know how you like it."

He took a long sip, paused, then shrugged. "Eh. Tastes like every other red wine."

I smiled at his inability to tell merlot from pinot. "Well, this vendor is making a six-figure donation, so pretend it's amazing."

He took another sip. "You know what? Best I've ever had." He set down the glass. "How is the charity? Neena mentioned she applied for a board position."

I bet she did. "Yes, I saw that she put in an application." I thought of our dinner with them last week, her not-so-subtle push for me to move her application through. It had been insulting, not to mention aggressive. I didn't need her schedule to be busier if I wanted my husband to spend less time with her. I could effect that on my own. He was *my* husband. If I didn't want him to spend time with her, he wouldn't.

"And?" He dipped a chunk of bread into the French cream sauce.

I cocked a brow at his interest. He'd never cared enough to ask about the wine charity before. Typically, his eyes would glaze over at the mere mention of their annual festival, which was their largest fundraiser. "And . . . ," I said carefully, "I don't think she'll be selected."

He frowned. "Why not?"

I let out a laugh that sounded more like a scoff. "Does it matter?"

"Humor me."

"She isn't qualified, for one."

"Qualified?" He grimaced, and I glared at him.

"Don't you dare."

"Fine." He raised his hands. "But there's a reason you're in charge of the board. The rest of those women—"

"And men," I reminded him.

"They're in it for the free wine and society-page mentions. It isn't exactly a crack bunch you have there."

"Oh, they're all drunk social climbers?" I accused. "You're right. That does sound *just* like Neena."

"Come on," he argued. "She's an intelligent woman."

"From what I've heard, she's a year out from being a secretary," I pointed out. "And I don't know how much impact she could be having at WT, considering she's spending all her time with you." The nag slipped into the conversation, and I hurried to cover up the remark. "Neena wants the social standing of being on the board, nothing else."

"She told me about a fundraiser she worked on at Plymouth Industries. She has the experience for it."

"I'm sorry." I cut into my lamb with vicious strokes. "Did I miss something? Are you guys talking about the team or yourselves in your meetings?"

"It was in passing." He paused. "Maybe you're right and she isn't a good fit for it."

"She isn't." I stabbed my fork into the tender meat. One meal. I wanted *one* meal where her name didn't come up. One meal where I didn't have to listen to some accomplishment or praise of her. She'd obviously pressed him into vouching for her. She had worked on something like this at Plymouth? *Whatever.*

I shoved the piece of meat into my mouth. She wouldn't be on the board. I'd already removed her application from the stack and fed it into the shredder myself. If I had to see her smug, pointy face every time I walked into a board meeting, I'd stab her to death with a vendor's corkscrew.

I met William's concerned look and bared my teeth in a smile.

CHAPTER 17

Neena

William's car growled down my driveway, and I was pleased to see that he'd chosen one of the exotic sports cars that lined his garage. It was a good sign. The tight quarters, the roar of the engine between our legs, the feeling of power and recklessness that he'd have behind the wheel . . . it'd all set the right tone.

I locked the side entrance behind me, letting my gaze sweep appreciatively over the car as I approached and opened the door. "Wow." I grabbed the handle and slid one stiletto into the footwell, making a careful entrance that exposed as much leg as possible.

He noticed. I could feel him stare, saw the tightening of his hand on the gearshift as he watched me settle into the bucket seat and pull the door closed. It felt immediately intimate, the engine's noise muting, the air conditioner stirring up the mixture of male and female scents, his cologne intoxicatingly close.

"Do you need more room for your legs? That seat moves back farther."

"Oh yes. That'd be great." I fumbled on the side, peering at the door and then feeling along the bottom of the seat, looking for the controls.

He chuckled. "It's not—may I?" He unbuckled his seat belt.

"Sure." I blushed, then stiffened as he reached in between my legs, the arm of his suit brushing against my knees as he reached under the seat and lifted a lever.

"Push back with your feet." His words came out against my left thigh, and I obeyed, the chair clicking back and giving me another six inches of room. He released the lever and straightened. Was it just my imagination, or was his face red? "It's old school. It's funny, you pay this much for a car, you'd think it would have power seats."

I smiled. "I like it. Now . . ." I looked at the seat-belt harness in faux confusion.

"Here, let me help you." He reached over, pulling the belt over my head. "You have to put your arms through—yeah. Like that." His eyes met mine, and it was the closest we'd ever been. His hands brushing against my blouse as he tightened the straps. His mouth, just inches from mine, his breath soft and warm against my lips.

"You smell good," he said quietly. "Really good."

With another man, this would be my moment. I'd grip his shirt. Let my eyes go soft, my lips part. Run my hand down to cup the bulge in his pants.

But this wasn't another man, and with William, he had to be the one to initiate things, or else I would never land him. I glanced down as if shy. "Thank you. And thank you for giving me a ride. I don't know what's wrong with my car."

He straightened up and reclipped his own belt. "We're going to the same place. It's no trouble. And if we didn't have this team meeting, I'd take a look at it." He frowned. "But Matt's good with cars, right? Didn't he restore that Corvette himself?"

Ugh. That Corvette. I *hated* that stupid muscle car. It was one thing to drive it around our old middle-class neighborhood, but he insisted we take it out on Atherton dates as well. "He did," I said lightly. "But I called the dealership. They're going to tow mine in and fix it under warranty. Do you mind bringing me to work for the next few days? I can get Matt to give me a ride home."

There was the sort of pause that a man makes when he doesn't want to say no but shouldn't say yes. Ned Plymouth once made that pause. It didn't turn out well for him.

"A few days?" He stalled. This hesitation was Cat, I knew it. I'd heard her in the background, huffing and puffing when I'd called—in an almost tearful panic—asking him for a ride.

"They said it should be fixed by Thursday, Friday at the latest." The dealership, which hadn't batted an eye when I told them I would be towing in my car for a full-service detail, had promised a twenty-four-hour turnaround time. I had pushed back, telling them to keep it until Friday, a directive they had happily accepted. "Thank you so much." I sighed in relief, taking the assumptive approach and silently daring him to combat it. "Can you believe this warm front we've had? It's amazing."

He paused, and I could feel him weighing whether to continue the conversation or let it ride. "Yeah, it's been nice." He shifted, putting the powerful car into second as he pulled out of our drive.

We moved around the curve, and I looked back at their estate, unsurprised to see Cat watching us from the front balcony, her arms crossed over her chest. It had been a risky move, the carpool play. But I needed some time with him away from the office. Inside that fishbowl, his guard was up and eyes were everywhere. Alone in this car, I could reach over and grab his hand and no one would know. We could kiss.

Not that I would do any of that yet. It was only Monday. I had an entire week to get him to let his prickly guard down a little. Who knew what things could look like by Friday?

William upshifted into third, and his hand brushed against my bare knee. I didn't move it away, and he kept his grip on the gearshift, our bodies connected through the contact. The breath tumbled out of him and, against my knee, the edge of his pinkie moved in just the slightest, smallest way. I knotted my hands in my lap as if I were nervous and turned my head to look out the window. I settled deeper in the seat, opening my thighs and stretching out my legs, inviting—begging him for—more.

After a long moment, his finger moved again. Farther this time, a drag of his index finger upward along my knee. This was it. William Winthorpe was *touching* me. Practically caressing me. It had taken over seven weeks of me working at Winthorpe. Slow-growing chemistry. Longer looks. Casual run-ins that I spent all day engineering. All worth it for this moment—the first crack in the facade of his monogamy. After this, things would be easy, a crumble of resistance until we were both undressed and William was falling fully into my trap.

Inside, my emotions warred between the possibilities he held. Maybe my fantasies over grilled cheese were possible, and he'd fall in love and make me the next Mrs. Winthorpe.

Maybe this would be just sex and pay off in orgasms and emotional superiority over Cat, followed quickly by blackmailing William and a big financial payday.

I didn't really care which path the trap took. I needed another stepping-stone up in the world, and William would give it to me. With or without love. With or without a wife by his side, or a husband at mine.

This was a chess match over my future, and—as with Ned—I was going to win.

CHAPTER 18

Cat

We built the Winthorpe Tech offices to suit our industry. Sleek, expensive, and highly functional. I was walking through the front doors when my cell hummed with a call from Tom Beck. I paused in front of the security desk, then took a seat at one of the lobby seating arrangements that overlooked the lake. Glancing around, I made sure I was alone, then answered the call.

Tom Beck dived right in. "Ned Plymouth has ignored my calls, but his new receptionist has been very helpful. Are you somewhere where you can view an email?"

I dug into my bag and pulled out my tablet, opening up my email and refreshing the in-box. "You've already sent it to me?"

"Just did."

The email appeared, and I opened it, then clicked on the attachment. "What is this?"

"It's a termination-of-employment contract."

I paused, the title sinking in. "I thought Neena quit that job to take this one."

"Part of this contract stipulates that they will continue her employment until she finds another job, provided that she does so within six months. But, during that time, she is not allowed on company grounds or to have any contact with Ned Plymouth, any of his employees or partners, or any member of his family, including his wife."

My stomach flipped with an odd combination of dread over what this meant to Winthorpe Tech and glee over the find. I scrolled down the page. "So, she gets the appearance of a friendly parting, and he gets . . . what?"

"Aside from the absence of contact, she also signed a nondisclosure agreement that forbade her from discussing anything that ever happened on Plymouth property or with Ned Plymouth."

"Do you think they had an affair?" I lowered my voice and glanced over my shoulder, making sure no one was around.

"Most definitely." He paused. "We never discussed why you hired me. Do you suspect that your husband—"

"No." I shook my head. "No." Maybe if I repeated it five more times, it would eliminate the possibility altogether. "I just want to know—"

"Cat." Neena's voice rang through the marble lobby, and I flipped the tablet over and stood as she approached. "What are you doing here?"

"Just stopping in to see William." I pulled the phone away from my mouth and gave her my warmest smile. "We have dinner plans, so I thought I'd save him the trip home and meet him here."

Her eyes hardened, even as she reached out her arms and clutched me in a hug. "Oh!" She pulled back, spotting the phone at my ear. "I didn't realize you were on the phone."

I held up a finger, asking her to give me a moment. "Tom, I have to run."

Neena watched as I said my goodbyes; then I put my phone and tablet back in my bag.

"Sorry about that. You didn't have to get off the phone." She tilted her head at me, and I noticed her hair extensions. They were a nice addition, her thin hair now a thick mane of platinum-blonde waves.

"It's fine." I zipped up my bag. "How's your car? You know, my BMW was the same way. Constant problems. I can call Bill Hopkins if you'd like. He owns the dealership. Could bump up your car in the lineup."

"Oh no." She waved off the offer, but I noticed the way her skin flushed, her eyes pulling nervously to one side. "They're working on it now. Should be just another day or so."

"Good." I met her eyes. "I'm sure it's disruptive, carpooling with William."

Her gaze didn't waver, and if she was doing anything underhanded, she was hiding it well.

"He's been so kind. But honestly—if you have a problem with it, I can always get a taxi."

"Or have Matt take you," I suggested.

"Sure, though he normally leaves by seven."

I was already bored with the conversation, well aware of the Ryders' conflicting schedules. William and I had already argued over the minute details of Neena's schedule versus Matt's during our fight, one where I had forbidden him to cart her into work each day, and he had deftly ignored my feelings in favor of not inconveniencing *her*.

Friends—if that was the path Neena was trying to go down with me—didn't cozy up to friends' husbands. Especially new friends. You had to earn that level of comfort, and I was growing more and more distrustful of our neighborhood's newest wife, especially after speaking to Tom.

"By the way." I touched her arm. "*So* sorry that you didn't make the cut for the wine-charity board. I really campaigned for you, but the other members didn't think you were the right fit."

"Oh?" The light dimmed in her eyes, and her smile fell for a moment before she quickly jerked it back into place. "Well. That's fine. Gives me more time to focus on work. William—"

"You know, I didn't understand it," I soldiered on, letting my voice carry. "I mean, all that experience at Plymouth? Truthfully, I think it was an issue of jealousy."

She didn't want to take the bait. I could see the hesitant sway of her body as she chewed over the tidbit. "What do you mean?"

I leaned forward and lowered my voice. "A few of the women on the board . . . they mentioned some rumors they've heard. It's all jealousy, like I said. I mean, you going after married men?" I let out an incredulous laugh that almost sounded genuine. "That's ridiculous! And I told them that." I patted her arm. "Don't worry. I'm watching out for you. I know how much you love Matt, and I know what this town is like. Rumors like that . . ." I winced. "They can kill someone's reputation."

There had been no such conversation. But between all my lies, there was a knife of truth—a rumor like that could absolutely kill Neena Ryder's future standing in Atherton. I met her eyes, confident that she was intelligent enough to understand the threat. "Now, I've got to find William. Do you know where he is?"

"No." She pulled self-consciously at the top of her dress. "I haven't seen him."

Ha. Why didn't I believe that? "Well, it was good to see you. Let's grab lunch sometime?" I extended an arm and gripped her generous chest against mine, giving her a parting hug. I inhaled her new fake-blonde curls, searching for the scent of William's cologne in the strands.

She pulled away sharply before I had a chance to finish. "I'd love that. Next week?"

"Anytime," I cooed. "I'm always around."

She stepped back and gave an awkward wave. "Well, until then."

I stayed in place and watched as her too-high heels clipped across the lobby. She hesitated at the elevator, then pushed into the ladies' room. I let her escape, then settled back into my seat.

I was closing in on her, and William was not the sixty-year-old horndog that Ned Plymouth was rumored to be. We were a team, William and me. We were a team, summer was our *fucking* season, and a sociopathic blonde with boundary issues wasn't going to bring down my house.

NEENA

Now

"Blackmail, Dr. Ryder, is a felony. Are you aware of that?"

"I wasn't blackmailing anyone." I took a sip of the coffee, then struggled to swallow the burned liquid.

"According to Ned Plymouth, you were. This is a copy of the check that Ned gave to you, and here are text-message transcripts that prove his case." Detective Cullen slid the pages toward me, rearranging them as if they were place settings on a table. Satisfied with the layout, she pulled her short-bitten nails back.

The damn text messages. I'd always preached at Ned to delete all evidence, advice that he had obviously ignored. Had he also kept the naked photos I'd sent him? The salacious texts detailing my so-called fantasies? I flipped through the pages, half expecting to see them there.

But no, these printouts were all about my leaving. The text where he called me psychotic. The one where I told him I'd slit his throat while he slept. My demand for him to rewrite my recommendation letter and make it better.

The woman tapped on one text message. "I must say, Neena—I think a jury would find these very interesting. These texts paint a different picture than your polished exterior."

Well, Ned could push a girl into violent territory. I'd like to see this woman fake arousal with Ned's flabby body on top of her, his sweat dripping onto her face, his ugly mug grinning down at her. It had been exhausting, all my moaning and praise. Exhaustion that had needed compensation, and naive Ned had thought a new salary and an Hermès handbag would be enough.

He'd never even planned on leaving his wife. That's what he told me, his voice dismissive, his attention back on his computer, our meeting already done in his mind. But I hadn't seduced Ned Plymouth for an extra six figures a year, and being a long-term mistress had never been part of that plan. I deserved more, and the seven-figure check he'd given me at termination had proved it.

"And then there's this." She rearranged her collection of photos until the check with Ned's angry scrawl glared up at me.

Ah. There it was. A million dollars. Could I have gotten more? Probably. Ten years ago, I would have taken it and run. Left Matt and used that money to start a new life with a wealthy husband. Ten years ago, a million dollars would have been all I needed. Now, it wasn't enough. William Winthorpe would have given me more. William Winthorpe would have made me queen of Atherton or paid ten times that amount to make me go away.

William Winthorpe had been the right mark, targeted with a well-oiled execution, but I had made the horrible assumption that I was the smartest person in this game.

PART 3

JULY

TWO MONTHS EARLIER

CHAPTER 19

Cat

I sat in one of four Adirondack chairs halfway down our long front yard. Blue lanterns were hung between the trees, stretching all the way from us to the gate. I kicked up my feet on a bale of hay and watched as William and Matt stood on ladders and worked to position a giant **Happy Fourth of July** sign across the drive. To the right, on the landscaped lawn, the staff prepared the croquet sets and stage while A/V teams laid the wiring for the speakers and lighting. While the club covered brunch, our house always hosted the evening watch party for the Atherton fireworks.

"Mrs. Winthorpe." A landscaper approached, cords of wood hanging from both shoulders and hands. "We were going to set up the firepit, if it doesn't bother you."

"Are you kidding?" I nodded to the stone enclosure before me. "Please. I'm dying for some warmth."

Crushed shells crunched down the drive as Neena approached, a bottle and two glasses in hand. "I must say, you guys certainly take your parties to a whole new level. You're making our front-porch flag look really pathetic right now."

I waved off the compliment. "You should see our Halloween setup. And Christmas. But don't worry—we'll give you Thanksgiving."

"Gee, thanks." She sat next to me, passing me a glass and working at the wine cork. "What do you do for big holidays like that? I know you aren't big on cooking."

It was a jab at me and not her first. There had been several pleasant comments, all designed to point out my rudimentary cooking skills. I ignored it and held out my glass, holding it steady as she poured the red wine. "We always go to the Hawaii house for Thanksgiving."

She stiffened. "Oh. I wasn't aware that you had a place there. I'm surprised you don't spend your summers there."

"You see what it's like for William. It's hard for him to get away for any length of time. We sneak over there when we can. We're heading there for my birthday, in two weeks." I almost added a bit about needing some alone time but swallowed the temptation.

"Wow." She poured her own glass, being generous with the portion. "You guys live the life. I could never leave work like that. You never know when someone on the team might need me. Plus, Matt's workload is crazy year-round."

I fought the urge to roll my eyes. She hadn't seemed too concerned about her team when she'd been fighting for a spot on the wine board. And Matt's workload? I could set my clock by the time he pulled in their driveway each night.

"So, it'll just be the two of you in Hawaii?" She crossed her legs, and I noticed her new Uggs, a shade darker than mine.

"Yep." I took a sip of the wine. At this point William would feel obligated to invite them. Neena's inquisitions about our activities were typically followed by a hurt silence, which he would fill with an offer to participate. Screw that. This was my chance for some much-needed one-on-one time with my husband. She could take her uncomfortable silences and gorge herself until she puked.

"Mrs. Winthorpe." Another man arrived, more firewood in hand, and I smiled in response to his greeting. The two stacked in tandem, creating a complicated pyramid of logs.

"I've never been there. Are you taking the plane?"

"Yep." I ignored the blatant hint for an invite and watched as William hammered his end of the sign into place. God, he was a sexy man. Smart *and* strong. In his T-shirt and faded jeans, he looked like he belonged in a Hugo Boss ad. On the other side of the drive, Matt swatted at a fly.

A match was dropped into the center of the logs, and the kindling ignited, a crackle starting. As the flames licked up the wood, she glanced at me. "How many neighbors normally attend this?"

I propped my boots on the edge of the pit, anxious for the warmth of the fire. "Around a hundred. We have viewing stations set up on the upper balconies, but most families prefer the lawn. They'll arrive around six, and the show is at nine."

She studied the barbecue grills, which were set up to the left of the driveway, just past the golf-cart parking area. The caterers had been smoking meat since morning, and the smell drifting off their smokestacks was mouthwatering. "Do you have enough food?"

"Oh yeah. We've done this for eight years now. It's one of our favorite events. You should see all the kids that show up." My voice shuddered a little, my composure wavering, and I brushed a bit of ash off my jeans, hoping she hadn't picked up on the slip.

She did, her next question hesitant as she extended the bottle of wine as if it might help. "Have you guys ever thought about having children?"

I took the merlot and topped off my glass. "Sure, at times." All the time, especially on a night like tonight. Family events were both a blessing and a curse. A reminder of what we didn't have, paired with the joy that children can bring. We had the perfect house for kids. I could host midwinter pool parties in the basement grotto. Movie nights in the huge theater. Constellation sleepovers on the massive balconies. I swallowed a deep sip. "What about you guys?"

She didn't flinch. "Of course, early on. But Matt had prostate cancer just out of college, which killed that possibility for us."

"I'm sorry," I said. "You could adopt," I suggested, sounding exactly like every nosy and insistent parent I hated.

"We didn't want to. Honestly, we're happy without kids." She studied me, and this was it. My turn. She'd been open with me and would expect me to be the same way with her. "Are you?"

Of course we were happy. We didn't need children to be happy. But William wanted children. I wanted children. And while he was building our life financially, it seemed as if I should be building it with babies—a job I was failing miserably at. "We're not interested in getting pregnant right now." The lie fell as smooth as the wine. "Like you guys, we like our life as it is. Kids . . ." I felt a frown pull at the edges of my mouth and hoped it didn't come across as grief. "Kids would change everything in our life."

Change everything. Inside my chest, my heart broke at the words, all the fantasies I'd ever had pushing to the forefront of my mind as if assaulting me with their strength. William, spinning our little girl into the air. A boy with his soulful eyes and my crooked smile, tearing across the deck and cannonballing into the pool. Sunday mornings, a pile of us in the bed, then chocolate-dotted pancakes.

"So, you don't *want* kids." She tilted her head, considering the concept. "It has nothing to do with . . ."

"No." It had nothing to do with my scarred ovaries, their surface littered with cysts, their reception to sperm . . . what word had the doctor used? Hostile? It had nothing to do with failed surgeries or hormone treatments, my percentage of conceiving just high enough to keep adoption talks off the table. I knew what William wanted—a baby with his bloodline. A surrogate was the next option, and I'd put off that step for as long as I could, desperately hoping my body would give me this one thing. I wanted him to see me pregnant. Cup my swollen belly. Hold my hand during labor. I wanted to be a *mother*, and having another woman birth my child seemed like a broken equation for our future family.

"Huh." That was all she said. *Huh.* As if she knew the truth. As if she saw my weakness.

I watched as William came down the ladder and fought the rising paranoia that he had told her about me.

~

"I'm sorry." I apologized for the fifth time and frowned, my hand on my stomach. "I've just got to go lie down. But seriously, thank you guys for all your help tonight."

"It was fun." Neena stepped forward and wrapped her arms around me in a hug. I squeezed her back, then moved toward Matt.

"I hope you feel better," he said gruffly, giving me an awkward side hug, then quickly retreating back.

"Sure we can't send some of this leftover meat home with you?" William offered.

"Well . . ." Neena glanced at the buffet table, still piled high with food.

"He's joking." I stepped in before she had a chance to take William up on his offer and stretch out this night by another half hour. "We donate it to the homeless shelter. The staff are already packing it up for delivery."

"Just don't eat anything else," she cautioned. "You don't want to make that stomachache worse."

"Thanks." I leaned into William's chest. "You guys have a good night."

There was another round of goodbyes and well-wishes, and I fought the urge to slam the door behind them, waiting until they were in their new golf cart and halfway down the driveway before I closed the door. I glared at William. "Do you have to invite them to everything?"

He frowned. "You're the one who asked them to come over. Remember? When we were at Morton's."

"I invited everyone in the neighborhood. And honestly, I would have skipped over their invite if Neena hadn't painted a request across her tits with steak sauce."

He sighed, setting the alarm and heading to the kitchen.

"And I thought they'd show up at six, like the rest of the neighborhood. They've been here since *one*." I glanced at my watch. "It's almost eleven. Why on earth would you invite them to watch movies with us?"

"We always watch *Jaws* on the Fourth of July."

"Right. When the guests leave at ten. Not after sitting and discussing the freaking Canadian economy for ninety minutes. Plus, *we* always watch *Jaws*. Not you, me, Neena, and Matt. I swear to God, we need to bail on this friendship. They're obsessed with us."

William opened the door to the wine cellar, stepping in and reaching up for a bottle.

"I don't understand why you aren't sick of them," I said.

"Matt's a good guy. He isn't like the rest of the pricks in this neighborhood. If I have to listen to one more discussion of the architectural review board election prospects, I'm going to hang myself. Plus, I work with Neena."

I sighed. "Yeah, I have employees, too. And you know what? I'm not hanging out with the maids on the weekends. There's a reason you're supposed to separate business and pleasure."

He shoved the bottle back into place and pulled out another. "Why are you so against her? Things are improving at WT. I've told you that. I need you to root for this."

I frowned. "I'm *always* rooting for the companies. But even if the team is making progress with her—it doesn't mean Neena and Matt have to dry hump our legs every other day of the week. I feel like I never get time alone with you anymore." I adjusted the thermostat in the cellar, making it a degree warmer. "And did you notice that the Plymouths didn't come?"

"Who?"

"Ned and Judy Plymouth, from Plymouth Industries."

He moved his focus away from the wine and to me. "Why would they come?"

"I invited them. Stopped Judy in the club last week and invited her personally." And, not to be bigheaded, but a personal invitation from Cat Winthorpe was paramount to an Oscar nod. I'd spent ten years building that clout, and the pasty-faced woman had flushed appropriately, gripping my arm with red-nailed talons, and *assured* me that they would come. I hadn't mentioned Neena and had been almost giddy at the thought of seeing her and Ned's reaction to each other. The anticipation of it had overcome any annoyance at her presence, and I'd stayed glued to her side, ready to watch their interaction. My excitement had slowly fizzled into disappointment at the realization that the Plymouths weren't going to show. His wife had been practically frantic to attend, so Ned must have been the stumbling block. Maybe he'd heard we hired Neena and was worried she'd attend.

"I don't understand what the Plymouths have to do with anything." William turned away from the rack and headed toward the door. "But look—I'm sorry I invited them to watch *Jaws* with us. Are you still in the mood for it?"

I scoffed, flipping off the light. "Always."

"Then let's go scare your panties off."

I stopped him before the entrance to the theater room and pulled him into my arms for a hug. He didn't fight the gesture or ask me about it. He wrapped his arms around me, a protective blanket of security, and gave his insecure wife the long moment I needed.

～

On the screen, the end credits to *Jaws* rolled. I lay back against William's chest, a cashmere blanket over our bodies, and tried to push Neena from my mind.

He ran his fingers over the top of my head. "You want to do another?"

I shifted into a more comfortable position and remembered the way she had hugged him goodbye, gripping him for a moment longer than was necessary. "Sure. Which one?"

He lifted the remote, scrolling through our July Fourth movie list.

I watched the familiar names roll by. "*Independence Day*," I mumbled.

He clicked on the link, and I turned to him, unable to hold back a final Neena question that had been bothering me. "Did you tell her about my cysts?"

He didn't say anything, but I could feel the tightening of his chest muscles underneath me.

I shifted to get a better glimpse of his face. "You did," I accused.

"I didn't tell her why we hadn't had children, just that we have been trying."

"Oh, right. So you didn't mention that it was me and not you?"

His silence answered the question. I propped up on his lap and turned to meet his gaze. "That's something personal, William. It should have stayed between *us*."

"I didn't mean—it just came out. We're both dealing with that. Her with Matt, me with—"

"Oh my God, stop." Any minute and the tears would come. "You can't—" The image of them together, complaining over their infertile spouses. Talking about the missed opportunities and the children they yearned to have. Two fertile individuals, both married to such sad excuses for a spouse. Had they considered the easy option, the one that would have been painted so clearly before them?

Embarrassment flooded through me. "Tonight, Neena asked me why we haven't had kids. I sat there and lied to her, and she knew it. Do you know how stupid I feel? Knowing that she thinks this is some secret the two of you share?" I shoved off him, and he caught my arm.

"When did this come up? How did this come up? Because it sure as hell doesn't have anything to do with Winthorpe Tech."

"I don't know." He frowned down at me. "It just did. In passing. I'm sorry."

"When?" I stayed in place, stubbornly fixated on the question. "Don't tell me you don't remember, because you remember everything." He was an encyclopedia of conversations and details, both insignificant and important. He'd be hell if he was ever called to a witness stand, and an absolute terror to have an argument with.

He swallowed, and I watched his Adam's apple bob with the motion. "At lunch, sixteen days ago."

"You didn't tell me you went to lunch with her." I yanked my arm free of his hand.

He grimaced. "We didn't go to lunch together—I was eating lunch, she stopped by the table, and we ended up eating together."

It sounded like a lie, but I was too emotional to sort out the details. "And?"

"And she asked why we haven't had kids. People ask, Cat. It's a normal question. Don't tell me you haven't gotten it."

People ask. How many people had asked him? How many times had he offered up the details of my infertility struggle?

I turned away, and when he went to follow, I stopped short and held up a hand. "Leave me alone. Just . . . leave me alone."

I moved silently through the giant house, my steps quickening as my hurt emotions flared. I heard him calling my name, his steps sounding up the stairs, then down the hall. I crouched beside the one place he wouldn't find me. Ducking into the dumbwaiter elevator, I curled into a ball on the polished wood surface and closed the heavy insulated door. Leaning back against the wall, I took a deep breath, then broke into tears.

CHAPTER 20

Neena

"You're going on a run?" Cat stared at me as if I'd just announced my plans to join the circus. Behind her, the warmth of the house curled out of the large front doors, tickling along my skin.

I offered her my best smile. "William offered to show me the neighborhood trails. I tried to find them on my own but couldn't."

"Really? The signs are pretty obvious." She knotted her arms over her chest.

"Are you feeling better? I was thinking, you know, that it could have been that July Fourth potato salad that made you sick. You didn't throw up, did you?"

Cat's face got that annoyed look, the one that twisted her beautiful features into a haglike pinch. "I don't think it was the potato salad."

William appeared beside her, a long-sleeve shirt snug on his strong chest, a baseball cap hiding his dark hair. In workout pants and Nikes, he looked good enough to eat. "Ready?"

"Ready." I gave her a cheery wave. "We'll be back in an hour."

"I—" She searched for an objection. "Will, do you need a water bottle or—"

"I'll be fine." He planted a quick kiss on her mouth, then moved out the door, lifting his chin in my direction. "Good morning."

"Morning." I turned my back to her and jogged down the steps. I reached the wide drive and bounced up and down in place, warming my muscles. "You want to lead the way?"

He nodded toward the main road. "Sure. We'll pick up the trail off Britnon. It's a four-mile loop, if that's okay with you."

I scoffed and flashed a cocky grin. "Just try and keep up."

I started down the long drive, and William ran easily beside me, his strides almost twice as long as mine. It didn't matter. My closet had a stack of marathon T-shirts in a dozen different colors. When I'd noticed him leaving on early-morning runs, I'd started pounding out miles on my treadmill, increasing the speed and distance until I was back in race mode. And . . . just like that, another check in the Neena Is Better Than Cat column.

I let out a huff of air, reminding myself to be patient with William. While our progress had been slow, it was beginning to ramp up. Our contact had transitioned from business to personal, my text messages answered with increasing speed, our inside-joke collection growing, my suggestions of lunch no longer met with stiff reluctance but quick agreement. He didn't recoil from my casual touch and had lost the stiff air and foreboding manner he typically carried with Winthorpe Tech employees.

We rounded the bend, almost to his gate, and I looked up into the ceiling of tree limbs and inhaled the crisp morning air, giving myself a mental pat on the back. This run was already a victory. I had been careful with Cat so far, but that flash of insecurity on her face as he'd joined me on the run . . . it had been unexpectedly enjoyable. Had she started to nag him about me yet?

All I had to do was remain innocent in his eyes. The sane to her crazy. The calm fun to her neurotic paranoia. A safe haven for his thoughts and fears. A support system who made him feel valued and protected. I'd be a better version of *her*, doused in the tempting light of the forbidden.

"What are you smiling about?" His arm brushed mine as we turned left out of the open gates and onto the street.

"Nothing." I looked down at the ground, suddenly aware of how my cheeks were split with the grin. "I was just thinking about the team members. I've had a bit of a breakthrough with them recently."

"Really?"

His focus was one of the things I was starting to love about him. It was as if he stopped everything in his life and turned his full attention to me. I felt it in my initial interview, and I savored it now as the pebbles crunched under our running shoes, his head turned to me.

"Yes." I continued my fictional story and hoped he'd see the parallels. "We've always had a distance, but recently they've begun to let me in." We moved up the hill, hugging the edge of the road, protected from the wind by an estate's stone wall. As we rounded the curve, the view of Palo Alto appeared through the morning fog.

We stopped at the park and stretched, my muscles now warm and pliable. I propped one shoe on the top of a bench and hopped back on the other foot, getting a deep stretch that he couldn't help but notice. I turned to him quickly and caught the moment before his eyes darted away. Was he imagining what else my limber legs could do?

I stretched my hamstrings and thighs, then nodded to the small grassy area underneath the trees. "Stretch my back?"

I lay back on the manicured grass and lifted one leg. He settled above me, his knees on the ground, his shoulder flush against my ankle. As he leaned forward, my leg moved effortlessly, my teenage years of dance still blessing me with the ability to do a split or straddle. His brows lifted in what I took to be appreciation, and he pushed farther, his body moving in tighter to mine. This close, I could feel the heat of his body, loved the grip of his hand on my thigh, the burn of every finger.

The risk of it hit me with delicious intensity. I pictured Cat's convertible curving along the road, the brake lights glowing when she saw her husband on top of me, his eyes on mine, pelvis pressed against my thigh. I looked up at him, and that handsome smile broke across his face, his eyes crinkling at the edges, his—

"Ready for the next leg?"

I nodded, and he settled back on his heels, placing one leg down and lifting the other. He returned to the position, and I tried to sort my way through his head. Was he on guard? He didn't seem to be. But skittish . . . yes. Still a little skittish. Wary on the edges of his appreciation. I thought of his finger brushing against my knee in the Ferrari. That beautiful moment of contact that had never been re-created. This, at least, was a move in the right direction. Touching. Proximity. It had to be pushing at the binds of his self-control.

He'd been harder to crack than I had expected, but that loyalty was one of the most attractive things about him. Every time he reestablished boundaries or held himself in check, I wanted him more. I appreciated him more. Cat griped at him when she should be thanking him. She would start needling him over our growing friendship when the smart woman would play the supportive and loving wife.

But that was what made this game so fun to play. I had the cards. I knew the hands. And she . . . she didn't even know the game.

He grunted a little, applying more pressure, my foot passing over my head, and I closed my eyes in bliss at the sound.

CHAPTER 21

CAT

Tom Beck's full report on Neena was thirty-two pages thick. I settled into the end of our couch, a cappuccino in hand, and flipped over the embossed cover page.

The first few pages were sad but unsurprising.

She'd been poor, even more than I'd been. A small-town beauty queen whose mom had run off when she was ten, her dad following suit seven years later. She'd won the town's sympathies while wearing the crown of . . . I squinted at a grainy photo of a young Neena with a crown and a sash, the newspaper caption barely legible. The . . . Strawberry Queen. Amusing. Not surprising she omitted that from her wine-charity board application. It looked like she'd lived with her aunt and uncle until graduation and then gotten married to Matthew Ryder.

From that point on, things grew boring. I quickly flipped through the pages of home deeds, credit card balances, and credit scores. All average. The medical-history section was where things got interesting.

I'd known she'd had some work done, but my mouth still dropped open at her list of surgeries. Arm lift. Butt lift. Tummy tuck. Breast augmentation. A second breast augmentation. Cheek implants. Brow lift. Eye job. Chin implant. Ear reshaping. Rhinoplasty. Neck tuck.

Labia and vaginoplasty. She was Frankenstein's monster, and I flipped quickly through the rest of the report, hoping for a before photo of the petite blonde. There wasn't any other than the newspaper clipping, and I returned to the medical-history section of the report.

Below the cosmetic surgery list was a section marked OTHER SURGERIES. I ran my finger down an appendectomy, wisdom-teeth removal, a broken arm, sprained ankle—my nail stilled on the last item, and I scanned the details, focusing in on the date.

Eight years ago. An abortion.

~

It had been three days, and all I could think about was Neena's aborted baby. All those probing questions when she knew I was struggling with my fertility. Eight years ago, she had been pregnant. Pregnant! Pregnant, and given it up. Was her story about Matt's prostate cancer even true? And if it was, that just reaffirmed my belief that she was a cheater. I pulled our lunch from the fridge and yanked open the lid to the lobster pasta salad. William's phone dinged, and I jerked my head to the side in time to see him silence the notification, his attention on the paperwork before him. It sounded again, and I reached across the kitchen island and grabbed it, unsurprised to see her name on the screen. Two new texts.

Brought some of my cookie dough bombs into the office. Hungry?

Are we still on for three?

I bit back the desire to ask why Neena was texting him. They had a standing meeting schedule. Mondays, Wednesdays, and Fridays at three. There wasn't a need to verify it. No need for chitchatty little texts at all hours of the day. He was growing more and more comfortable with her, and my nerves were fraying with every single ding of his phone.

Their encroachment into our lives had passed any level of social norms. Matt and Neena seemed to be everywhere we were, all the time.

You've got a box at the 49ers' stadium? We loooovve football.

Oh, how funny to run into you at the market. Join us for lunch!

Sorry to pop in, but we accidentally bought extra wine that happens to be your favorite!

We're eating some nasty healthy crap for dinner. Why don't you guys come over and pretend to like it?

Okay, so that last one wasn't verbatim, but I'd read between the lines. Add in Neena and William's new biweekly runs, and I couldn't turn around without seeing her ridiculous face. And now, with him home for lunch, she was still interrupting us. I flipped his phone to silent and tossed it back onto the counter. "I'm *exhausted* by her. I swear to God, I'd just like one day without seeing her face or hearing her ridiculous laugh."

"Who?" William flipped to the next page, his pen skimming over the lines of a contract.

"Neena," I snapped.

"When did you become so vicious?"

"Excuse me?"

"There's nothing wrong with her laugh. Or her outfits, or whatever else you feel the need to bitch about." He scrawled his signature along the block at the bottom of the page and dotted the *i*'s in his name with a little more intensity than needed.

I turned away, pulling plates from the cabinet and shoving them onto the counter. "So you're defending her now?"

"I just don't understand why you're so hostile toward her. She's doing the best she can. She's not like you, Cat. She doesn't have everything in life."

I let out a strangled sound. "I'd love to know what *that* means."

He abandoned the contract and stood, rounding the edge of the counter. Leaning against the marble, he attempted to pull me away from the food and against him. "It means that you're beautiful."

I resisted, standing before him, my arms crossed.

"And she's not. You don't have to work, and she does. You're the queen of this social circle, and she's excluded from it. It's got to be hard on her, trying to compete with you—with us and our world." He closed the gap between us, hugging me despite my crossed arms, the awkward positioning of our bodies breaking my stern composure as he tried to jiggle my arms loose.

A smile cracked across my features, and he took advantage of the break and gave me a kiss on either cheek.

I forced a scowl back into place and pushed away from him, my mind turning over Tom Beck's report and wondering how much of it to share. "Giving me compliments doesn't excuse the fact that she has no boundaries. Coming by here and asking you to get a *bird* out of her house? She doesn't know how to shoo?"

"She was petrified, Cat. When we were in the room with it, she was trembling."

I snorted. "Oh, please. And wanting to carpool to work? It's called a loaner car. I called the dealership. They have plenty of loaners there. She had to specifically decline one, and why would she do that?" I smacked my forehead. "Oh, right. Because she wants to spend time with you. She's *a snake*, William. A *snake!*" I inhaled sharply, unsure of why I was suddenly screaming. I turned back to our lunch and ticked through the necessary menu items, then reached for an avocado from the bowl.

"Cat."

I ignored him, pulling a knife free of the block and halving the fruit on the stone cutting board. She had been pregnant. Hadn't she realized what a blessing that was? She could have an eight-year-old child by now, but she didn't. She had thrown it away, and I couldn't even manage to

A.R.Torre

wrangle up a miscarriage. I felt a sob push up my throat, and I swallowed it down, blinking hard to keep the tears at bay.

"Please ease up on her."

I stacked the quarters and ran the knife tip over their lengths, slicing through the avocado's flesh. I gave myself a moment, then spoke. "I don't want you running with her again."

He coughed out a laugh of incredulity. "Wow. You're that insecure about this? You want me to fire her, too? Is that what you want? Should we move to a different house?"

I pinched pepper pieces together and worked the knife furiously against their strips, cubes of red and green flying along the cutting board.

That blonde bitch had backed me up against a wall, and I hated it.

CHAPTER 22

Cat

"Good morning, Mrs. Winthorpe."

"Good morning." I smiled at the chef and poured a cup of coffee. "I'm going to walk through the gardens. If William comes down for breakfast before I get back, please let him know."

"Certainly." Philip nodded, and I took my mug and stepped through the back door, inhaling the crisp morning. The hydrangeas were in full bloom, and I took a moment to appreciate the neat pockets of color set off against the roses and grass. The gardens stretched between our home and the pool, then picked back up at the entrance to the orchard at the rear of our lot. I'd spent years cultivating the perfect mix of apple and lemon trees, set off by spice and strawberry bushes.

The privacy hedges between us and the Ryders ended at the edge of our home, the back of their home exposed if you walked deeper into our gardens. I wove around a bed of white roses and glanced over, spotting Matt on their upper balcony, his own coffee in hand.

He leaned against the railing, and even from here, I could see some dark chest hair peeking out of the top of his white robe. "Good morning!" he called out.

"Morning." I moved closer and lifted my hand in greeting. "It's actually warm out!" The prior few days had been miserable, the air thick with humidity, the skies dark and gray.

He laughed. "I don't know about warm, but I'll take it."

An awkward silence fell, the distance too far for real conversation. Still, the effort should be made. "The pavers look great."

He came to my side of his balcony and leaned forward, cupping his ear. "What?"

I worked my way around a bed of lilies and leaned against the low stone fence between our two backyards. "The pavers!" I pointed to the new white bricks that circled their pool. The color would be impossible to keep clean. I'd told Neena that, but she'd ignored the advice, picking a crisp bone color that would require bleaching and weekly pressure cleaning. I made a thumbs-up sign.

He nodded, then turned, a guilty expression flashing across his face. The door behind him opened, and I saw Neena appear, her obligatory workout outfit on. She'd probably already pounded out five miles on the treadmill, then jumping-jacked her breakfast off.

"Morning!" I called, waving up at her.

She came to stand beside Matt, looking down at me without returning the smile. "Cat." Turning to her husband, she said something I couldn't catch.

His head dipped, and he gave me an awkward wave. "See you later."

I lifted my cup in response, my gaze settling on Neena's face. She glared at me as if I'd pissed in her cereal. I kept my expression light, my voice sunny. "Can you believe this weather?"

She knotted her arms over her chest. "It's fine."

"Matt looks *great*—that keto diet is amazing." I rested my forearms on the fence, a bit of chill coming in through the gap in my robe. "Maybe I should get William on that."

She blinked at me, and I could see the inner struggle she had with a response. She was probably warring between telling me to keep my eyes off her husband and reacting to the reference to William.

"How was the wine-festival meeting?" she finally managed.

I was surprised she knew about it. Then again, I wasn't. It was funny she had asked, since she had come up as a topic of conversation. Valerie Cortenza had mentioned she had seen William leaving Bevy's Sandwiches with Neena on Tuesday. I'd found that information very interesting, since I hadn't been aware of that lunch. I'd returned home and examined my calendar. I'd had an early dinner with William that night, and he hadn't mentioned a word about a lunch meeting with her.

"It was good. Again, *so* sorry you didn't make the board." I frowned in mock regret.

I pushed off the fence and lifted my coffee to my lips, making sure to use the hand with the diamond, the huge stone impossible to miss. *He's mine.* "Have a nice day, Neena."

"You, too." She smiled, and I smiled, and the morning chill didn't have anything on us.

CHAPTER 23

CAT

"I can't believe I'm not there." William cleared his throat, his exhaustion audible even through the phone. "I miss you already."

I stretched out on the master bed in our Hawaiian home and kicked the expensive sheets loose. "I know. How's everything there?"

He groaned. "I can't even go into what a screwed-up situation this is. I'm crunching numbers to try to salvage the deal, but it doesn't look good."

"I'm sorry." I fluffed the pillow under my head. "We should have canceled the trip." He'd been on his phone since the minute we'd headed to the island. Half of my conversations with him were ignored, his fingers tapping across his phone, the sound of his text-message notifications driving me insane. He'd left two dinners in the middle of our entrées, stepping outside the restaurant for calls, then returning after I'd already polished off dessert.

"Even the brief moments were worth it. I just owe you another trip after I fire every member of my acquisitions team."

For once, the issues hadn't been with Winthorpe Tech, but with Winthorpe Capital. William had been midacquisition of an accounting firm when a whistleblower in upper management revealed that half of the due-diligence documentation had been altered. This morning,

William had left the jet in Hawaii and taken a direct commercial flight at nine. He'd gone straight to the office from the airport and buried himself in work. I'd heard from him sporadically throughout the day, his energy level waning with each call.

I yawned into the receiver. "I could have come back with you. I'd be dragging you to bed and forcing you to get a few hours of sleep."

"As tempting as that sounds, I'm glad you're there. Someone needs to enjoy that view."

I looked out the open french doors at the turquoise waters, the gentle sweep of waves barely audible. "I'd rather look at other things."

"Just enjoy the next few days. Get lots of massages and run up our credit card. I expect you to come back tan, spoiled, and ready to punish me for our foiled vacation."

"What kind of punishment are you thinking of?"

He groaned. "Something filthy. Wear that black-lace number I love so much."

I grinned, rolling on my side and stuffing the feather pillow under my head. "Don't give me any ideas."

He chuckled, and even exhausted, he was lethal on my heart. I wanted nothing more than to have him beside me, his warm body curled around mine.

"Have you talked to Matt or Neena?" I pulled the sheet higher on my body.

There was a pause I didn't like, a hesitation before he responded. "No. Why?"

"I was just wondering if they knew that you were back." I closed my eyes, pushing off my paranoia. He was at the office. There wasn't a safer place for him to be on a Sunday evening in terms of women or temptation. "Are you planning on sleeping at all?"

"Once I figure out the real numbers and talk to the legal team, I'll lie down for an hour. What is it, eleven thirty there?"

"Yeah." I yawned. "I'm in bed now."

"In California, you're already a year older."

"Ugh." I curled onto my side. "I prefer my Hawaiian age."

"Happy birthday, sweetie. Call me when you wake up. I'll be a little more sane then."

"I will. Love you."

After he hung up the phone, I lay there for almost an hour, my mind festering on my increasing age, his empty side of the bed screaming at me. Why had I agreed to have him travel back home alone? It went against every foundation our relationship was built on. We did everything together, yet I'd let him talk me into being here—on my birthday, all alone.

~

The next morning I opened up a bottle of chilled champagne and poured a healthy amount into my orange-juice glass. It was funny how birthdays, with age, grew more painful.

First, there were the obligatory gifts, which were an art in our social circles, each item carefully selected to send the right message and each requiring a perfectly worded thank-you card. Just the act of giving and receiving was a social minefield that had taken me years to navigate properly.

Then there were the calls—coming from my parents, my sisters, my friends, and a dozen business and social connections. All well intentioned but unwanted, especially on a day like today, when I only wanted William, grinning at me in the Hawaiian sun, a thousand miles away from Neena. This was supposed to be our time to reconnect, to have four days without her smug little smile, her foil-wrapped plates in the center of our counter, her opinions cropping into William's conversations with me. If I heard *Neena said* one more time, I'd clench my hands around my ears and snap them off.

Even worse than William's mention of her was his silence. I could feel him retreating from me. His phone had become an almost-constant attachment, his emails and text messages dominating our time together. We'd been together for thirteen years, and I'd never seen him this distracted. Something was wrong, and I'd started to count down the days to our trip with a secret plan to put us all back together on the island.

And look how well that had turned out. William was back home, and I was scrolling through Facebook messages from strangers wishing me birthday cheer. As if getting older were something to celebrate in my world. One day, would I be too old for William? I had never considered it, always so cocky in my view of our marriage. But lately, with Neena breathing down my back, I was questioning everything. I tilted back the glass, my empty stomach rolling in protest of the bubbles. Setting down my phone, I looked at the water and considered walking down to the beach and finishing the bottle in one of the waterside hammocks.

My cell rang, and I picked it up, seeing my mother's face on the display. "Hey, Mom."

"Happy birthday, honey."

An unexpected swell of emotion hit. In the background I could hear my father's voice and the sound of baseball on the television. I pictured him in his recliner, an afghan laid across his legs. I settled into the closest chair and listened to my mom chatter about the day's events, getting updates on my sister's family and their kids. She asked about our trip, and I stretched the first two days into four, playing up the weather and the decadent meals we'd enjoyed.

"Put William on. I want to tell him hi."

"Oh, Mom, he's in the shower. I'll tell him when he gets out." The lie stuck in my throat, my pride too strong to admit that I was spending my birthday alone.

I rushed through the remainder of the call and hung up, immediately dialing William's number. It rang once and went to voice mail, as if he was on the phone. I sighed and ended the call without leaving a message.

My mind was starting to spin in dark ways, my solitude in this oceanfront home giving my doubts, insecurities, and paranoia free range to work overtime. The fear grew. Festered. Was something wrong between us?

I'd felt this way before. Six years ago, I'd had a similar feeling. William had been spending more time at the office, and I grew suspicious of the little changes. A cologne he began wearing with steadfast frequency. A new workout regime he was sticking with. An enthusiasm about the office I hadn't seen before.

I'd remotely accessed his work computer one day and spent hours wading through emails before I found the potential culprit. First, an email between him and his assistant, where she called him Mr. President. That, while a little odd, wasn't completely out of left field. He *was* the president and managing member of Winthorpe Companies. But in his response, he called her Ms. Lewinsky.

I'd stared at the words until they blurred, hot tears pricking the corners of my eyes, their presence quickly wiped away and replaced by something stronger—anger.

I'd printed every email between them since the start of her employment and gone crazy with a highlighter and Sharpie, underlining incriminating lines and scrawling notes with lots of exclamation points. By the time my clueless husband came home, every surface in his home office was covered in furious white pages, and my bags were packed and sitting by the door.

I had been like a baby snake, unable to control my venom and striking out with everything on the initial hit, no reserves left for the dumpy brunette who'd crossed the line with my husband.

And she *had* been dumpy. That had been the most alarming thing of all. I'd spent our marriage on high alert for the sex kittens, the glamour queens, the pinup models masquerading as pencil pushers. I'd known his type—leggy brunettes with great bodies—and had blocked every potential threat with precise accuracy. He was a sexual man, one who appealed to practically every woman out there, and I'd spent the first few years of our marriage playing badminton with beauties until I'd found secure footing in his fidelity. But when he had strayed, it had been with the most ordinary of women. Brenda Flort. Forty-two years old to his then thirty-five. Chubby around the midsection, she wore pants a hair too short. Glasses because "contacts made her eyes hurt." Her hair was in a perpetual messy bun. She was a woman whom William should never have given a second glance to, yet he had. He'd risked our marriage over his flirtation. And I made sure that the minute he'd walked in the door, he understood it.

It hadn't gone well at all. I'd expected tearful remorse, a shuddering of composure, and him begging me to forgive him, to give him another chance.

Instead, he'd turned haughty, dismissing my emails as nothing. He called me crazy and brought up innocent acquaintances of mine, painting them with the same brush.

We'd fought for hours, our throats growing hoarse. They'd developed nicknames for each other after a conversation on a Lewinsky news piece. That was *it*. She was old, for Christ's sake. Did I think he was sleeping with her? Was he not allowed to be playful with his own staff? Was I that insecure in our relationship? Had he ever, in seven years, given me any reason to doubt him?

I'd deflated and begun to question every word I'd read. I'd cursed myself for not doing more research—following him and gaining more evidence than just emails. Was I wrong? Had it been just innocent wordplay?

I'd fallen silent, and when he gathered me into his arms, I allowed it. I took his reassurances and swallowed my concerns. The suitcases returned to our closet, where they were unpacked by the home staff the next morning, our perfect life back in place by noon.

I'd caved, but despite my carefree comments to Neena, I'd never fully trusted him again.

~

I was down at the surf when my phone chimed. Moving away from the water, I dug in the pocket of my robe and pulled out the cell. "Hey, love."

"I hate that I'm not there to celebrate with you." William sounded guilty, and I ditched any thoughts of sharing my pity party with him.

Adopting a breezy tone, I told him about my morning, playing up my lunch, telling him about the beachfront café and an intact conch shell I found half-buried in the sand.

"You sound like you've been drinking."

I glanced down at the champagne bottle, almost empty in my hand. "I have been. Remember that bottle of Dom we had for tonight? And the chocolate-covered strawberries?"

"Ah." He sighed. "That's right. I had big plans to lick it all off your body."

"Don't tease me. We've got another two days before we see each other. I'm already planning to tackle you the minute I get home."

He was silent for a long moment. "I'm miserable without you. I don't want to ruin all of your fun, but . . . I need you here."

He needed me. It was a sentiment uttered frequently between us, but my starved emotions chugged it as if hearing it for the first time. I tossed down the bottle, watching as a bit of the champagne sloshed out the top and fizzled on the sand. "Call the airport and tell them to prep the jet. I'll go upstairs and pack. I can be on the way there in twenty minutes." I calculated the time in my head. A five-hour flight . . . I could be there by midnight, California time.

"Thank you." His voice was gruff, heavy with need and love. "I promise, I'll bring you back to the island and we'll do it right."

"I know you will." I made a kissing sound into the phone and stumbled up the soft sand toward the house, anxious to pack and get back to my husband. There was something I didn't like about being apart from him. Especially with Neena right next door. Watching. Waiting. Did she already know he was home?

CHAPTER 24

NEENA

The chicken was missing its left drumstick. At the open door to the oven, I glared at the one-legged bird, then turned my head and cursed Matt's name. He continued rummaging through the fridge, unperturbed by my yell.

"Honestly, I'm going to kill you." I slammed the oven shut and opened the lid to the garbage, immediately spotting the evidence, half-wrapped in a dirty paper towel.

He pulled out a container of yogurt and peeled back the top, ignoring me.

"You *know* I like dark meat," I complained, forcing the lid back on the trash and cursing when it didn't fit correctly.

Of course he knew. I always claimed the drumsticks and thighs. He'd probably eaten it out of spite over my refusal to add some NFL package to our cable account.

"The chicken's not even done yet. It still has another twenty minutes to cook." Maybe he'd get salmonella and die. I'd have his five-million-dollar insurance policy and no more headaches. I warmed to the idea and, for not the first time in our marriage, added it to the list of potential retirement scenarios.

Moving back to my prep of the broccoli-cheese bake, I paused at the sound of my phone, buzzing by the mixer bowl. Licking a chunk of cheese off the tip of my finger, I grabbed the cell.

I had to come back early. Don't be alarmed if you see lights on over here.

I stared at William's text. *He'd* had to come back? Had he left her there? I thought of Cat's smug announcement that they'd be in Hawaii getting some "alone time" for her birthday. Ha! She'd probably stuck birthday candles into a heap of solitude. I leaned against the counter and texted him back.

Me: When'd you get back?

William: Yesterday, but I've been at the office nonstop.

Me: Everything okay? Can I bring you some food?

"That's the smile I love." Matt rounded the corner, coming up beside me and pulling me into a hug. I held the phone out of harm's way and gave him a quick kiss. "What, did you find the perfect recipe?"

"No, just got a text from an employee. A breakthrough with the device." I slipped the cell phone in my back pocket and smiled at him. I could invite William to eat with us, but where would the fun be in that? His attention would be on Matt, and while I was turned on by their close union, I was starting to think that their friendship might slow my progress with William.

And I needed that progress. My focus on him had increased tenfold with Cat's recent betrayal, delivered on wine charity–board stationery this Monday. *We regret to inform you . . .*

As if they were a fucking Ivy League school. A bunch of lacrosse moms and Ambien addicts, that's all they were. I could have brought intelligence to the group. I was a *doctor*. They should have waved me through, no questions asked.

But I hadn't even made it to the reduced list of finalists who'd received board interviews. My friendship with Cat should have gotten me *that*, even if I didn't have any other strengths in my favor.

It was clear that she'd sabotaged it. She didn't want me on there and had slashed through my name with one perfectly manicured nail. I'd let her know how important it was to me. I'd even offered to reduce my interactions with William, but she hadn't cared. Selfish, that's what she was. Selfish and shortsighted.

Cat had done more than remove me from the candidate pool. She'd drawn a battle line in the sand and added a new incentive for my seduction of William.

"Go sit down." I pointed to Matt's recliner, a revolting piece of his-and-her furniture I had lost the battle over. The ugly thing was annoyingly comfortable, its siren call almost soothing on long days. "If you distract me, I'll burn everything out of spite."

His grin crooked up, revealing the chipped tooth from a sixth-grade fistfight. "And mar your perfect culinary record? You wouldn't dare."

It was sweet how much he loved me. I'd wager to say he loved me even more than William loved Cat. She thought she was queen, but her castle was made of sand. One perfectly timed blonde wave and . . . whoosh. Slow erosion at first, then a cascade.

The phone buzzed against my butt cheek. Watching Matt sidle over to his chair, I fished out the phone and checked the text.

> I wouldn't be able to eat it. I'll be at the office until I pick up Cat from the airport around midnight. But thanks.

I knew what he wanted, the hints practically painted across a billboard. I typed one-handed as I dumped the shredded cheese over the broccoli spears.

I have to run into Palo Alto on an errand anyway. I'll drop by a plate in a few hours, assuming it's not a bother.

This would be perfect. Late night. The empty office. The two of us, paper plates in hand, enjoying each other's company. It was an opening, and I'd be an idiot not to take it.

Not a bother at all. See you then.

I smiled and turned up the oven's heat.

~

"So, their revenue was fabricated?" Two hours later, I perched on the edge of the private boardroom table and watched as William dived into my food, his enjoyment clear. I watched as his throat flexed, his Adam's apple bobbing. He hadn't shaved in a week, his skin was tan from his time in Hawaii, and he was overdue for a haircut. The end result was addictive, his wild edges only enhancing his chiseled good looks. His intelligence, the power, and the looks . . . I leaned closer, unable to maintain a respectable distance.

"At least part of it. I'm having to rework the deal with the data we can verify and see if there is still profit to be made."

"And if there's not?" I pushed off the table and picked up his empty bottle.

He watched as I moved to the minifridge to get him another water. "Then I walk. This was an opportunity to expand our footprint, but it wasn't necessary. I won't risk everything on an unknown."

I won't risk everything on an unknown. I glanced at him. Was there a hidden meaning in the words, or had he just given me an unintended peek into the inner workings of his mind? Maybe he considered me a wild card, one with an unknown reaction if he made a move.

It was interesting to see the evolution in him over the last two months. He used to flinch when I touched him, and avoid prolonged eye contact. Vomited Cat's name whenever the conversation turned away from work. Now, I noticed his eyes lingering on me, his gaze warmer when he smiled, his tongue looser to confess. He didn't bring her up very often, and when he did, he rarely used her name. All tells. Little tiny arrows pointing in the right direction.

I bent at the waist over the low minifridge, keeping my legs straight, my butt out. "You don't seem to want to walk away from the deal."

"I don't. If I did, I wouldn't be back here crunching the numbers. I'd be screwing my wife on a beach in Hawaii."

I straightened and came closer, pausing just before him, the crude reference spiking my competitive arousal. "But instead you're here."

"Yes." His eyes lifted to me. "With you."

With me.

He reached for the bottle, and his fingers brushed against mine as I released it. William Winthorpe was an alpha male, one who enjoyed the chase, and I'd fostered that challenge in every way I could. A flirtatious look countered with a small insult. A casual touch followed by a mention of my husband.

Sometimes I wondered if he was doing the same thing with me. A compliment on my dress, a long kiss with his wife. Quick responses to my morning texts but nothing late at night. If it was a game, it was one he played very well and seemed to enjoy. I smiled at him and could feel the lines of our relationship blurring.

Neighbors. Boss. Employee. Friends.

We were circling each other, each rotation growing closer, and was this the moment? Our eyes met, and he stood. "Why did you really come here, Neena?"

"You're hungry," I said quietly, not stepping back, our proximity already too close to be professional. Around us, the empty building lay dormant and silent.

He set his water on the conference table and reached out, his fingertips settling on my waist and tugging me forward until I was flush against him, my thighs to his, hip to hip, the warmth of him branded along my body. *This was it.* His hand slid up my back and twisted around the length of my hair, tugging it back until my chin was lifted, my face turned up to his. *It was happening.* His gaze dropped to my mouth. I held my breath.

And then . . . he lowered his mouth, and his lips met mine. A soft brush, the hair around his mouth tickling mine. A second kiss, this one deeper, our lips parting, his tongue meeting mine. His mouth was warm, his kiss tender, almost hesitant. The great William Winthorpe in a moment of moral indecision. I pulled at the back of his head, strengthening our kiss, and he responded, pushing me back until I hit the wall of the conference room, his hands exploring and gripping—

He pulled away, his hands raised as if protesting his innocence. I sagged against the wall, my footing uncertain, and waited, my lips tingling from the contact.

"That shouldn't have happened." He turned and rested his palms on the table, his strong shoulders hunched over. One hand shot out, a quick movement that startled me, and the water bottle flew across the room and bounced off the wall. He cursed. "You need to go."

"I—ah." I struggled to find the right thing to say. "It's okay, William. No one will ever know."

"Go," he bit out.

I crouched, picking up my bag, and hurried out of the chilly room, my flats tapping softly along the floor until I reached the elevator, my ears pricked for the sound of his call.

It never came, but it didn't matter. I had felt the electricity between us, the passion, the surge of his need. This wasn't the end—it was the beginning, the blurring of lines between professional and friendly, appropriate and not.

Blurred lines. Smear enough of them together, and you could change the color of everything.

His marriage.

My life.

Everything.

CHAPTER 25

CAT

It had been a week since I'd returned from Hawaii, and I still hadn't adjusted to the cool shift in temperatures. I was submerged in the heated pool, sitting at the bottom of the shallow end, when I heard the muffled sound of a yell. I immediately pushed off the rock floor and broke the surface. Blinking the water out of my eyes, I saw Maria, our head of landscaping, kneeling at the side of the pool and waving frantically at me. "What's wrong?"

"It's next door," she whispered. "The new neighbors. There is a man screaming for help. I didn't want to go in case police are needed."

I pushed out of the pool and shivered in the chill of the morning air. Wringing the water from my hair, I took the robe she offered. In the distance, I heard a pained yell and spun my head to the sound. "Who is home? *¿Quien está aquí?*"

"No one. Just us."

"Okay." I yanked the robe on and pushed my feet into my flip-flops.

"Here is your phone." She looked at me worriedly. "What can I do?"

"Nothing. Thank you for letting me know." I ran along the cobble-stone path toward the Ryders' home, my teeth already chattering in the cold. I should have swum indoors today but had relished the idea of a hot-tub session after my swim, and possibly a snack of prosciutto and melon as I enjoyed the smell of fresh-cut grass and roses. I eyed the low wall between our properties and then skirted it, finding an opening in the bushes big enough to slip through. "Matt!" I called out. "Matt! Are you okay?"

"I'm over here!" His voice came from the pool deck, and I sprinted up the deck's side steps and skidded to a stop when I spied him.

I inhaled sharply. "Matt. Don't move."

He lay awkwardly on his stomach in the grass, his arm bent back at an impossible angle, his face gray with pain. Beside him were pieces of an iron railing. I glanced up and spotted the hole in the upper balcony. Pulling my phone from the robe pocket, I quickly dialed 9-1-1.

"I'm getting an ambulance, Matt. Try not to move."

I wrapped my arms around my chest, hugging the material to me as I told the operator their address and what had happened. I ended the call. "They're on their way. Said less than five minutes."

"Call Neena," he rasped.

I was already dialing her number and growled in frustration when it went straight to voice mail. I ended the call and tried again. Same result. Glancing at my watch, I called the main receptionist at Winthorpe Tech, relieved when William's assistant answered the phone.

"Ashley, it's Cat. I need to speak to Neena. Do you know where she is?"

"Of course, Mrs. Winthorpe. She's in a meeting with your husband. I was told not to disturb them."

I frowned. "Are they in his office?"

"No, the boardroom."

The boardroom. The only location in the building, except for the closed labs, where visual privacy was afforded. Was it a coincidence? "I need you to interrupt them. There's been an accident, and I need to speak to Neena immediately."

"Certainly, Mrs. Winthorpe. May I put you on hold? I'll get her right now."

CHAPTER 26

NEENA

I stood behind William's boardroom chair, the heavy leather piece pulled away from the conference table, and kneaded the taut muscles in his neck. "That's it. Inhale slowly and hold." I counted to three in my head. "Now, exhale as slowly as possible."

I found a knot of tension and kneaded it with my thumb, the tight bundle of nerves uncoiling. He finished his exhale and groaned. "God, that feels good."

Of course it did. If I had him naked, I'd work over his entire body. He'd be moaning my name and swearing allegiance to me for life. *Soon,* I promised myself. Soon. I glanced toward the locked boardroom door and wondered how much sound carried outside it.

"Tilt your head back against the chair." He obeyed, settling his long frame against the leather, and I placed my hands on top of his head, softly running my fingers through the thick chunks of his hair, my nails scraping lightly against his scalp. "Let the tension leave through your head. Release any stress or fear and send it up to the universe." I kept the rhythm slow and methodical, giving him just enough and letting him want some more. Lifting my hands from his head, I circled the chair and stopped before him. "Close your eyes."

"Always ordering me around . . ." He sounded drugged, and I applauded myself for taking the next step and introducing him to meditation. I'd been working with the team on positive affirmations and the law of attraction—and William, while slow to accept the idea, was gradually coming on board.

I tugged on his hair gently, and his eyes dragged open. In those dark depths, I could see the need, a fissure of chemistry flaring between us. I reached forward, trailing my fingers down on his lids, a little surprised sparks didn't fly where my touch landed. His mouth fell slightly open, and I imagined it skimming across my skin, over the new lingerie I was wearing. I picked up his wrist and turned his large hand over in mine, his watch sliding down his wrist. He tensed a little, the cords in his wrist flexing, all senses tuned in to my touch.

"Keep your eyes closed," I ordered. "Breathe shallowly. Repeat your mantra."

I set his hand down on the high arm of the chair and ran my fingers along the folds and seams of his sleeve, bringing more of his tension out the tips of his arms. "Release your stress through my fingers. Any worries, any fears. Just let them go. Everything is as it should be, and everything will be okay."

I repeated the action with his other arm, and there was no tension now, his limbs loose and fluid. His breath slowed, his chest barely moving below the mother-of-pearl buttons on his stiff blue dress shirt. I bumped his knees with mine, opening them. When I gently sat on his right thigh, I watched his face, but there was no response, no objection—another boundary easily crossed when patience was used.

This morning, I'd dressed for him. A knee-length pencil skirt with a slit on one side. Hosiery that stopped at my upper thigh. A knit sweater that hugged my large breasts.

I ran my fingertips in soft patterns across his face, tracing the lines of his strong nose, his fierce features, his masculine jaw, the stubble of a missed section of his shave. I moved in small circles across his forehead, wide and gentle strokes over his cheeks, and whisper-soft brushes across his lips.

His eyes opened, and I could see the flecks of darkness in his brown eyes. Darkness and need. Want fighting with hesitation. I forced my fingers to keep moving, to trace the line of his mouth, to zigzag over the rough texture of his lips.

"I can't . . . ," I whispered, knowing that it would spur him on, give him the challenge, let my unsurety distract him from his own.

His gaze sharpened, and I felt his hand as it crept off the arm of the chair and curled around my back, bringing me closer to him. "You can."

There was a moment of stillness, a pause, our faces close, and then he tugged me forward and I dropped my hands from his mouth and clutched at his shirt, yanking him toward me. Our lips met, crashed, and molded, his tongue giving under mine, his hands tightening on my waist as he deepened the kiss.

It was everything I wanted and left our first kiss in the dust. Hot and needy, my body grinding into his as I panted against his mouth, my hands fisting along his shirt as I fought his kiss with my own, our chemistry ratcheting up as the heat level in the room increased.

We jumped apart at the sound, a rapid rap of knuckles against the door. I breathed hard, my lungs expanding as his assistant's voice rang out, her tone insistent as she called my name.

The *bitch*. I pulled away from William and held his gaze, reassuring him with my eye contact as I smoothed my outfit into place. Glancing at the mirror above his credenza, I checked my makeup and hair. Still perfect. Everything in place. I flipped the lock on the door and opened it with a scowl. "Ashley, we still have fifteen—"

"It's your husband," she interrupted me, her features pinched in worry. "He's hurt."

CHAPTER 27

Cat

Neena and William arrived at Matt's house together, her lipstick fresh despite the traumatic news. I watched as they climbed from his car, Neena running past the ambulance to her husband on the stretcher.

"What happened?" William asked as he approached. He frowned at my wet hair, tsking as he pulled my robe tighter, then wrapped me in his arms.

"Looks like he was leaning on the railing and it gave way. Deputy Dan is here looking at it. He said Matt's lucky he landed in the grass. A foot over and he would have hit the pavers."

William winced. "Are you okay?"

"Just chilly." I rested my head against his chest. "And I had to listen to an earful from Dan over speeding in the neighborhood."

"Poor girl," he chided, planting a kiss on the side of my head. "Troublemaker."

"Well, this heroic act should give me some leniency. I told him that." I looked over my shoulder at our neighborhood security officer, a retired detective who took his job way too seriously. "He's convinced this is more than an old railing. You know Dan."

"Oh yes. Let me guess—insurance-policy scam? Or is he thinking murder attempt?" He laughed. Last year, Dan had been adamant that

Mrs. Vanderbilt's torn window screen had been a foiled home-invasion plot. He'd peppered our mailboxes with best practices to avoid intruders, held a special homeowners' watch meeting, and doubled our nightly neighborhood patrols. Behind closed doors, we all mused that should a serial killer ever decide to target Atherton's residents, Dan would spontaneously orgasm at the thought.

"Murder attempt, I think." I smiled. "You know . . . young wife, frumpy husband . . . I bet Neena's got an insurance policy that would leave her comfortable. Add in an affair, and he'll have all the motive he needs."

Was it my imagination, or did he stiffen against me? I looked up in time to catch the uncomfortable look on his face, right before it smoothed into a smile.

"Cat." Neena's steely voice came from behind me, and I turned to see her arms crossed over her balloon chest, the toe of one peep-toed stiletto tapping the floor. "Thank you for coming to Matt's aid. I think we're good here. I'm sure you'd like to go home and"—her gaze slid distastefully over my thin robe—"get some dry clothes on."

"I just want to make sure he's okay. Thank God he didn't fall on the pavers."

"Yes, we're all very grateful," she said tartly.

"Do you need a ride to the hospital?" My husband stepped forward, and I looked at him in surprise.

"Yes," she said quickly. "That would be . . ." She blew out a breath of air, and I watched her closely, curious if there was an actual person under all that plastic. "That would be wonderful. Thank you, William."

Thank you, William. As if he would be driving her to the hospital alone.

"I'll run back home and change." I looked at him. "Swing by and pick me up on your way?"

"Oh, do you mind staying here?" Neena glanced back at the ambulance. "I hate to leave the house open with all these people here. It would be a big help if you could keep an eye on things."

My gaze darted between her and him, and my stomach cramped at the idea of them going to the hospital together. It would be hours of one-on-one waiting time, my husband in easy reach of her manicured little claws. "Sure." I forced a smile. "Anything I can do to help." I wrapped my arms around William, burrowing into his chest, and rose on my toes, giving him a kiss on the neck. "If you need to get to the office, just let me know. I'll come up and relieve you."

"I love you," he said gruffly. "Don't stay out here with that wet hair. Go inside." He nodded to their house. "You can watch things from there."

Neena delivered a stiff smile. "Thank you, Cat. Will, I'll be in the car when you're ready."

Will? I kept my features mild at the nickname. After all, what was three letters? Pushing my thumb along my ring finger, I touched the diamond, reassuring myself of its presence. She headed for the car, and I met William's eyes.

"Don't give me that look," he groaned. "What? What are you worrying about?"

"Ashley said you two were in the boardroom." I shrugged. "What was wrong with your office?"

"I had a meeting prior with a large group. I stayed in the room. After Neena, I would have met marketing in there." He frowned at me. "You don't have anything to worry about. You know that."

"I know that you have four different companies to run, and there's plenty of other people who could take her to the hospital. Me. Maria. A friend, if she even has one."

"Cat, I—"

"Look. Matt is your friend. I understand that. And I want to be here to support them. But you've just been so busy lately, I feel like I haven't gotten any time with you. And yet, now you can ditch everything to go sit in a hospital? You know it's going to be hours, right?"

"I can call—"

"I already called the hospital. They're ready for him, and they'll get him right in. Best and quickest of everything. But still, it's going to take time." I wrapped my arms around his neck, kissing him on the lips. "Just . . . be good."

"I'm always good," he said against my mouth.

I pulled away from him and wished I could believe it.

CHAPTER 28

NEENA

I fastened the seat belt, straining to hear Will's conversation with Cat, one that involved lots of frowns and head shakes. She wrapped her arms around his neck and gave him a kiss. I watched as her hand curled into his hair and fought the wave of jealousy that ripped at my chest. He shouldn't be kissing her. Not when he'd kissed *me* just an hour ago. Not when my husband was in the ambulance and the attention should be focused on getting *me* to the hospital. He lifted his mouth from hers but stayed in place, their heads close, words quiet.

Looking for a distraction, I reached forward and quietly opened the glove box, snooping through the contents. I spotted some eye drops and grabbed them, glancing back out while I twisted open the top. They were still in place, her body clinging to his. Lifting the small vial, I tilted back my head and dripped the saline solution in both eyes, then pocketed the container, flipping the glove box closed. They turned to me, and I managed a pained smile, hoping that they could see the faux tears. I blinked, and a drop dribbled down my cheek.

He kissed the top of her head and left her side, rounding the front of the vehicle and opening the door. "You okay?" He settled into the seat and closed the door, starting the car.

"Yeah." I wanted to reach over and hug his arm, lace my fingers through his, and lean into his warmth—but I didn't. I faced forward, lifting a limp hand in parting as we pulled past Cat. This was an odd part to play—the emotional almost-widow. I tried to think of a take that would endear him to me, one that would make him jealous of Matt. It wasn't a clear path to navigate, especially given the powerful one we'd already been on—the one that had been going so well until *this* interruption of it. What could have happened in the next fifteen minutes of that meeting? Would I have straddled his hips, his hands roaming underneath my sweater? Just the thought of it made me a little light-headed, and I pinched my knees together, shifting on the seat.

"Did they tell you about his injuries?"

I needed to decide what to do when he mentioned the kiss. With our abrupt halt, I wasn't able to follow the plan—one where I would reluctantly tell him that we shouldn't keep this up, all while spurring him on. At the end, I had planned to focus the conversation on keeping the secret versus what we had done. I could probably still follow that plan, but it would be less effective with his mind clear.

"Neena?"

I looked at him. "Yes?"

"Do you know how Matt is? How badly he's injured?"

"Oh." I swallowed and turned a little in the seat to face him, hoping he saw the moisture on my cheeks. I should have been a little more aggressive with the drops. "They said a broken arm and probably some fractured ribs."

"Thank God Cat heard him screaming."

"Yeah." Thank God for Cat. What would I do without her? Oh, let's all praise Cat and her ability to swim laps in her million-dollar pool and hear my husband's cries. I bet she lay all over him when she was helping him out. She probably loosened the tie on her robe and let it fall open, revealing her bikini-clad body. Had he looked at her? I dug my nails into the seat belt, imagining it was her throat. I didn't have much in this life, but Matt was one of the few things that was solidly mine. It was out of line for another woman to lounge all over him during an injured moment when he couldn't move away.

And besides, it wasn't like she saved his life. Chances were, I would have come home after my meeting with William and found him. And if I hadn't—it was a broken arm and some ribs. He could have eventually crawled inside and called his own ambulance. Or, heaven forbid, driven himself to the hospital. Honestly, I don't know why she took it upon herself to call 9-1-1 instead of just calling me.

William paused. "Cat's close with the head of the hospital. She called her already, so they'll take good care of Matt."

I hadn't been aware, until Cat rubbed my face in it, that the Winthorpes had paid for the new east wing of the hospital. She'd assured me that the staff would bend over backward for Matt if they knew "our connection."

She had no idea of connections. No idea of what was growing between her husband and me. William was on the hook. I just needed time—without her or Matt—to reel him in.

"Look . . ." And here it came—the mention of the kiss. I could already hear regret coating his words, an apology hovering on his lips.

I cut him off at the pass. "Don't worry about it." I watched him turn at the light, storefronts and street signs passing, the morning sun streaming through the front windshield. I flipped down the visor and resisted the urge to raise the seat, the height set for Cat's long legs and torso. "It's between us. No one has to know about it."

He said nothing, his eyes on the road. As he made the turn into the hospital, I unclipped the seat belt and leaned forward, grabbing my purse off the floorboard. "Mind dropping me off up front? I'll let the reception desk know we're here."

He nodded, pulling up to the grand front entrance and stopping at the curb. He shifted the vehicle into park, and I leaned toward him, half crawling over the center console as I wrapped my arms around his neck in a hug. "Thank you," I whispered, hoping he could smell the scent of my new perfume.

I felt his hand slide around my back, squeezing me against him for a brief moment. "I'll park and come find you. Call me if you have any trouble."

I pulled away and opened the door. "Thanks. I'll see you inside."

There was a moment before I stepped out—a break of time where our eyes met and I felt the undercurrent of chemistry still taut between us.

Stepping out of the vehicle, I couldn't help but smile.

CHAPTER 29

NEENA

Matt was awkward in the car. His cast was too bulky, bumping into the door with a loud clunk as he tried to adjust the seat belt. From the back seat, I watched him fumble and swallowed a sharp remark.

"Thanks for the ride," he said to William, then turned his head in an attempt to see me. "Neena, why didn't you drive your car?"

I looked out the window, grateful that he couldn't see me from his position. "I was so worried about you. We thought it'd be safer if William drove."

Matt bought it as easily as every other lie I spoon-fed him. I listened as he went on and on, re-creating the yawn-worthy scene for us.

Coffee in hand. Black, like always.

The weather almost too cool to be out on the porch.

Saw a hawk on one of the trees.

Was leaning against the railing, as he always did, when it gave way.

"I swear, I've never cursed those high first-floor ceilings in my life. What do you think they are, eighteen feet?"

Silence hung, and I realized he was talking to me. "Uh . . . yeah. Eighteen feet."

Matt chuckled, and I don't know why he found that funny. "Thank God I hit the grass. You know, they say you should go limp when you fall, and I *knew* that, but I stuck out my hand like an idiot. Good thing I didn't land feetfirst. I'd have snapped my weak ankles like twigs."

He did have weak ankles. We used to laugh about it. I once put an anklet of mine on him and it fit, though a bit snugly, the gold chain tight around his hairy leg.

"Doc gave me three weeks of staying at home and letting my ribs heal."

I made a face at the thought. Three weeks of tripping over him in the house? I'd go mad. And it was his right arm, of all things. He was high maintenance already—would be much more so with a crippled dominant hand. I reached forward and rubbed his good shoulder, making sure that William caught the action. "I'll take good care of you, baby. Spoil you rotten. You're going to hate it when you finally heal enough to get back to work."

He turned his head and kissed my hand, and he really was sweet. It would be hard to re-create the amount of love and naked trust that Matt had for me, paired with his ability to overlook all my flaws.

William's cell rang, and I saw Cat's name light up on the dash. He hit the screen, and her voice broke through the speakers.

"Hi, love. Where are you?"

I hated the way she spoke to him. It was filled with such ownership, such familiarity and confidence. I'd been with Matt since high school, yet somehow—whenever I saw them together—it felt as if we were inadequate. I couldn't wait to knock her off her perch and destroy that casual arrogance.

"We're headed to the house now." The stoplight ahead turned yellow, and William gunned the engine, slipping through as it flashed red.

"Great. I'll head over and meet you. I threw the pieces of the balcony in the trash and put some tape up between the posts."

"That's great, Cat." Matt craned forward, as if he needed to get closer to the delicate speaker in order for it to hear him. "Thank you so much."

Oh yes. Thank you so, so, so much. I thought of her passing through our bedroom and onto the balcony. She probably judged us with every step through the house. Thank God I'd made the bed.

"I'll put up a temporary railing," William offered. "I can do it tomorrow evening. That'll tide you over until you can get a replacement piece."

"That would be great." I reached forward and squeezed his arm, letting my hand trail over his bicep. "That's so kind of you, Will."

On the other end of the phone, Cat said nothing, and I knew that this—me with both of our men—was killing her. I sat back in my seat and smiled. "Will?" I called out sweetly. "Would you mind stopping on the way so we can grab something to eat?"

"I've already got food here," Cat broke in crisply. "William, Philip just made lobster rolls and those cheese biscuits you love."

William perked up, she blabbed on and on about their gourmet lunch, and I was ready to gag by the time they finished their *I love you*s and hung up the phone. It wasn't natural, how often they said it. As a semi–health professional, I could recognize the insecurity in the gesture, the constant need to verify the feelings a giant red exclamation point of concern. If I were a marriage counselor, I'd tell them to hold back the words and show their love more with actions. I'd also pull William aside and make it clear that he could do much, much better.

We started up the hill, into the neighborhood, and I looked out the window, watching as the landscape passed by. In the front seat, the men started a heated conversation about the 49ers' chances of a playoff run. I listened to them talk, laughter and insults slinging between the front seats, and wondered if William felt guilty toward Matt, about our kiss. Or was he like me and turned on by the close association and risk?

I didn't know yet, but I would soon. If there was guilt, I'd massage it. I'd invent and provide a justification for our actions. And if it aroused him, I'd play up that angle, too. Increase the danger and heighten the stakes.

Either way, he didn't have a chance.

NEENA

Now

"According to employees at Winthorpe Tech, you and William Winthorpe started to spend more and more time together and conducted most of your meetings in the boardroom." The detective looked up from her notebook. "Were you meeting in the boardroom because it was more private?"

I thought of the first time we'd had sex, just one week after Matt's fall from the balcony. My skirt pushed up around my hips. His dress slacks unzipped. A pen rolling off the table. It had been quick. Dirty. Sexually unsatisfying but emotionally breathtaking.

"I'm not sure what you're trying to allude to," I said stiffly. "You already know that we had an affair. If you missed it somehow, you need a new job. Cat has made sure that everyone in town knows." They say that hell hath no fury like a woman scorned, and Cat had been a shining example of that mantra.

"You're right, Neena. We have proof that you seduced Ned Plymouth. Proof that you seduced William Winthorpe. Let's jump right ahead to the meat of the matter." She sat on the edge of the table, close enough to touch me, and folded her arms over her scrawny chest. "When did you decide your husband needed to die?"

PART 4

AUGUST

ONE MONTH EARLIER

CHAPTER 30

CAT

"I swear, I literally couldn't listen to another one of that woman's stories. They were disgusting. If you'd been stuck beside her on an international flight, you'd have done the same thing."

William shook with silent laughter, the glass never making it to his lips before he had to set it down. Holding up a hand, he tried to speak. "I—I wouldn't have. I would have smiled politely and listened to every story."

"Oh, bull," I sputtered, leaning back as the waiter set a strawberry shortcake before me. "You would not. During the playground orgy story, you would have found an excuse. Maybe not a ghost on a plane—"

"Definitely not a ghost on a plane." He brought the chocolate torte closer to him. "I would have gone to the bathroom."

"I did that," I pointed out. "I went to the bathroom, came back, and she dived right back into her stories."

I dipped my fork through the six layers of shortcake and cream, watching as the white-gloved staff set down more desserts. After two days of a juice cleanse, we'd thrown caution to the wind and proclaimed ourselves deserving of a drinks-and-desserts date. Two bottles of champagne in, we were laughing through a memory of a promiscuous grandmother

I'd gotten stuck next to on an eleven-hour flight to London. Running out of options, I started screaming that I saw a ghost sitting in her lap. The flustered first-class flight attendants had assured me that there was no ghost, but I'd stuck to my guns until they moved me to a different seat.

He lifted his glass to me. "Here's to being blacklisted from American Airlines."

"Well worth it." I tapped mine against his. "Plus, it prompted the jet purchase." I grinned at him. "Which may have been my evil plan the entire time."

He smiled. "I love you so much."

I leaned over the table and stole a kiss.

We were watching the bananas Foster presentation when he dropped the bomb. "I've been thinking, and I'm ready to think outside the box with starting a family."

It was such an unexpected statement that I choked, a chunk of strawberry lodged in my throat. I took a long sip of water and managed, my stomach coiling in protest against whatever he was about to say. I couldn't do a surrogate. I couldn't. Not yet.

"I'm willing to consider adoption."

The contraction in my stomach eased, and I let out a shuddering breath, switching to champagne as I processed the information. "Are you sure?" I studied him. "You've always been against—"

"I've been stubborn. You know, male lineage and pride. But I want a family, and let's face it, I'm getting old." He grimaced.

"You're not old." I reached for his hand, pulling it across the table, and tried to decide if I was happy or hurt by the realization that he was giving up on my ovaries.

He smiled at me. "I want to see you as a mom. And Neena said that the adoption process can be as quick as a few months."

Any percolating enthusiasm immediately withered on the vine. "What does Neena have to do with anything?"

"Well, you know—with Matt, they can't have children. They've looked into adoption in the past. She's the one who brought it up and pushed me to consider it."

"So you two discussed my infertility *again*?" I pushed the plate away, nauseated by the thought. She'd thrown away her baby. Kept it from reaching a family who might want to adopt. And yet he was discussing it with *her*. Getting advice from *her*.

"No, it wasn't—" He stopped. "Please, I don't want to ruin our evening. I thought you'd be happy."

"I find it interesting that she and Matt looked into adoption, considering that she had an abortion eight years ago." I clenched my jaw, immediately upset with myself for showing the trump card I should have held on to longer. But I couldn't keep the words inside, not when they had clawed up my throat and out of my mouth. She had killed her baby—she didn't have the right to adopt another.

"What?" He flinched, and maybe it hadn't been wasted after all. "Where did you hear that?"

"It's true. I have proof of it." I crossed my arms and rested them on the white linen surface. "So, if Matt's shooting blanks, then who do you think the father was?" I raised one brow and waited for a response.

Beside his spoon, his phone lit with a notification. He glanced at the screen, and it was all I could do to keep from reaching over to see if it was her. "I'm not going to ask why you're digging into Neena." His gaze flicked back to me. "But I just told you I was open to adoption, something you've pushed for for years, and you're turning this conversation into a fight about her."

"I want you to fire her." I straightened in the seat, surprised a little by my own suggestion, one I'd fantasized over for weeks but had never intended on broaching. "She isn't healthy for our marriage."

"I can't fire her," he argued back. "We're within weeks of FDA approval. We're getting bombarded with requests and offerings—I need to have the team cohesive. I can't rip Neena away from them now."

"She cheated on Matt. Why in the hell would I want her anywhere near you?" I lowered my voice, aware of the close proximity of the waiter, our bananas Foster almost complete. "Don't put the company before us."

"Don't put your insecurity in the way of something I've worked four years on." He reached for my hand and gripped it, leveling me with a stare that would intimidate anyone but had never worked on me.

"*We've* worked four years on," I corrected him. "I was right there beside you. Supporting you. And if I thought Neena's presence had a single iota of an effect on WT's success, I—"

"She has an effect. It doesn't matter if you don't see it."

I pulled my hand free, looking away as the waiter set the sizzling presentation before us. She *didn't* have an effect, not on Winthorpe Tech and not on him. Three months of team building and employee quizzes didn't replace thirteen years of marriage.

"Cat, let's focus on what's important. We're about to get the device in a marketable place, and then I can work less. Focus on our family. A family I want to move forward with, even if it is through adoption."

Even if it is through adoption. A substandard solution, but acceptable in order to achieve his end result. He was always a businessman at heart and oblivious to the knife he wielded with such careless accuracy. Was I a crucial element to this equation, or a component that could be easily replaced if faulty? I used to swear on our allegiance. Now, with his refusal to fire Neena, his constant attention to his phone, his increasing detachment from me . . . I didn't know. I didn't know anything.

I smoothed my napkin on my lap and tried to fit my thoughts into neat boxes that would make sense.

"William, I'm excited that you've warmed to the idea of adoption, but I feel like you've been growing apart from me. Neena is wedging herself in between us. You think it's all focused on Winthorpe Tech, but it's more than that. Her interest in you . . . it's unhealthy."

"That's your insecurity and paranoia talking. She gives the same amount of focus to every other team member."

I rolled my eyes. "Really? She's jogging with the biologists? Is she popping into any other employee's house with their favorite cookies? You don't understand. She's going after you."

"Just stop." His voice was louder than it should have been, and I glanced sharply at the other tables, worried his voice had carried. "Can you focus for a minute? I'm trying to talk to you about our future."

"Look, if you want to start the adoption process, then I'm in."

His features calmed, and I hurried to finish the thought.

"But the *minute* we have FDA approval, Neena's done at Winthorpe. Give her a big parting bonus if you have to, but I want her desk cleared and her security badge returned. I want to go back to a normal relationship with my neighbors, one where she stays on her side of the hedges and we stay on ours. Okay?"

He beamed at me. "Sure."

"I'm serious," I warned. "She's gone after FDA approval."

He laced his fingers through mine and pulled me in for a kiss. "Deal."

It should have felt like a win, but it didn't.

CHAPTER 31

NEENA

Something had changed with William. I sensed it in our morning team meeting, the way his gaze stubbornly stayed at different points around the room but never in my direction. I saw it in his doodle along the edge of his notebook during my group visualization exercise. I felt it in the silence that followed my text messages, his chatty behavior suddenly reduced to a stony quiet.

I watched him warily and tried to understand the source of the chill. Was it Matt? Guilt over our kisses? Cat? I pulled up her social media profiles and scanned the posts, looking for a hint. Club events. Charity galas. Professional-quality photos of her morning coffee, their gardens in the back. A new pair of heels, the angle not-so-innocently including a glimpse of their walk-in closet, the racks of color-coordinated shoes lit and displayed like jewels on velvet shelves.

"I need to see you in the boardroom." William spoke from my office doorway, his tone curt. Without waiting for a response, he turned and walked down the hall, heading for the private conference room.

Closing the internet browser, I grabbed my phone and notebook and followed. I glanced both ways down the hall, making sure no one saw me, then went in.

"Close the door behind you." He stood by the windows, his hands in his pockets.

I did, then moved hesitantly into the room, preparing for whatever he was upset about. My best defense, I decided, would be to blame everything on—

"Cat told me you've had an abortion. Is that true?" He turned to me, his gaze sharp, and I floundered, the accusation one that I hadn't anticipated.

"Uh—yes." Out of everything I had done, the procedure had barely registered in my history, and I tried to piece together what he must be thinking and how that nosy bitch had found out. "I—"

"I don't care about the abortion. Do what you want with your body, but it does bring into very clear focus that you're a disloyal wife. I don't need to be romantically seduced, Neena. We're two adults here. If you want me to have sex with you, just say so."

I cleared my throat, trying to understand the stiff brace of his shoulders, the curtness in his words. He was an alpha male. He should want the chase, the game. I looked at the floor and tried to readjust my strategy. "I'm . . . not sure what to do. I've never felt—"

He moved closer until he was directly before me and forced my chin up, my eyes on his. "Cut the crap, Neena. I don't buy your sweet-and-innocent routine. Either you *want* this or You. Don't. Which is it?"

"I want it," I whispered.

"Fine." He dropped his hand from my chin. "Skirt up. Panties down. And if you feel the need to scream, don't."

CHAPTER 32

CAT

I perked up at the view of delivery trucks and vehicles at the Vanguards' house, ready for my summer of isolation to end. Turning into our driveway, I waited for the gate to open and placed a call to Kelly.

It was answered midyell, her voice rising as she lectured her son on sunscreen, then huffed out a hello.

"Looks like they're prepping the house for you. When are you coming home?"

"In six days, and I tell you, Cat—I'm looking forward to it. I'm done with South America. Next year, I told Josh, we need to go to Paris. Don't they always say Paris in the summer?"

"I thought you hated Paris."

She blew out an annoyed breath. "Whatever, we're just not coming back to Colombia. It's like they're unfamiliar with the concept of flat steamed milk."

"Sounds like a rough life."

"Oh, shut up. You're as spoiled as the rest of us; you just hide it better. But yes, we're coming back Friday and shipping the horses over tomorrow. Don't say anything snarky, but one of them has my name on it. I just couldn't resist his big doe eyes."

I laughed, and the cold rock in my chest warmed slightly at the idea of her return.

"Once we get back, I'm thinking a party is in order. Something casual, maybe just a few couples over for the Stanford game."

"Count us in." I pulled down the drive and parked in front, leaving my key in the ignition. Once I was inside, someone would move it into the garage after doing a top-to-bottom detail. Was Kelly right? Was I as bad as all of them, or even potentially worse? I hadn't visited a gas station in a decade, hadn't set foot in a grocery store for close to as long, and thought nothing of freshly ironed sheets, a bath already drawn for me when I returned from tennis, or of having a social assistant on salary.

"What are you doing for tonight's game?"

I groaned and pushed open the front door, stepping into the quiet interior and setting my purse on the large round entrance table, next to a towering arrangement of fresh-cut daylilies. "Going to Neena and Matt's. Apparently our husbands have bonded over football." Another association formed while I was trying my best to yank our two couples apart.

"How are things with the little blonde? Was I right? Social leech?"

"You were right about that . . . and more. She's become much closer to William than I would like."

"You've got to nip that in the bud before it becomes a problem. Remember Josh and that nanny? Best baby nurse I'd ever seen, but I wasn't about to let that fresh-faced girl live in our house, not with everything she and he seemed to have in common. I mean—fantasy football? How did I end up with the only woman on earth who enjoys fantasy football?"

I put her on speakerphone and settled down on the couch, checking social media and then my email. My thoughts slowed upon seeing the email from Beck Private Investigations. "Kelly, I've got to run. The game is at six, and I haven't even showered."

"Okay, but listen—bring Neena over to next week's game. Josh wanted to talk more with her husband anyway, and I'd like to spend some time with her."

I clicked on the email. "Why does this sound like I'm leading her to slaughter?"

She let out a laugh. "Oh, honey, you know me too well. But I'll behave. After all, you've got to know your enemy before you can destroy them."

I smiled at the sentiment, one that echoed my thoughts exactly. "Fine, I'll suffer through tonight's game with them and extend the invite to your house for next week's."

"Perfect. I'll see you then. Give a hug to William for me."

I ended the call and scrolled through the email, which included a link to the invoice and a few photos. I expanded the images.

William and Neena, on the neighborhood trail, half-obscured by a tree. They were standing by the overlook, her hand on his arm, his face tilted toward hers. Casually innocent, but the proximity sent a knife through my stomach.

A photo of the Winthorpe Tech parking garage. Clearly at night, the exit sign glowing in the dark, only two cars parked beside the security guard's cart. His Porsche and her BMW. I studied the photo with trembling fingers, finding the time stamp in the upper right-hand corner—8:44 p.m. It didn't make any sense until I saw the date. July 14. My birthday. I thought of my solitude in Hawaii . . . his time alone at the office . . . and looked back at the photo. *Not* alone at the office.

I sat down on the closest chair, my chest tightening in a sharp pain. I took a deep breath, trying to calm down, but this was too much. I heard William's car pulling down the drive and quickly logged out of my email.

William knew about the abortion, but the rest . . . I quickly checked my face in the mirror beside the door, making sure that my eyes were dry, my expression calm. I needed to be smart with this information, and with everything in Beck's report. Play my cards closer to the vest. Line up the dominoes and then let them fall.

I'd already tapped the first one, but no one knew that yet. I opened the front door and beamed at my husband, admiring his strong profile as he strode around the front of the glossy car and up the steps toward me. He planted a quick kiss on my mouth, then lifted me up and swung me in a small circle. Gripping him fiercely, I looked across the dark-green lawn, the tip of the Ryders' roof just visible above the row of cypress trees, squatting on the low lot like a bad child in time-out.

CHAPTER 33

NEENA

In my kitchen, I adjusted a stack of cardinal-red napkins and topped off a glass of wine. "Can you turn that down?" I snapped. "I can't even hear myself think."

Dutifully, Matt raised the remote and adjusted the television's volume, not moving from his place in the living room.

"And put these items on the buffet. They'll be here any moment."

He lumbered out of the recliner and to his feet, making his way slowly toward me. "The food and the drinks?"

"Just the food. Use a hot pad underneath them."

I glanced over the dishes with a critical eye. Glazed meatballs. My famous chili. Steak and blue cheese bruschetta. I might not have a private chef, but there was nothing here for Cat to turn up her nose at. I opened the fridge, verifying that a dozen bottles of William's favorite beer were lined up and ready. At the counter, Matt struggled to lift the heavy chili pot with his good arm, and I sighed, batting him away. "I'll get that one."

It'd been four days since our sex in the boardroom. Four days when William had stayed in his office and away from mine. Our Wednesday and Friday meetings had both been canceled by him, his assistant emailing me the update without an excuse. I'd almost expected a no-show today, but Cat's texts had been bubbly, friendly, and cancellation-free. My texts to William had gone unread.

Postsex was normally the time men hounded me, desperate for reassurances of their sexual performance. William had zipped up his pants, tucked in his shirt, and walked away without a word—then completely ignored me. I'd blame it on the unsatisfying sex, but while he had neglected my pleasure, he certainly seemed to have had enough of his own.

Or maybe I was wrong. Maybe he'd hated it. Maybe his quick finish had been a hurried attempt to bail out on a mistake. My insecurity warmed to the idea, then panicked, offering up suggestions and criticisms in chaotic repetition. I had to fix things before the self-doubt became a permanent obsession.

I set down the pot of chili, centering it on the hot pad, and took a deep breath. It was normal, I reminded myself, to have a period of cold feet after a big action. It had nothing to do with the dimple of cellulite I'd seen when pulling up my panties, or the believability of my faked orgasm. It couldn't have. William had an addictive personality, and addicts were a very predictable breed who followed a standard pattern.

Act.

Enjoy.

Regret.

Push away.

Yearn.

Obsess.

Justify.

Obsess.

Turn against those who keep them from their addiction.

Obsess.

Act.

My father had proven that cycle again and again. With gambling. With women. With alcohol. With abuse. And maybe there was more of him in me than I wanted to admit. After all, I'd formed an addiction of sorts to William Winthorpe. The slow construction of building and creating *his* obsession with *me* . . . that was the job I hadn't finished, skipping over a few crucial steps in my haste for the prize. But it wasn't all for naught. I had played my role well during the last four days. I'd stayed away. Been nonthreatening and temptingly aloof. Now I just had to play tonight's interaction the right way. Follow his cues. Keep him off balance. Set the hook in his gills deep enough that later, when I started to reel him in, he'd be helpless to do anything but flop toward me.

I adjusted the shimmery gold V-neck top that innocently displayed a bit of my bra when viewed at the right angle. Reaching into my bra, I adjusted my cleavage, bringing it forward before picking up the platter of veggies and dip. Following Matt to the buffet table, I eyed his placements before nodding in approval.

"Knock, knock!" Cat called out, easing open the side door.

I glanced over, smiling when I saw William step in. "Hey, there. I was about to call you. It's almost kickoff."

"Oh, you know how things go. We got . . . distracted." She gave a coquettish giggle and reached over, gripping a handful of William's butt as if she were a twenty-dollar hooker. I took a quick sip of wine to keep myself from gagging.

She swept forward and hugged me, and I returned the gesture, making eye contact with William over her shoulder.

"William." Matt approached, and William's face broke into a warm smile. "Ready to watch Stanford lose?"

"Not likely," he responded. "But if they do, I plan to soothe my anguish with that twenty-one-year-old tequila you've been hiding from me."

My husband laughed as if it weren't true, as if he didn't squirrel away the Fuenteseca every time company came over. "Let's break it out tonight. I have a feeling you'll need it."

178

I watched as Matt stole William away, leading him toward the living room.

"This food smells fantastic," Cat mused. "We skipped lunch, so we're starving. And . . ." She pulled a wrapped gift from the interior of her bulky designer purse, the same one looped over every celebrity's arm. "I brought you this. Happy birthday."

I paused, stunned. "How did you know it was my birthday?"

"You had it on your club application. My social coordinator keeps track of everyone's birthdays and sends me reminders. I'm sorry it's a day late." She settled in at the bar top, setting her bag on the granite counter.

Had William known as well? Had he intentionally not said anything on Friday? Had he seen the huge rose arrangement that Matt had sent to the office? Surely he had. I'd put them on the low file cabinet by my desk, in clear view of the hall.

"You didn't need to get me anything," I said helplessly, taking the beautifully wrapped box she held out. "I didn't get you anything for your birthday."

"Oh, shut up and open it." She smiled and worked her way out of her thin coat. She was dressed like it was winter, complete with a cream scarf and matching gloves. "Come on. I've been waiting weeks to give this to you."

Under her coat was a vibrant red wrap dress. On me, the color would have highlighted my pale skin, but against her olive tan and dark features, her toothpaste-ad smile . . . she looked like a million dollars.

The gift was small, and I tried to guess at its contents. Maybe a watch? I glanced at my own timepiece—a Cartier lookalike that I'd found on Black Friday years ago. I pulled away the thick cream wrapping paper, unveiling a red box.

"Shake it," she urged. "Guess what it is."

I obeyed, feeling like a child as something rattled inside. "Um . . ." I tried for something conservative. "A paperweight?"

She let out a delighted trill. "Oh, you're terrible at this game. Just open it."

Setting aside the paper, I worked open the lid to reveal a product box, one cradled atop red tissue paper. My thoughts stalled at the image on the front. Not a watch. *Definitely* not a watch. I glanced up at her. "Is this—"

"Oh my God, you're going to love it," she gushed with a furtive look over her shoulder at the men. "We call it the six-minute orgasm."

"We?" I turned over the box, the small handheld device looking more like a face massager than a pleasure deliverer. "Who's we?"

"Well, you know." She took the torn wrapping paper and gift box from me, and I stared at the vibrator, trying to formulate an appropriate response.

By the time I looked up, my mind still blank, she had worked off her first glove and was getting off her second. A flash of sparkle caught my eye, and I grabbed her wrist, taking a closer look at the gigantic ring on her finger. "Wow. That's new."

She blushed. "A surprise present. William gave it to me last night."

I thought of his lack of texts. His guilt. I turned her hand, examining her new wedding ring in the light. The center stone was at least ten carats. Perfectly cut, with a diamond-covered band. "What'd you do with your old ring?"

She shrugged. "I think I'll get a matching stone and have earrings made."

Said in the casual and annoying way of a woman with more diamonds than she knew what to do with. Jealousy twisted my gut, and I fought the urge to hide my own ring. It was barely two carats, a size I used to be joyous over—but it was starting to feel smaller and smaller with time.

"It's beautiful." I stared at the stone and tried to see the positive—every time I saw it, I could remember what prompted it. *His guilt over sex with me.* It was a mini trophy in the battle between us. I just couldn't tell if it had my name on it or hers. Should I be feeling triumphant or defeated?

"He *proposed* to me when he gave it to me. Asked me if I'd marry him all over again." She blinked, and I was surprised to see tears beginning to mat the lashes underneath her eyes.

I yanked a napkin off the top of the stack and offered it to her. "Here." *He asked her to marry him?* That was a bad sign. I thought quickly, trying to understand his current mindset.

"And I wanted to thank you." She grabbed my forearm and squeezed it, the action awkward, considering I still held the sex-toy box. "I don't know what you said to him, but he says he's ready to adopt."

"Really?" My heart fell. Maybe she was lying. After what William and I had just done, there was no way he was talking to her about children. Nausea swelled at the thought of her scooping up a running toddler, his face filled with pride.

He'd be a great dad. Hands-on. Loving. Lots of fun. The kids would go to him for anything they wanted, and he'd let them have it all. They'd never know the slur of his voice when he ridiculed them, or the weight of his body, throwing them against a wall.

That wasn't how that conversation had been meant to go. When I'd brought up adoption last week, it was with the intent of pointing out Cat's infertility, planting an image in his head of an alternate future he could have with me—carrying his own baby. A true Winthorpe, not some trashy woman's rejected infant.

Cat sighed. "I have to admit, you've done an amazing job—with the team and with him."

Something wasn't right about this. Cat was too warm, too accepting, and I didn't like the sudden jump in support of my work. She'd all but laughed over my job before, and now she was gushing? Was this all because of the ring? Or was it the new possibility of having a family?

Her arms crushed around me, and I added another likelihood—she was drunk. She pulled away, and I felt unsteady, too many factors suddenly added to this game.

"Anyway . . ." Cat dabbed at her bottom line of lashes and gestured to the vibrator. "I really love mine, and I thought you'd like one, too. You know." She smirked. "For when Matt is out of town."

"Oh." I looked back down at it. "Thank you."

She studied me for a minute, her beautiful features pinching. "Oh God. I weirded you out, didn't I? I'm sorry."

I stopped her. "You didn't weird me out. Honestly. It's a great gift. It's just . . ." I shrugged, grateful for the change in subject. "Thank you." *For this trashy, cheap sex toy.*

"Oh, it was nothing." She pushed off the stool with a big smile. "Now, sit down and let me fix you a drink. We've got four hours of time to kill, and I've got the juiciest gossip about one of the security guards at the north gate."

I glanced at the men and opened our junk drawer, slipping the vibrator in among the scissors, pens, and Scotch tape. Following her deeper into the kitchen, I watched as she opened up cabinets and got to work with our drinks. When she dropped the queen-bee act, there were times when she was almost likable.

She reached for a bottle of vodka, and I straightened.

"Oh, wait—I have something chilling for you." Crouching down, I opened the wine cooler and pulled out the bottle of limoncello that I had purchased for her. I twisted the cap. "I already opened it—had to try a little last night to see what the fuss was all about." She'd gone on and on at dinner one night about a limoncello vintage that was—in her words—to *die* for. Both Matt and William had expressed dislike over the lemon liqueur, which I'd never had.

"Wow! I can't believe you found this." She swooped forward, picking up the rare edition, which I had spent hours tracking down. I'd ended up ordering it from Italy, the shipping price more than triple what the bottle had cost. "Did you love it?"

"I have to side with Matt and William on this one. It was too sour for me. So—" I gestured to it. "Please, drink up. It's all for you."

"Thank you so much." She beamed, then squeezed me in another hug, and I almost felt guilty for what I was doing. *Almost.*

~

Two hours later, the game paused for halftime, and we took the opportunity to sit outside. It was pleasant, looking over the lit pool, the twinkle lights on, our firepit crackling. Though he had done it slowly and complained about his ribs and arm the entire time, Matt had actually gotten off his butt and helped out. With the recent injury, he'd grown more needy, as if his good arm were as useless as his bad. Still, his injury had an upside—his inabilities had given me several opportunities to ask William to come over and fix things or lift heavy items. And while my husband had many shortcomings, ignorance was still one of his strengths.

I passed through the arched opening and spotted our husbands already by the firepit, glasses in hand, the ice drenched in something golden. "That better not be tequila," I warned the pair as I slipped my arms around Matt.

"Let's pretend it's not." Matt smiled at me, and I rose on my toes, gently planting a kiss on his lips.

I stole his glass and peered at him over the rim, playing the sexy, coy wife. "Let's pretend I'm not going to steal it from you." I tipped back his glass and was rewarded by a chuckle from William. A chuckle I ignored, turning my head to call out to Cat. "Need any help?"

From the kitchen, she scooped a slice of my blueberry pie onto a plate and hummed along with the Stanford fight song. "Nah. Just find out who's eating."

I glanced at William. "Are you going to eat any of my pie?" I kept my expression blank and innocent, devoid of the playfulness I'd given Matt.

He studied me, trying to understand if I heard the sexual innuendo in the words. "Sure," he said finally. "I'll have a piece."

I would have preferred a comment about how much he loved my pie, but I still chalked it up as a step in the right direction.

~

A round of pie later, I was in the kitchen struggling with a bottle of champagne when William came in, two plates in hand, and gave me an awkward smile. "Here. Let me get that for you."

"Thanks." I sighed. "This cork is a pain."

He took the heavy bottle, our arms brushing, and I forced myself to take a step away. Grabbing a dish towel, I dried off my hands as I watched him. "Look. About the other day . . ." I glanced toward the back deck, Cat and Matt still involved in a heated debate over whether a stop sign was needed at the Rolling Pine intersection. She cupped her glass to her chest, and I was pleased to see the bottle of limoncello beside her, over half of it gone. Were her words slurring yet? "It was a mistake, and all my fault. I'm sorry. It won't happen again—it *can't* happen again."

He nodded. "I'm glad to hear you say that. I feel the same way. I—"

"Good. That's a relief." I blew out a breath and managed an awkward laugh. "I was worried that you would want to . . ."

"Wanting shouldn't be part of the equation," he said quietly, his forearms flexing as he popped the cork, the sound adding an exclamation point to the end of the statement.

"No," I agreed, letting my own voice fall to match his, and injected a hint of yearning into the single syllable. I cleared my throat. "So, we're agreed. Never again."

"Never again." He nodded, holding my gaze, and I warmed at the sexual tension that crackled between us.

Wanting to end on a high note, I turned to the cabinet and plucked out a fresh flute. I took my time in pouring the champagne, listening as William's steps rounded the island and headed toward the sofa, the kickoff in progress.

Another woman might have seen the conversation as a fail, but I knew exactly what I was doing.

I stuck my head out the back door to call Matt in, and paused, my back stiffening as I saw him take a sip from Cat's glass. He paused, then took another. I heard her giggle and strode out to the pair. "What are you doing?" I snatched the glass from his hand and shoved it at Cat. "You hate limoncello."

"Aw, I convinced him to give it another try. Like I said, this one is amazing. It's like candy." She put her hand on Matt's arm, and I stared at the contact, hoping her fingers would turn black and rot off. "Isn't it? Tell me that you didn't enjoy it."

He blushed under her attention, and I glared at him, daring him to agree. Catching my look, he straightened. "It's, uh, still not for me. Too sour."

"The game's back on," I said sharply. "We should get inside."

"Oh, sure." Cat stood, reaching for the bottle. She misjudged the distance, and I flinched when the bottle tilted off the table and fell toward the tile. There was a sharp crack as it landed, and I jumped back as glass and liqueur shot in all directions. Cat cursed and whirled to me with an anguished expression. "Oh, Neena, I'm so sorry. I must—" She swayed to one side, and I wished William were here to see what a mess she was.

"Don't worry about it," I bit out. "I'll clean it up. Go sit in the living room and keep William company. Matt, you, too. I don't want you to miss the game."

"But you went to all that—that workkkk to find it." She slurred the word and sank into a wobbly crouch, picking up glass shards and collecting them in her palm. "I'm so sowrrry."

"Seriously, stop." I pulled on her arm and got her upright. "I've got this."

Matt stepped carefully over the broken bottle, his cast held high, as if he were wading through waist-deep water. Coaxing Cat into the living room, he led the way, pausing to assist when she tripped over the transom.

She should really go home. She couldn't be feeling well. After cleaning up the mess, I'd suggest it.

I took my time sweeping the broken pieces into a dustpan, then went over the floor with a dry mop, then a wet one. By the time I made it back to the living room, Cat was curled into the right side of the sofa, her heels off, feet tucked underneath her. Her face looked almost gray, and I studied her carefully as I took the chair closest to William. "Are you feeling okay?"

"Not . . . great, actually." She put a hand on her stomach.

"Would you like to lie down in the guest room? Or head home? Please, don't feel like you have to stick out the game." The offers were delivered perfectly, with just the right amount of concern.

"I think I will actually head home." She reached down and grabbed her shoes.

"Really?" William leaned toward her, concern pinching his features. "Is it your stomach or your head?"

"It's more like—" She stood, and whatever she was about to say was lost in the forward heave of her body, one that shot a projectile of bloodred vomit all over the front of William's shirt.

CHAPTER 34

Cat

The vomiting didn't stop. I left Neena and Matt's with a paper bag in hand, William running next door to grab our car and pick me up out front. Neena cooed with concern as William opened my door and carefully helped me into the front seat. My vision blurred, and I clutched at his shoulder, relieved when he helped with my seat belt.

"She probably just needs to lie down," Neena said to William, so quietly that I had to strain to hear the words. "She's drunk. She'll sleep it off and be fine in the morning."

She was wrong. My freshman year of college, I held the chugging record of our sorority. I've gone shot for shot with grown men on Valencia Street. I knew what drunk felt like, and this was something else. This felt like, if I took dear Neena's advice and went to sleep, I'd never wake up. This felt like my stomach was tearing into two and rotting from the inside out. All this had been a mistake. Coming over today. Drinking so much. Eating that nasty chili and stuffing my face with meatballs.

"I'm going to take her to the hospital to be safe."

"We'll come with you." Matt, sweetheart that he was, spoke up without hesitation. "I can follow you in our car."

"The hospital?" Neena said with an awkward laugh. "William, she's *drunk*. Or maybe she has a stomach bug. And Matt, there's vomit everywhere. I need to clean that up before it sets."

"We're going to the hospital," Matt said firmly. "William, I'll bring you a clean shirt, unless you want to grab one from my closet before you go."

"If you can bring one, that would be great. I want to get her there as soon as possible. Neena, thank you for the food and drinks."

She protested again, but William was already rounding the front of the car and opening the driver's door, settling in the seat next to me. He reached over and grabbed my hand. "Sit tight, sweetie. I'll have you at the hospital in just a few minutes."

A cramp hit my abdomen, and I gasped in pain. "Please hurry."

~

"Poisoned?" An hour later, William squinted at the doctor as if he didn't understand the word. "With what?"

I lay back on the hospital bed and stared at the doctor, trying to keep up with the conversation.

"We'll know in a few hours. We've sent off the stomach contents for testing. In a case like this, we would normally contact the authorities before sharing the information with you. That being said, we understand that this is a delicate situation and wanted to present you with the option of whether to include the police."

A delicate situation. What an interesting way to refer to the millions of dollars we donated every year. If I had a broken arm and black eye, would we be afforded the same privilege? William looked at me, and we had a long moment of silent communication. I returned my attention to the doctor. "Can you tell how long ago I ate—or drank—whatever made me sick?"

"Sometime in the last few hours. You're lucky you came right in. We were able to pump out what you didn't vomit up before the body had a chance to metabolize the chemicals into toxic acids. Once that happened, you could have gone into metabolic acidosis."

William nodded, as if that jumble of words meant anything, and to him, it might have.

"So, the last twelve hours." I glanced at the clock on the wall. Eight thirty.

"You had a bagel at breakfast," William reminded me.

"Right. With coffee and fruit." I struggled to remember the contents of the plate, which I'd enjoyed on the garden balcony along with my new novel. "Mango and blueberries. There was, um . . . avocado and a poached egg on the bagel."

"We skipped lunch," William remarked. "I remember you mentioning how hungry you were on the way to the Ryders'."

"How did you feel during the day? Any loss of coordination? Fatigue? Headache? Nausea?" The machine beside me began a series of beeps, and the doctor reached over, pressing buttons until the sound ceased.

I frowned, thinking. After a period of time, I shook my head. "I really didn't start feeling off until halftime of the game. I remember going to the bathroom and feeling queasy." I gave a rueful laugh. "I thought it was just the alcohol going to my head."

"The Ryders—those are your friends out in the hallway?"

We both nodded, and the doctor made a notation on his clipboard. "What did you eat at their home?"

"Meatballs and chili. And limoncello." William answered for me, then tilted his head, thinking. "Did you drink anything other than the limoncello?"

"A glass of water, once." Neena had extended the glass with a knowing look, as if I were making a fool of myself and needed to slow down.

I thought of her new couch, now splattered with my vomit, and hoped it was drying in the creases, staining it forever.

"I'm not saying that ethylene glycol was the culprit, but it has a very sweet taste. It could have been in food but was most likely in your drink. Limoncello would have easily masked it."

"Antifreeze?" William blanched. "You think she drank antifreeze?"

"We'll be able to confirm the exact culprit soon. But that's the most common." The doctor looked at me. "Do you want me to call the police? They could go to the Ryders' and test the food there."

"No." I shook my head, thinking of the dropped bottle of liqueur, any evidence lost. "We'll figure this out on our end. Thank you for your discretion."

The doctor left, and William sank into the chair beside my bed. "What do you think happened? Is there any chance you—"

"Accidentally drank antifreeze?" I choked out a laugh, then winced at the pain it created in my sore abs. "No. But I also don't want to accuse Neena and Matt of anything. I mean, Matt drank the limoncello, also. Not a lot of it, but a sip or two. He seems to be okay."

"You had a lot more than a sip or two of it," William said carefully. "The doctor said it tastes sweet. Do you think some could have been in it?"

"Honestly?" I sighed. "I don't know. But William . . . if the limoncello had antifreeze in it—how? Who?"

His hand tightened on mine. From outside in the hall, I heard Neena's voice.

I closed my eyes and tried to shift on the hospital cot, rasping out a cry of pain at the motion. "I can't deal with Neena right now. Could you make some excuses for me? Get them both out of here?"

"Of course." He leaned forward and kissed my forehead. "Give me a few minutes." He squeezed my hand and stood, moving quietly out of the room, the door pulled tight behind him. I heard the muffled sound of his voice, then Neena's and Matt's.

I wanted her out of here and far away from me. I remembered her arguing that I was fine, telling my husband to have me sleep it off. If I had, I could have died. Was Matt okay? Did he have any symptoms?

Her voice rang out again, and I fisted the sheet, straining to hear what they were saying. William's voice grew louder, and when the door to the room creaked open, I turned my head and met his eyes.

"They're leaving now."

"Thank you." I relaxed back against the bed. "How long before I can go home?"

"I'm having a private doctor sent to the house. We can leave anytime, but I'd like the ambulance to take you home, just so they can continue the fluids and monitor you during the ride."

"Have them prepare the guest suite for the doctor—"

"The house staff is already working on it. Don't worry about any of that. Just get better." He looked down at me, his face tight with worry. "God, Cat. If I ever lost you . . ."

"You won't," I swore, and closed my eyes, comforted by the grip of his hand on mine.

CHAPTER 35

NEENA

I stared out the window as Matt pulled the car out of the visitors' lot. The seat belt cut into my stomach, and I knew I should hit the treadmill before bed and burn off the extra thousand calories our little get-together had caused. The bruschetta had been a mistake. I hadn't been able to stop myself from taking one after another, the blue cheese–topped calorie bombs barely helping my nerves as Cat had downed glass after glass of the expensive limoncello. William hadn't even *looked* at me in the hospital. He'd dismissed me as if I were one of his employees, as if we hadn't shared a dozen special moments, a unique bond, a *sexual* history. Pulling at the waist of the seat belt, I stewed over the brush-off.

Matt put on the blinker too early, and the tick-tick-tick filled the car. I listened to the maddening sound for a half minute, then reached over and flipped it off. "There's no one around," I said tersely. "Just turn."

He turned, and I stared out the window, watching as a runner stopped at the intersection, jogging in place. I should have run this morning. I'd been so stressed over everything with tonight that I'd skipped it. "I should have just stayed home. I could have cleaned up the mess. Now her vomit is going to be caked on."

Honestly, with the staff that Cat had, *she* really should have sent over someone to help. I didn't have the money or inclination to bring in a professional crew just to clean up her mess.

"I don't think you're understanding what has happened." Matt spoke slowly, as if I were mentally handicapped. "William said that Cat ingested something that made her sick. That she was poisoned."

"Oh, please," I sputtered. "*Poisoned?* Matt, you don't believe that. That's Cat being dramatic."

"You saw her. She looked terrible. She threw up everywhere."

"So, someone *poisoned* Cat? Who? Why?"

"I think William thinks that we did," Matt said quietly.

I flinched. "He doesn't think that. Maybe she thinks that, but he doesn't. He'd never think that of—of us." I almost said *me* but caught the pronoun just in time.

"You act like it doesn't matter if Cat thinks that!" My passive husband exploded, and I was reminded of the fact that—beneath his very sweet and calm exterior—there did lie a killer. "That is a big issue, Neena. A *huge* issue."

He suddenly gripped the steering wheel, his face tightening. "Oh my gosh. I think I'm going to be sick." He retched, and I glared at him.

"Don't you *dare* throw up in here. You shouldn't even be driving. You've been drinking all day." Between him and Cat, I might as well put *vomit patrol* on my forehead. "And I don't know why you drank the limoncello. You hate limoncello." Fresh anger burned at the thought of her cozied next to his side, her hand on his arm, my guileless husband's mouth on her drink.

"Do you have anything for me to throw up in?"

"Are you serious? Pull over, I'll drive."

He yanked the wheel unnecessarily hard to the right, and I opened the door in time to hear him retch.

I stomped around the front of the car and glared at him, waiting as he emptied his stomach into the thick grass. "Done?"

He didn't respond, just straightened and walked around to the passenger side. Stepping over a pathetically small pool of vomit, I moved the seat forward and fastened my belt.

"I need to know if you put anything in that liqueur." Matt closed the door with his good arm, the motion awkward around the cast.

"I didn't put anything in it." I yanked the car into drive and flipped the headlights on.

"Neena."

I hated when he said my name like that. As if he knew everything and I knew nothing.

"I didn't," I insisted.

"If you did, and the police find out—"

"I *didn't.*"

"I won't protect you. This isn't like before. What I did . . . I can't go down that path again. It just about killed me."

I pulled out into the street and accelerated past a minivan. "I didn't do it," I repeated, my voice softening.

He said nothing, and inside the stuffy car, the distrust between us grew.

CHAPTER 36

Cat

Two days later, I spotted Matt easily, his fluorescent-orange cast standing out in the brightly lit hospital lobby. "Hey!" I smiled warmly at him. "What are you doing here?"

"Getting my cast off." He lifted the bulky appendage. "I've been counting down the days. You?"

"Oh, just a follow-up on my stomach. I'm actually on my way out. Is Neena with you?" I kept my face blank, as if I didn't know about the all-employee meeting going on in the WT offices, one that would tie up his wife for at least two hours. I'd spent the entire morning hanging around the hospital lobby, waiting for this moment to catch him alone. While I did have a follow-up appointment on the books, it wasn't for another two days. In the meantime, I needed to share something with him. Something important.

"Nah, she's working. Are you feeling better? You look good." He froze, a look of panic crossing his face. "I mean, you look healthy. Better. Less sick." Poor guy. Neena probably had a noose around his neck that automatically tightened whenever she sniffed out flirtation.

I smiled to put him at ease. "I'm feeling much better, thank you for asking. Plus, I've lost six pounds, so"—I shrugged—"that's great news. I should drink limoncello every day."

"Yeah." He shifted uncomfortably. "You know, I don't know how anything got into that drink, but we've called the company, and they're testing the facility to see if there's any contamination—"

"Oh, I know you guys didn't have anything to do with it. Did you feel okay after that sip or two you took?"

"Actually, I threw up, too." His chubby cheeks tinted pink. "On the way home from the hospital. But I'm fine now."

"I am wondering if we're all jinxed. You know, they say trouble comes in threes. With the limoncello and your fall . . . I just hope there isn't anything else. I was thinking about that railing last night. Did you guys ever research it further?"

As if on cue, his face turned blank. "Research what?"

"The railing on your upper balcony. The one off your bedroom. Didn't Neena tell you?"

"Tell me what?"

"Well, most of the bracing for the railing was tight and secure." I let out a short, awkward laugh. "*Overly* secure. It wasn't going anywhere. But on the far end, by where you fell, there was only a single screw holding the railing in place, and a pretty loose one at that."

He frowned.

"And it was odd, because the posts had the holes in them, as if there were screws at one time, but they were all missing. I found that strange, so I told Neena about it. She told me to throw away the damaged items and that she'd show them to you later, before they were picked up by trash collection." I peered at him. "You did see them, didn't you?"

"Yes," he said slowly. "Yes. Of course. I forgot." He hit the side of his head lightly with his palm. "I've gotten so absentminded lately."

"Well, you've been working so hard. I thought you'd slow down with the broken arm, but I see you heading out to work almost every day. You should give your body a chance to heal. Maybe take a vacation. You know, we have a house in Hawaii. You guys should head over there for a week and have a romantic getaway. Relax on the beach and enjoy the last bits of summer."

He sagged a little in place. "You're so wonderful. And you're right. I'm working too much. It's just, with this big house, we're a little stressed over the costs. Atherton is expensive." His face tightened. "Though, don't tell Neena I said that. She wouldn't—"

"No worries. Stays between us." I gave his good forearm an affectionate pat. "Now, go get that cast off. I'm sure your arm is dying for a good scratch."

"Thanks." He lifted the cast in parting.

"And be careful," I added, almost as an afterthought. "No more falls off high buildings."

"No problem," he said. "I'm drinking my coffee inside now."

I waved and watched as he made his way to the sign-in desk. He was a good liar, but I knew the truth.

Neena had never told him about the missing screws. She couldn't have.

CHAPTER 37

NEENA

When I got home from work, my husband was standing on the balcony, his cast arm pale and scrawny. He was staring down at the rudimentary balcony rail that William had constructed for us. The new ironwork would take months to arrive, but I had to say that I liked the temporary solution. I had really enjoyed the view of him putting it together, his shirt slightly sticking to his build as he had lifted boards and hammered things into place.

I opened the french door and joined him on the balcony. "What are you doing?"

Matt didn't turn, his attention still on the railing post. "Why didn't you tell me that the railing was missing screws?"

"What?"

"When I fell, someone had removed almost all the screws from this post. It's why the railing gave way so easily."

"Someone removed all the screws? What are you talking about? That railing has always been a little wobbly."

"Yeah, a little." He turned to me, and I flinched at the suspicious look on his face. "But the day I fell, it gave way almost immediately."

"So it loosened up. Why are you staring at me like that?"

"Cat told you that screws were missing from the post. Why didn't you tell me that?"

"She didn't tell me that," I said, straightening up with indignation.

"So, you didn't tell her to throw away the broken railings?"

I hesitated. "I don't remember what I told her, but I know she didn't mention missing screws—are you listening to yourself? Missing screws, someone poisoning Cat?" I gave a hard laugh. "You're paranoid."

"I'm not sure I am." He moved past me and into the house, his shoulder knocking against me in the process.

A stab of fear hit me, one I hadn't felt in years. "Matt." I hurried after him. "Matt. Where are you going?"

"To the office. I need to check on some things." He jogged down the winding staircase, his boots loud on the stairs.

"Wait." I caught him just before the back door and wrapped my arms around him. "Matt." I pulled him around to face me and pressed my body against his, my hands stealing around his neck, my mouth sweet and eager on his lips. He was slow to respond, but he softened, his hands finding my waist, his mouth responding to my kiss. I considered initiating sex but discarded the idea, my energy not up for the laborious task. Instead, I curled into his chest. "I love you," I whispered.

He returned the sentiment gruffly, his hand sweeping over the back of my head, and I felt, in the sigh of his embrace, the buying of a little more time. But how much? I squeezed him tightly and recalculated things in my mind.

CHAPTER 38

HIM

It was amazing how useless security guard gates were if you were on foot, dressed in black, at night. All it had taken was one distraction, a car pulling up to the pair of officers, and he had scaled the low part of the wall undetected, shielded by a large willow tree. A half mile later, past ridiculous homes and million-dollar landscaping packages, he was moving down the driveway and settling into a dark corner of the yard.

There, he waited. Hours passed. The chorus of crickets and frogs came. Lights in the house extinguished, room by room. Once everything was dark, he waited another hour and a half, then stood, pulling on gloves.

He unlocked the back door and moved in quietly, blue surgical booties already pulled over his shoes, his steps silent on the wood floors. He headed for the staircase and kept to the far side, avoiding weak spots that might make noise. Above him, like the lull of a pied piper, a man snored.

His instructions had been clear, and he followed them to the letter. The master bedroom was at the end of the hall, the door ajar. The pale light of a television flickered through the crack. His heartbeat increased, and he removed the small handgun from the clip on his belt and held the weapon in front of him like a sword. Pushing gently on the door, he eased it open and paused, taking in the scene.

There were two humps in the bed, one large and snoring, one silent and small. On the television, an infomercial about a treadmill played. He stepped sideways, moving around the giant king bed until the man's face came into view. Chubby. Mouth open. Eyes closed. Features slack. He looked as if he were already dead, the illusion marred by the guttural wheezes that eased out of him. Moving closer, he carefully worked the barrel of the pistol into the man's mouth.

Brown eyes flipped open, his lips tightening on the cool barrel of the gun before gaping back open. The intruder carefully flipped off the safety with his thumb. As the prone man's eyes pleaded with him for mercy, he let out a slow breath and pulled the trigger.

CHAPTER 39

NEENA

The police came in silently, their sirens off, three cars in total. From my perch at the window, I watched them pull up to our house, the knot of unease growing in my stomach. This was bad. I didn't even know what had gone wrong, but this was *bad*. I followed Matt as he opened the front door, meeting them as they came up the wide brick steps.

"Mr. Ryder?" A female detective flashed her shield, then introduced the other uniforms, all in the standard black garb of the town police department. "I'm Detective Cullen. You said on the phone that the intruder has left?" She had a thick New York accent and the aggressive posture to match it.

"Yes." Matt straightened to his full and unimpressive height of five feet nine inches. "I heard him leave through the front, and I searched the house. He's not here."

She looked down at the stoop. "He left through here?"

My husband nodded, not realizing the issue of three officers trampling through the exit. "Yeah."

"Dammit," she swore. "Donnie, get back. All of you, get back and watch where you're stepping. We just screwed ourselves in terms of footprints."

I hung back in the warmth of the house, the night chill trickling through the open doorway, and watched as the cops attempted to maneuver inside without damaging evidence. "I'll open the side door. You can come in through there."

"Thank you." The woman lifted her flashlight, shining it in my face. "You Mrs. Ryder?"

"Dr. Ryder," I clipped back, holding up my hand to block the flashlight's glare. "Do you mind?"

"No problem." She clicked off the lamp and gave me a hard smile. "We'll meet you around the side."

~

I leaned against the left side of the house, my hands tucked into the pockets of my robe, and felt like a criminal. The scene was eerily familiar. Suspicious looks. Probing questions. Before, they'd only done a brief glance through the house, then ushered me into the back of a police car. Before, I'd been given a series of gentle questions paired with sympathetic looks. Now, I was being drilled. An army of uniforms was moving into my house. Matt and I were being kept outside and questioned as if we were suspects.

The detective pointed down the dark stretch of our driveway. "Your front gate out there—does that fence go all the way around the property?"

I shook my head. "Just the front. The neighbors have fences that make up the sides. Well, most of the sides. And we leave the front gate open. The motor is broken on it."

"And the back of the property?"

"The back doesn't have a fence due to the steep hill. Past the tree line, there are other homes."

"So, someone could have gotten in that way?"

"Sure, but those homes are in the neighborhood, also. They'd still have had to get past the main entrance gate."

She turned to the garage's interior door, examining the lock, then nodded to the security keypad mounted on the wall. "Your security system go off?"

"It doesn't work. It's from the last owners."

"You have any security system at all? Cameras? Motion sensors? A Ring video doorbell?" Her voice rose with each item, and I bristled at her incredulous tone. She probably lived in a townhome. Something low rent, in a neighborhood that might require a security system. This was Atherton. We were paying the highest property taxes and home-owners' dues in the state for a reason.

"No." Seeing her raised eyebrows, I pushed back. "You know, most people in the neighborhood don't even lock their doors. The Winthorpes leave theirs wide open most of the time. We had planned to get some sort of system in place, but we're renovating. Did you see the new landscaping?"

Maybe we should have pushed an alarm further up the to-do list. The security company had given a thorough presentation of the different safeguards available. Window sensors, motion-activated cameras, a schedule of interior lights that would give the appearance of constant activity. I'd seen the estimate and taken a few giant steps back at the cost, deciding to invest in an outdoor seating set instead. And the weather-friendly sectional had been a valuable and impressive investment—until Cat had splattered limoncello all over it.

She pointed at our side door. "Was this locked when you just came out of it?"

"Yeah. It's a dead bolt. I flipped it to come out."

"Let's step in there for a moment." She opened the door with a gloved hand and moved into the secondary foyer. She let out a low whistle, and I stiffened at the critical way her eyes moved over the space.

Excessive grandeur, that's what Matt's mother had called it, her afternoon pop-in perfectly timed when I was exhausted from unpacking and too emotionally fried for verbal assault. *Way too fancy for the likes of you two,* she'd said, running her hand over the velvet chair with an unimpressed sniff. *That chandelier come with the place, or did you guys buy it?* She liked to remind him that I grew up in a shack and had been perfectly happy in my Kmart sundresses before I started wearing designer lines. She was wrong, of course. I may have smiled the night I met her in my cheap sundress, but I had never been happy. Not while my father was home, and not until I was out of that horrible town and had my first taste of financial stability. She thought I changed Matt, but his lifestyle had been what changed me. He'd given me a taste of the good life, and I'd binged on each middle-class bite until I'd developed more expensive tastes.

From behind us, an officer wiped his boots on my mat. "No one's on the property. I've got lights moving through the back woods, but that's a wild-goose chase. There are at least six different directions he could have gone in. Right now uniforms are tightening up security and doing vehicle checks at each neighborhood exit."

She nodded. "Go next door to the Winthorpes'. See if they've seen anything, and make sure they're all locked up."

Oh, poor Cat. She was probably still feeble from her "poisoning." I hoped the gunman didn't go in their often-unlocked door. I hoped he didn't find his way to their bedroom. I hoped dear little Cat hadn't been a casualty of his panic. *Gag.*

She glanced at me. "You know anything about the property on your other side?"

I shook my head. "The Rusynzks are gone for the summer."

The officer nodded. "I'll check windows and doors on both places," he offered.

"Look for cameras. If they got 'em, get footage."

"Will do." He turned and pulled the door closed behind him, his hand casually resting on the butt of his weapon.

The detective stepped farther into the house, rounding the corner and entering the great space. Looking down at her pad, she flipped over a page. "Mrs. Ryder, we're going to bring your husband inside and go through a few questions together."

~

My shoulder rubbed against Matt's, and I don't know why he didn't change his shirt before they got here. He was in a thin ribbed tank top, his slight man boobs sagging, the fat of his underarms squishing against his sides. His skin felt clammy and slid against my deltoid in a disgusting way. I shifted a little to the side, wanting to break the contact, and felt the detective's eyes follow the action.

"I woke up with the gun in my mouth." Matt swallowed hard. "It was pressing against my teeth, shoving my head back."

"And then he pulled the trigger?"

"Yes. There was a click, but nothing came out. A misfire. He looked at the gun and then ran."

"You're lucky," the detective remarked. "Both of you are." She glanced at me, and I tried to assume a look of gratefulness.

Oh yes. *So* lucky. One shot and Matt could have died. I would have been a widow. Instead, we were here, dealing with all this, a crowd of strangers trampling through our house, my husband fully intact beside me, not a single hair harmed on his head. So lucky.

Detective Cullen moved down a list of questions, and I stayed quiet, listening to Matt's responses.

An accent? *No.*

Did he sound familiar? *No.*

Was he tall? Short? *I couldn't really tell. I was in bed, looking up at him. Maybe six feet tall? Maybe?*

How was his hair? Short? Long? Bald? *He had on a hat. Wait, a ski mask.*

Did he move smoothly? Limp? Have any distinguishable characteristics whatsoever?

No.

No.

No.

As she moved through the questions, she grew more and more frustrated at how inept Matt's observation skills were. *I know,* I wanted to chime in. *You have no idea how many affairs I've carried on right underneath his nose! I'm not surprised he had a gun stuck in his mouth and still didn't manage to pay attention.*

"Is something funny, Mrs. Ryder?"

I sat straighter in my seat. "No."

"You're smiling," she pointed out. "Surely you don't find this amusing."

Matt was looking at me now, his features pinching in annoyance. A burst of anger popped in my chest. It was three in the morning! How was anyone supposed to keep their wits about them at this ungodly hour? "I'm exhausted." I rose to my feet. "Can we finish these questions in the morning? I didn't even see the guy. Or hear him."

"Yes . . . ," she said slowly. "Because you 'slept right through it all.'" She put air quotes around the last part of the sentence, and I gawked at her nerve.

"I told you what happened. I woke up with Matt screaming at me to call 9-1-1 as he ran downstairs." I glared at her and dared her to call me a liar.

"Mrs. Ryder—"

"Dr. Ryder," I corrected, unable to let another flub pass.

"This is going to take some time. Perhaps you could get some coffee while I finish up with your husband?"

"Fine." I moved away before she had a chance to change her mind. Spotting a handsome uniform dusting the back doorknob for prints, I ran my fingers through my hair and decided to detour by the bathroom and take a moment to freshen up.

Inside the bathroom, I tried William's cell, but for the third time that night, he didn't answer.

~

Detective Cullen found me in the dining room, one of our mugs in her spindly hand. I eyed the coffee and wondered if Matt had offered it to her or if she'd helped herself. Brushing off the thought, I gestured her closer and lowered my voice, making sure Matt wasn't nearby. "I've been thinking, and it's possible Matt imagined this entire thing. A stranger, in our house in the middle of the night? No forced entry? He put his gun in Matt's mouth and then the thing misfired?" I clutched my own coffee cup, the contents now lukewarm, and glanced at the evidence teams scattered across every area of our home. "Have you found *any* evidence there was anyone here? Any bullet holes? Fingerprints?"

The woman nodded slowly, considering the idea. "So, you think your husband made the entire thing up?"

"He takes sleeping pills at night." I shrugged, encouraged by her open reaction. "Maybe he thought it happened and it didn't."

"On the 9-1-1 call, you said there was an intruder." Her voice was hardening, incredulity beginning to coat the syllables.

"It was dark in the bedroom. I woke up to him yelling at me to call 9-1-1. I was half-asleep during that call. But we have no security footage, no footprints, and Matt's given you a hazy description that could fit anyone from Pee-wee Herman to Arnold Schwarzenegger." I stood from the seat, my voice rising in vigor. "You could be looking for someone that isn't out there. Wouldn't you rather go home? And besides—are you even allowed to be looking through all of our things? Don't you need a warrant for that?"

"Neena."

I stiffened at the flat sound of Matt's voice and turned to see him standing just inside the back door, his features eerily still, his eyes dead. "May I speak to you for a moment?"

CHAPTER 40

CAT

I stood on the upper balcony and watched as the cars clogged the Ryders' long lot, black-and-whites with the official seal of Atherton, their lights on, sirens silent. In the dark, black figures with sweeping white beams of illumination moved, their progress partially hidden by shrubbery and trees, their canvass slow and methodical.

"What's going on?" William stepped out of our bedroom, his chest bare, his silk pajama bottoms on. He shivered in the cool night air and crossed his arms over his chest, his attention immediately caught by the activity next door.

"I don't know. There's an ambulance, but they haven't put anyone in it. I tried to call Neena and Matt, but they didn't answer. I'm waiting on a call back from the chief."

As if beckoned, my phone lit up, the Atherton chief of police's private cell number displayed. I answered the call and put it on speakerphone so William could hear. "Hey, Danika."

"It was a home invasion," she said without preamble. "Or armed robbery gone wrong. We aren't sure yet. Someone in a ski mask came in the home and attempted to shoot the husband."

I inhaled sharply. "Is he okay? And Neena—"

"No one was harmed. The gun misfired, and the husband chased or scared the man out of the house. But we haven't located the intruder yet. So it's important that you stay inside and lock all your doors. We have officers headed to your house now, but please arm your security system, if it's not already."

William pulled on my arm, glancing around as he ushered me inside. Shutting the french doors, he flipped the locks.

"I'll go open the front gates so the cops can get in." He gave me a stern look as he pulled on a worn Stanford T-shirt. "Stay here."

I waved him on and moved to the window, parting the curtain and scanning my eyes over the dark stretch of lawn. When the bedroom door clicked shut behind William, I took the phone off speaker and lowered my voice. "Danika, there are some things about the Ryders your detectives should know."

~

By the time I pulled on clothes and made it downstairs, an officer was present. I rounded the bottom of the staircase, and the man nodded at me. "Good evening, Mrs. Winthorpe."

I smiled in greeting but didn't recognize him. We sponsored the department's annual Christmas party, along with the Care Fund—generous donations that granted us a special decal to put on our license tag, our names at the top of every donation list, and an open invitation to the station. Every uniform in town knew our name, our vehicles, and would look the other way if they spotted us, tipsy and sluggish, stepping into our car. But while they all knew us, I could only recognize a handful of them. Chief McIntyre, of course. A few of the captains and inspectors. Tim, the main patrol on our side of the city.

"Is everything okay?" I asked. "Are Matt and Neena all right?"

"They're both fine," he said. "But we haven't located the intruder and wanted to see if you'd seen or heard anything."

I stepped past him and out onto the front porch, my bare feet curling against the polished wood. Craning my neck, I tried to get a better look at the activity, but the fence blocked the view.

"Cat," William protested. "Please come in. It's not safe out there."

The detective cleared his throat. "Have you seen anyone on your property this evening? Heard anything? Has anything out of the ordinary happened?"

I turned back to him. "No. It's been a quiet night. I heard their garage door open about twenty minutes ago. It woke me up. But nothing else."

He glanced up at our porch eaves. "You got a security system?"

"Yes." William waved him toward the kitchen. "I'll show you."

The officer nodded and pulled off his hat, his black hair fringed in gray. "Thank you."

Following the men inside, I pulled the front door closed and locked it. In the kitchen, I started a pot of coffee as William pulled up the security app, the content accessible from his phone. "The cameras are both interior and exterior and triggered by motion or the window and door sensors. We turn the interior motion sensors off if either of us comes down in the middle of the night. That's why you aren't seeing them now."

"Can I view exterior footage from tonight?"

I gave a regretful frown. "We have the exterior motion sensors turned off the majority of the time. Between the rabbits and the opossums, plus the fox that likes to visit our yard, the alerts were almost constant. I now only have them triggered by a door or window opening—or by the front gate." I leaned forward and clicked on the folder for tonight. "Here's when you pulled through the gate." There were several clips showing his car moving down the drive. Him stepping out and putting on his hat. An adjustment of his pants before he took the steps up to the front door. A moment when he glanced in the front window, then rang the bell.

William spoke. "We were pretty security conscious when we moved in, but over time we've grown comfortable. Most of the time we don't arm the alarms or lock the doors."

"Well, please make sure that all your cameras are on and doors are locked, at least until we apprehend the suspect." He stuck out his hand to William, and I hurried to the coffeepot, wanting to at least get him a cup to go. "Here's my card, with my cell number on it. If either of you think of anything, please call me."

"Do you know how this guy got in their house?" I pulled a disposable cup from the coffee butler and filled it to the top. "Cream? Sugar?"

"Um, neither. Thank you. And no, we don't see any evidence of forced entry."

"They might have left a door unlocked," William remarked. "And they didn't have a security system. I remember the neighborhood deputy scolding them for it when Matt had his fall."

"Yes, it seems Mr. Ryder has had his fair share of bad luck." The man glanced at me, and I wondered how much Chief McIntyre had told him.

"I'm gonna head over there." I passed him the coffee cup and moved to the coat closet, pulling out a long cashmere cardigan. "I need to see Neena. She's got to be freaking out."

"I don't know if that's a good idea," William said. "If they haven't found—"

"Did you see how many cop cars are out there? There's not a safer place in Atherton right now. Wherever that guy is, he's not coming back to the scene of the crime."

"Just—give me a second." William stepped toward the hall. "Let me put on a pair of jeans. I'll come, too."

~

We approached the Ryder house together, my hands stuffed in the deep pockets of the cardigan. Above us, spotlights moved through the dark, white circles of light illuminating the trees. I moved closer to the officer and glanced behind me, grateful for the well-lit driveway. "Where have they searched so far?"

"The Ryders' property and the surrounding lots. The back drop-off is pretty steep, and the guy has a fifteen-minute head start on us, at least."

I glanced at the dark sky. "Could you bring in a helicopter? Search that way?"

He chuckled. "Not for this. If there had been an actual homicide? Maybe. But murder attempts kind of fall into a budgetary gray area." He caught a glimpse of my face and hurried to reassure me. "Which isn't to say that they won't do everything they can to catch him. But things like a helicopter are a bit overkill at this point. Don't worry. We've got a set of dogs on the way. They'll be able to track his path." He herded us toward the driveway.

William frowned. "Murder attempt? I thought this was an armed robbery."

"I'd have to let you get the details from the detective." He shrugged in apology. "I don't have the full scope of the investigation so far."

I walked faster, anxious to be inside the house and closer to some answers.

We stepped into the open garage, and I skirted Matt's Volvo, heading for the interior door. The officer grabbed my arm just before I touched the knob. "Mrs. Winthorpe?"

I turned and noticed the bright-blue tissues he held out to me. He nodded to my shoes. "They're booties. We'll also need both of you to wear gloves."

"Oh." I let out an awkward laugh. "Our prints are throughout the house already. We're over here all the time."

"Still, we have to preserve the scene as best we can."

I pulled the booties over my shoes and could see, through the glass panes in the door, more officers inside. Neena had to be flipping out over the intrusion. I worked the gloves on and nodded at the man, holding up my palms to prove my adherence.

When we stepped inside, the first thing I heard was Matt's voice, muffled, but clearly raised in anger.

CHAPTER 41

NEENA

Over the last sixteen years, I had seen Matt run through every gamut of emotion. Pride. Fear. Pain. Love. And he had been mad, even furious upon rare occasion. But I'd never seen the look of hatred he wore when we stepped into the office and closed the door.

"Did I just hear you tell her that you think I *invented* this entire thing?" His voice was very calm, but the glint in his eyes was that of a man pushed to the edge.

"That wasn't what I was saying to her," I protested. "I was just saying that I was tired and that I didn't see anything. That for all I knew, there wasn't anyone in our room."

"Look at me, Neena."

I did. I looked into the eyes of the man I had married at nineteen and wanted to divorce by twenty-two. It wasn't his fault. Over the past twenty years, he'd gained an extra forty pounds and lost half of his hair, but he was the same guy. Loyal. Dependable. Hopelessly in love with me. I was the one who'd changed.

"Have I ever made *anything* up?"

No. He was annoyingly honest. Once, when he'd bought a used car and found a hundred dollars tucked in the manual, he'd tracked down the prior owner just to return it. It was freakish and unnatural, and I couldn't help but think that some of it was guilt over a then-five-year-old crime.

"I didn't say you made it up," I insisted.

"Yes, you did. That was exactly what you were saying."

"They're going through all our stuff, Matt. I'm exhausted, and I'm ready for them all to leave, and there's a big difference between a psychopath standing in our bedroom versus a thief. If someone was in our room, it wasn't to kill us. He was robbing us. You're being overdramatic, and it's causing them to look at this in the wrong way." *To look at me in the wrong way.*

"I came *this* close to dying." He held his thumb and his forefinger a hairbreadth apart. "You haven't even reacted to that. You haven't even asked if I'm okay. To be frank, I'm not sure you even care. You're *exhausted?* Could you make this any more about you?"

I flinched at his words, the hatred delivered with a spray of spit, his face turning red as his voice rose in volume. When he stopped, I raised my hands in surrender. "Okay, sorry. Please keep your voice down. You want all these people here? Fine. Let them cover our house with fingerprint powder. But don't forget what's in that safe upstairs." I stepped forward and hissed out my words at a volume that only he could hear. "We *cannot* let them search the house. Do you understand me?"

A conversation sounded from the hall, and I stiffened, holding up a hand to stop his response. Listening closely, I recognized the voice and pulled open the door, a tremor of excitement zipping through me.

William was here.

CHAPTER 42

CAT

"Mr. and Mrs. Winthorpe?" The female detective approached us. "I'm sorry for interrupting your night, but this is a crime scene. We're going to need you both to stay in this dining room to avoid contamination of the scene."

William moved forward. "We understand, and no need to apologize. Our house is yours if you need anything. A base of operations, a bathroom, a snack, anything. Just come over. We're bringing in the staff now to prepare breakfast sandwiches and coffee for your officers."

She acknowledged the offer with a curt nod. "Thank you, but that's really not necessary. We hope to be out of everyone's hair shortly."

"William." Neena appeared, followed closely by Matt. I scanned him quickly, relieved that he seemed unscathed. "And . . . *Cat*." The edge of her mouth curled in distaste. "How nice of you both to come by. The police are almost done, so all this . . ." She gestured to the mess. "It'll be gone shortly."

"Actually"—Detective Cullen turned to face them—"your home is considered a crime scene and will need to be thoroughly processed, especially the master bedroom. We're also processing the paperwork for a full search warrant, which will include your computers and phone records."

Neena stiffened. "What?" she spat out. "I thought you were just looking for evidence of the intruder. Fingerprints and shoe prints and stuff. You told me it wouldn't take long."

The detective didn't flinch, and if I had to guess, she wasn't a big fan of Neena Ryder. "And . . . then I got a call from up top. We've upgraded the focus on this. Just to make sure we don't miss anything, we're going to take a closer look."

Call from up top. Upgraded the focus. See, this was why we shelled out six figures last year for the police department. If a man broke into my home and painted the living room walls with the blood of eight different children, I could have the FBI present within fifteen minutes, or my house to myself one hour later. There are rules and policies, but there are *always* ways around and through them. Which was why, in my call to the chief, I'd told her to use *every* means necessary to get to the bottom of this situation. I'd explained about my poisoning and Matt's suspicious fall, and she'd promised to treat it as if her own family's safety were at stake.

It was a conversation William never needed to know about, and one that would enrage Neena, but our home was less than a hundred yards away from theirs. I'd spent part of this weekend in a hospital gown, the taste of vomit in my mouth. I didn't care if Matt's or Neena's privacy was violated. I needed the police to find answers and to see what—if any—connections could be made.

Detective Cullen's eyes met mine, and an unspoken knowledge passed between us. She knew about my call to the chief. I took a sip of the coffee and swallowed a shudder at the now-cool liquid.

"As I mentioned to you both earlier, this is a crime scene."

"You didn't mention phone records and computers," Neena seethed. "I have privileged client files on my computer. We have personal emails—I'm not having you rip apart our lives for—"

"This isn't a discussion, Dr. Ryder. It's a fact. We're treating this with the same diligence we would a homicide. Be grateful it isn't one." She closed her notepad with a snap of finality.

Neena hesitated, then threw up her hands. "This is ridiculous. I'm suing all of you for this." She turned, sweeping her arm across the kitchen counter and knocking over the collection of coffee cups. I watched as mine shot off the edge of the counter and hit the oven door with a spray of chocolate-colored liquid.

I shrugged. "Mine was cold anyway."

She kicked a stool to the side, and Matt winced. Impulsively, I reached out and gave him a hug.

"Are you okay?" I asked him softly.

His lips tightened in one of the saddest expressions I'd ever seen. "I am. Thank you—thank you for asking." He inhaled deeply. "I'm a little shook up. I woke up when he put the gun in my mouth."

"Jesus, Matt. You're lucky to be alive," William muttered.

"I'm so glad you weren't hurt." I gave him another tight hug. "Why don't you guys come by the house and get some breakfast? We've got the guesthouse if you want to get some privacy and sleep." I looked at the detective. "Do you need them here? They've got to be tired."

"Oh, I don't know." Neena looked at William. "Are you sure we won't be a bother?"

Detective Cullen nodded in approval. "As long as you're close by, it's fine for you to leave. Mr. and Mrs. Ryder, please keep your phones on."

A forensics tech called Detective Cullen's name urgently from the top of the stairs, and she glanced at us and held up her hand. "Wait for a minute. We may need you for this." Striding out of the room, she climbed the stairs two by two, disappearing into the upper level and toward their master bedroom.

I caught the look that passed between Matt and Neena, a furtive glance that immediately raised my suspicions.

"You guys go on home," Neena said quickly. "We'll come over as soon as they finish with us."

"Are you sure?" William asked. "We can—"

"We're sure," Matt said. "We'll be there shortly."

We nodded and said our goodbyes. On the way out, I glanced back at the couple, who stood apart, their gazes both stubbornly off each other.

CHAPTER 43

NEENA

The cash was stacked in three neat rows along the bottom of the hidden cavity. I stared down at the display and tried desperately to come up with an explanation for its presence.

It was in the floor of our master bedroom, the hole cleverly hidden under a trapdoor that fit seamlessly into the wood planks, the pattern hiding the outline of it. I'd found it when we moved in and had quickly put a rug over the find. Matt . . . Matt had never found out about its existence. Now, he crouched and tested the trapdoor lid, the hinges operating without a sound.

"We found this a few hours ago." Detective Cullen nodded to the money. "What's all the cash for?"

"I don't know." I held up my hands. "I didn't even know that compartment was there." Too late, I noticed the fingerprint powder on the top of the inset handle and cursed the oversight.

Matt reached forward, then hesitated. "Can I touch the money?"

Detective Cullen passed him a set of latex gloves. "Wear these." She held out a pair for me, and I shook my head, stepping back. Matt got the gloves on, then picked up the closest stack of cash, the bills bound with a two-thousand-dollar wrap. He thumbed through the ones underneath it, then tapped his finger along the rows, counting.

My mind calculated along with him. At least eighty thousand dollars, assuming each row held the same. All underneath our cheap rug from Bernie's Furniture.

"It's not yours?"

I hesitated, wondering if the cash could be taken from us, depending on my response. "I may have put it there," I said carefully. "And forgotten it."

Matt's head snapped toward me, his eyes narrowing in suspicion. I glared back at him, unsure of how he didn't see the importance in claiming this small fortune as our own. There was a long and quiet battle of eye contact, then he looked back at the cash, his focus zeroing in on the red box sandwiched beside the green stacks of bills. I followed suit, taking in the familiar red square. "What's in the box?"

The detective nodded at it. "Open it."

My chest tightened as Matt reached for the lid, and I wanted to shout at him that this was a trap, to step back, to not touch—

He leaned forward and stared into the box. Despite myself, I navigated to the side to see the contents from his viewpoint.

It was filled with photos. A stack of them, varying in size, the original photos cut into varying sizes. He pulled out the stack and flipped through the glossy prints.

They were all photos of William. Some blurry, some crisp. Some taken in our house, the angle odd, his attention elsewhere. Others showed him in New York, smiling for the camera, or covered in mud, at a runner's event of some sort. It was the ones near the end that were the hardest to see. I saw the tightening of Matt's back, the stiffening of his neck, his movement slowing as he looked at each of them in painful slow motion.

William's wedding photo.

A selfie with him and Cat, obviously in bed.

Him at a football game, his arm around her.

Another with the two of them, laughing on a Hawaiian beach.

In each of those, Cat's face was scribbled over in black marker, and a careful cutout of my face was glued atop the scribble, my bright smile next to William's. Looking over his shoulder, it looked like the work of a crazy person. *Me.*

The last three photos were the worst. Shots of the four of us. Poolside at the club. At the Winthorpe Foundation charity golf tournament. At the Fourth of July party. In every single one, Matt and Cat were beheaded, drops of blood painted in red marker around the crude hole where their heads used to be.

He dropped the photos as if they were poisoned, his fat knees scooting back on the floor, his breath wheezing as if we'd just had sex. He turned to me, and the pain and hatred that emanated from him made me step back in defense. "You—you're obsessed with him."

"What?" I shook my head. "I'm not. I didn't—I didn't do that, Matt. Come on! I love you." I sank onto my knees before him, abandoning any thoughts about a life without him. I couldn't lose him, couldn't have him look at me like this, not when he was the only person in my entire life to look at me as if I had worth, to cherish me as if I were a prize.

"Have you slept with him?" he gritted out.

"What?" I gasped. "*No.* Matt." I grabbed his hand, clutching it between mine. "Matt, I love you. This—this is all a setup. Someone else put those photos in there. I didn't do that. I don't love him. I don't even like him. I love you." The lies mixed with the truth, and I prayed that he would believe them all. He had to.

"For twenty years, I've bent over backward to be a perfect husband," he seethed. "I've dealt with your jealousy. I've supported your career, your plastic surgeries, your insecurities . . . and for what? Eighty thousand dollars underneath our bed and an obsession over our neighbor? I'd thought it was Cat, all this time. Cat you hated. Cat you wanted to be like. Cat you were obsessed over."

"I'm not obsessed with Cat," I spit out. "I *hate* Cat."

"Then why have we spent so much time with them? Why all the dinners? Why the stupid pop-ins? Admit it—Neena. It was because of *him*." He stared at me with a look I couldn't escape two decades ago and was helpless to avoid now. "Look at me, Neena, and tell me the truth."

"He's my boss," I said quietly. "Anything I did was to keep my job and to give us new opportunities." Like a weed, the idea immediately grew. William could have forced himself on me. Made inappropriate comments. Touches. No one knew what happened in that boardroom. It'd be my word against his. Maybe tonight was all William. Maybe he'd grown obsessed with me and hired a hit man to kill my husband. It could work. And even if it couldn't, the threat of it to William's empire would be enough to get something. Some additional reward for all this.

"There was this, also." The detective crouched beside the open cavity and pulled out a picture frame, one that had been under the box. She held it out to me, and Matt flinched, recognizing the carved wooden frame that used to hold our wedding photo. As if pulled to the spot, I looked at the dresser where it had previously sat.

"The frame is ours, but the image . . ." I shook my head and lied. "I've never seen that photo before." It was a solo picture of William, a candid shot where he was smiling into the camera. The photo was from an African safari that he and Cat had gone on—the photo one of hundreds on her Instagram feed.

"These pictures are all of your neighbor." She tapped the glass, her short nails dotting William's face. "William Winthorpe."

I cleared my throat. "Yes, but I didn't do any of these. I've never seen *any* of this."

"You just said that you might have put the cash here."

"Well, I lied. It's not my money."

"Were you aware of this compartment in the floor?"

My chest grew tight, panic running like a fever through my chest. My fingerprints had to be on that handle. I hesitated. "Maybe."

"Maybe?" Matt repeated. He stared down at the photos, and I needed to get him alone before the images of me and William were seared on his brain forever. He pushed himself to his feet.

"Are you feeling okay, Mr. Ryder?" The detective's words floated from somewhere to my left, and I stared up at Matt, alarm rising as I saw the gray pallor of his skin.

"Honestly?" He held the side of his chest, and I thought of his heart, the thickening of his ventricles that had shown on his latest ultrasound. "I feel like I'm about to vomit. I didn't know . . ." He swept his hand across the display. "About any of this."

"Neither did I," I snapped, frustrated with everyone's inability to believe me.

The detective also stood, moving toward Matt with a concerned look. "Would you like some water? To use the restroom?"

He shook his head. "No. I just—am I done here? Did you have more questions for me?"

Detective Cullen's gaze swung to me. "No . . . ," she said slowly. "You can go. But Neena, we have more questions for you."

Matt brushed by me, his steps unsteady as he went for the door, and I followed after him. "Matt, you know I didn't put that there. You know I don't—"

"I don't know anything about you anymore." His voice was low, but each word punctured through me like a bullet. "Stay away from me." Just before the door, he paused and looked over his shoulder. "And, Detective? You might want to look in our safe."

I opened my mouth but could find nothing to say. Inside me, everything catapulted and twisted, my biggest fears tunneling into one slow and silent scream of agony.

My husband, my sweet, stupid husband, had betrayed me.

CHAPTER 44

CAT

We were in the kitchen, surrounded by a quartet of staff who had rallied, making the twenty-minute drive at three thirty in the morning without complaint. There were a few wrinkled uniforms, and our chef had yawned twice during the last ten minutes, but we already had french toast sizzling in skillets, our guesthouse fridge stocked, the beds turned down, and fresh flowers being clipped for arrangement. I inhaled the scents of coffee, butter, and roses and had a moment of nostalgia for my own early mornings back in high school. I'd leave the house by five thirty, two hours clocked feeding horses and mucking stalls before school each day. My father would always shuffle into the kitchen before I left, a few minutes stolen over coffee and buttered toast, his proud smile boosting my spirits on the way out the door.

I'd come a long way from that scratched kitchen table and slightly burned toast. I met William's eyes from across the room, and he smiled, setting down his fork and moving over to me.

Pulling me into his arms, he pressed a kiss on the top of my head. "I love you."

I returned the sentiment, my hands stealing around his waist.

"This is so crazy," he said quietly. "What if this guy had come to our house instead of theirs?"

"Then our security system would have gone nuts, and we would have been in the panic room and on the phone with the cops before he even got in the front door." I rose on my toes and kissed him. "Assuming I could keep you from storming downstairs and trying to tackle him."

"I am an excellent tackler," he admitted. "And it's been a long time since I got to use anything other than my sharp tongue in a confrontation."

"Well, it's a very talented tongue," I teased, grinning up at him. "I can personally attest to that."

A throat cleared, and we both turned to see Matt standing at the open side door, his arms limp at his sides. William frowned and stepped toward him. "Are you okay?"

"Is there anything going on with you and my wife?"

My gaze snapped to William, who stayed silent. "William?" I prompted, dread coating my heart at the anticipation of what he would say.

"There are no feelings between Neena and me," he said finally.

"No *feelings*?" Anger whipped, sudden and fierce, as my insecurities and emotions were validated in that simple yet horribly evasive response. I came around the counter and stood beside Matt. "What does that mean?"

"Have you ever *touched* my wife?" Matt asked, each word pushed out as if he were having trouble breathing.

"Yes." William's response ripped my attention from Matt's health and to my husband. "Once. It meant nothing."

It meant nothing. I choked on the words, vaguely aware that we had an audience, the kitchen staff falling quiet as my husband pissed all over our marriage. He had risked our marriage over something that meant *nothing*? What did that say about us? Our life? Its worth to him? I gripped the edge of the counter to keep myself from sinking to the floor, my response silenced by Matt's next words.

"You might want to tell my wife that." Matt's upper lip curled in a sneer, the expression foreign on his consistently cheerful face. "It may mean nothing to you, but from what I just saw in my bedroom, it means a lot to her."

~

"I can't believe he didn't tell us what was in their bedroom." William stood at the bank of side windows in our dining hall, his hands on his hips, and watched as Matt's car moved around a forensic van and down their drive.

I stood at the entrance to the room and waited for William to turn, waited for some acknowledgment of what he had done to our lives. He stayed at the window until after the car disappeared, his profile stubbornly turned away, his face hidden.

I used to think of him as a god. When had he fallen? When had he changed, so definitively, from the man I had married? Was he really this weak and helpless against basic human desires? *It meant nothing.*

"That was not how I expected you to find out. If you ever found out." He turned his head to the side, his profile visible but his eyes still elusive. "I'm sorry you had to hear it like this."

"So, you . . . what? You had *sex* with her?" I knew. I knew before he even opened his mouth. I could taste it in the air. Could taste *her* in the air, feel her presence as if it were clogging the air ducts. "Tell me you didn't."

"Cat." My name was a broken syllable on his lips, and when he turned to face me, his face was a mess of emotion.

"Please," I begged.

"I'm sorry."

Maybe I was wrong. Maybe—

"It just happened. She—"

I picked up the closest item, a glass bowl we'd picked up in South Africa, and threw it across the table, the delicate piece shattering across the polished surface. It felt good, the ability to destroy something. "She *what?*"

"She's been relentless. I tried to hold her off, but I—"

"I *told* you," I hissed, pointing at him, my voice rising. "I told you that she was obsessed with us. I told you she was getting too close. And you told me to trust you. You acted as if I was crazy. You *let* her do this to us."

"I fucked up," he said quietly, trying to reach for me. "I have no excuse. I—"

I shoved at his chest. "She tried to have Matt killed. You realize that, don't you? And she poisoned me at their house. I could have died. Did you know what a lunatic she was?"

He sank into the window seat and cupped his head. "I didn't know anything, Cat. I was being selfish, and insecure, and stupid."

"And risking us in the process," I said quietly. I hesitated. "Tell me you used protection."

He didn't answer, and his silence confirmed what I already knew. *He had been bare inside her.* What if she was pregnant with his child? Had he thought of me once during the act?

I thought of the way he'd walked back in the door after work each day and kissed me on the lips, as if everything were normal. "Do you love her?" This question was softer, and it was the one I was most terrified to voice.

"No." He stood up and moved toward me, his face breaking. "I don't . . . I don't even know what the hell I'm doing—*was* doing—with her." He grabbed my wrist, and I stepped back.

"I can't—" I inhaled sharply. "I can't do any better than us, William. We're happy. We've been strong. If you can't be faithful to me now, what will happen in our hard times?" I felt the tears in the moment before they came and rushed to finish before I broke into sobs. "You were my *everything*."

"Cat," he said softly, his voice breaking in a way I'd never heard from him. Not when his father had died, not once in our fourteen years together. "Cat, please. This was a stupid thing." He gripped my arms, pulling me against him, my struggles failing as he forced me to look into his face. "I need you to forgive me. I can't live without you. Please." It was a gruff, fierce plea, his voice shaking with the intensity of it. He dropped to his knees, clawing me closer. "Please don't leave me." It was as much an order as a beg.

I didn't move. I didn't respond. I watched him, and when he looked up at me, I studied the depths of his eyes, the love and heartbreak in them.

Of course I wouldn't leave him. That was why, after all, I had done all this.

CHAPTER 45

NEENA

"What's in the safe?" The detective was flanked by three uniforms, all of them staring at me, suspicion heavy in their eyes. I glanced back at the doorway. Matt was already gone, and I wanted to scream at him to come back. He couldn't leave me with these cops, not after opening Pandora's box and shoving me into its teeth.

"Neena?" Detective Cullen stepped forward, her gap tooth peeking through her chapped lips. I studied her greasy hair, pulled into a tight ponytail, and stayed silent. "What's in the safe?"

I shouldn't have put it in the safe to begin with. Though the alternative, the cavity hidden in the floor, had proved just as insecure. I eased toward the door that Matt had escaped through and was blocked by a fat officer in a uniform a size too small.

"The safe's in the closet." Another male officer spoke up from behind me. "It's locked."

"You can give us the combination, Neena, or we can drill out the lock." Detective Cullen shrugged. "It makes no difference to us."

"Or we can just call your husband," the fat one suggested. "He sounded like he'd be willing to give it to us."

I glanced at the detective. "Does your warrant cover the safe?"

"Your husband just gave us permission to search it. We don't need a warrant."

I clenched my hands into fists. "I'm not giving you the combination. I don't remember it. Call Matt if you want to. He's not going to know it, either." And he wouldn't remember the complicated six-digit combination, but he'd probably remember where we stored it—the Post-it stuck in the top drawer of our bathroom vanity.

"We will," Detective Cullen promised, glancing at one of the other officers. "Go get Matt Ryder's cell phone number and text it to me." She pointed at me. "And you, Dr. Ryder—you just stay right there."

Five minutes later, after a quick call to my treacherous husband, getting his verbal authority to open the safe and oh-so-helpful guidance to the yellow sticky note that held the combination, the chambers of the large safe clicked into place, and the heavy iron door was wrenched open. Detective Cullen flipped her Maglite on and shone the beam into the velvet-lined depths.

I think she said something, but I wasn't sure. At that moment, I swayed, my knees buckling as black spots dotted across my vision, and I fainted.

~

"I got to tell you, I've been in this business a long time and have only had two suspects faint on me." Detective Cullen knelt in front of our coffee table. She wiped a pale napkin across her mouth as she took a bite from the breakfast sandwich clutched in her nail-bitten claws. I blinked slowly, focusing on the sandwich and wondering if it had come from William's chef. Had Detective Cullen seen William? What had she told him? Did she tell him what was in the safe? I glanced down at my hands, surprised to see that they were free, no handcuffs in sight.

"I think she's okay." Detective Cullen waved at someone, and I followed her motion, surprised to see a paramedic crouched beside my recliner. How had I gotten downstairs? This was Matt's chair, not mine. I sat upright, and the man hurried to assist.

"Take it easy. It'll take a few minutes to get your bearings."

"You've been out for a while," Detective Cullen said cheerfully. "Fainted and then went right to sleep. You missed all the excitement." She tapped the folder next to her. "We cataloged everything in the safe. I got to say, Neena, you got me excited about the contents, but there's not a whole lot there."

I stared at the folder, unsure of what mind game she was going through. I didn't have the mental stamina for this. If she had opened the safe, then she had me. I should be in handcuffs and headed to the station, not sitting here listening to her crunch through a bacon-and-egg sandwich as if it were her job.

"We went through everything." She licked the tip of her right index finger, then did another mouth swipe with the napkin. "And I think I found the source of your anxiety."

She flipped open the top flap of the folder and shuffled a few pages aside. "You really do have a wonderful husband."

I thought of Matt, his face red, features angry as he had wrapped his hands around my father's neck. The silent gape of my father's mouth. The wild swing of his arms. The bulge of his eyes as he had stared at me, begging me, all the way until the moment they rolled back into his head.

"Yes," I managed, "I do."

"How long have you and Mr. Winthorpe been having an affair?"

That shut me up, and I hated the way she said the word. *Affair.* As if it were something fleeting and dirty. This was a righting of the axle, the putting of everything into place. I *belonged* with someone like William. And furthermore, I *liked* the emotional chess game that stealing Cat Winthorpe's husband entailed. I was going to have him as my husband or his money as my cushion—before today anyone could have looked at the playing board and seen it all.

I pondered which angle to attack this from. "You're confused," I finally managed. "William Winthorpe is my employer. Any relationship we have is strictly a professional one."

"As is so clearly evident by your photo montage upstairs," she said dryly. "Now"—she flipped over another page—"five million dollars. That's a nice little parting gift to leave a wife."

It took me a moment to understand that she was talking about Matt's life insurance policy. "So?" I shrugged.

"So . . . when we look at your obsession with William Winthorpe, that life insurance policy, and *this*, it equals motive."

This seemed to be indicated by the paper she slid forward. Matt's will and testament. Unlike mine, it was a simple one-page document, devoid of any confessions and secrets. His was entirely focused on the distribution of all his assets, his demolition company, and his life insurance policy. It all went to me, which made logical sense.

I paused, waiting for more. Waiting for my own will to be slid beside his, the guilty beside the innocent. Nothing came, and I stared blankly at her. "That's it?"

The detective smiled thinly, and there was a dot of pepper in her teeth. "I'm sorry, Dr. Ryder. You seem to be struggling to catch up, so I'll spell out the elements of motive." She held up the index finger of her left hand. "Money. You stand to inherit a five-million-dollar life insurance policy and significant assets upon Matt's death. That alone would be powerful, but you're impressive enough to have a second motive." She flipped out her middle finger to join the first, making a peace sign. "Your obsession and pursuit of William Winthorpe. With your husband out of the way, you could go after a richer, better-looking one, though I do have to say, you're barking up a formidable tree that is guarded by Cat Winthorpe."

"But . . ." I stared down at the papers before her, still stunned that this seemed to be all they had. "But you don't have anything."

She let out a strangled laugh. "I would hardly say that. Granted, from your husband's broad declaration and your resistance to opening the safe . . . I had expected something a *little* more incriminating, but it's more than enough for me to bring you down to the station for questioning."

"Questioning for *what*?" I still wasn't following this. Where was the gold envelope with my will? Why wasn't she going over it line by line? Calling in cadaver dogs and cold-case files? If they hadn't found that envelope, what were they arresting me for?

"For the attempted murder of your husband." She cocked her head at me as if she were confused. "Should we be questioning you for something else?"

CHAPTER 46

CAT

Kelly called me twice, her voice mails filled with concern and giddy intrigue over the police presence dotting the Ryders' property. This would be the most exciting thing to happen to Atherton since the Bakers' disappearance. Add in the fact that this was on the same property, and we officially had the most notorious block in the neighborhood. We might need to buy and bulldoze the house just to retain our property value.

I deleted her voice mails and watched as the police car containing Neena pulled out of the drive. She had been put in the back seat, handcuffs on, in the rigid pose of the detained. Their garage door was still open, her SUV in its spot, Matt's car still missing. Where had he gone after he had confronted William? Our guesthouse was prepped and empty, but I had a feeling he'd rather sleep in the street than on William's property. I pulled out my phone and scrolled through my contacts, finding his name, and the number I had never used. I typed out a text.

I don't know where you are, but if you're up for a drink, let me know.—Cat

I sent the text and turned to face the dining room table, where Randall James sat. Our Tennessee-born attorney had a full spread before him and was digging enthusiastically into a blueberry-and-whipped-cream-topped crepe. Across from him, William was on the phone with the Human Resources director of Winthorpe Tech, discussing termination possibilities for Neena. Firing her had been my first demand, coupled by the quick requirement that he never, ever speak to her again. No texts, no emails, no calls. A complete dissection of her from our lives. He had quickly agreed, then tried to pull me in for a kiss—one I had refused. Punishment for this crime had been too long coming to be dealt swiftly. Neena was experiencing a mountain of it. William barely had to deal with a molehill.

"No severance package." My husband slid his chair back from the table and met my eyes. "Yes, effective immediately. I want her locked out of everything."

Randall tapped a piece of paper and slid it toward him. William glanced at the document and nodded.

"Yes, I'm aware of that risk. If she threatens anything, you have her call Randall. He'll handle it. And we have a release form she needs to sign. Tell her that her final paycheck is contingent on it."

"Not until Monday," I said quietly. "Lock her out now, but don't fire her until Monday. In the meantime, send out an email that looks like it's going to the entire team but only goes to her. One that says the office is closed today and tomorrow."

"Will she believe that?" Randall settled back in his seat and straightened, his checkered orange tie resting on his generous belly.

"She won't have the mental energy to question it," I said, turning to the window and looking across our yard at their house. In the light of day, there were only two police cars present. The forensic van and search dogs had left, their work done. The dogs had followed the intruder's path through three yards and over a low place in the neighborhood's fence, then lost the scent when he got into a vehicle. Poof, gone.

"Why wait until Monday?" William questioned, the phone pulled away from his mouth.

"She's been hit with a lot," I said. "Losing her job in the middle of a police investigation—it might be too much for her to handle." I said it with an air of kindness, but my motives were far from altruistic. She needed to properly understand the ramifications of her actions, and right now, her firing would just be one more thrown stone. Better for that blow to come when she would feel the sting of its impact.

I met William's gaze and raised my brows, daring him to question me. He held the eye contact for a moment, then relayed the instructions.

From the front of our yard, movement caught my eye as a police SUV made the turn into our drive. I cleared my throat. "Randall, they're here."

~

The doorbell rang, and the attorney stood and wiped at his mouth. "Both of you, just stay right here."

I leaned against the wall and silenced my phone, which was ringing with another call from Kelly, who must be watching the excitement with binoculars. Randall's smooth accent boomed through the entry hall as he flirted shamelessly with Atherton's female chief of police.

"Cat. William." Chief Danika McIntyre appeared in the open doorway. "Good afternoon."

I rounded the edge of the table and smiled, accepting the hug that the tall woman provided. Danika McIntyre had been our chief for eight years and had, during that time, coordinated several toy drives and charity projects through our Winthorpe Foundation. "I'm sorry about the middle-of-the-night call."

"No apologies needed. I'm sorry it's taken so long for me to get here. But don't worry, we've been very busy on this case. I had a judge sign off on the warrants as soon as the courts opened, so we've been able to get quite a lot done in the last ten hours."

I spoke before William did, hoping that he wouldn't question the purpose of warrants. "That's great to hear. Please, sit down. Have you eaten? I can have a plate fixed for you—anything you want." From behind her, I spotted two officers hovering in the foyer, and I paused.

Following my gaze, she gave a regretful smile. "Unfortunately, this isn't a pleasure call. Mr. and Mrs. Winthorpe, this is Detective Cullen and Officer Anders."

I shook both of their hands, as did William.

"They need to speak to you, Mr. Winthorpe. Privately. If you'd like your legal counsel to join us, that is certainly within your right."

"You can question me here, in front of Randall. And I'd like Cat to stay. We have no secrets." He hesitated. "Not anymore."

What a laughable statement. He may not have any secrets from me, but I had a mountain of them from him.

"Very well." The chief pulled out one of our linen-wrapped chairs and sat, gesturing to the other uniforms to follow suit. "We need to ask about your relationship, or lack thereof, with Neena Ryder."

"We had a friendship, one that felt inappropriate at times. She made it clear that she was interested in a physical relationship. I declined her advances, for the most part."

"For the most part?" Detective Cullen spoke up. "What does that mean?"

"Don't answer that," Randall drawled. "The extent of William and Neena's relationship has no bearing on this conversation."

"Did Neena ever speak to you about a future between the two of you?"

"No."

"Do you think she believed that there was a chance of a real relationship between the two of you, if Cat or Matt were out of the picture?"

He frowned. "I don't know what Neena believed, but I never led her to think that there was any possibility of a relationship. I love my wife, and I made sure Neena understood that."

Oh yes. I'm sure he was just *gushing* about me in that private boardroom. I'm sure Neena never even considered the possibility of stealing him away from me.

"We did uncover some unsettling items in the Ryders' bedroom. Photos of William, some of both of you." The second officer produced a file and pulled out photos, sealed in protective bags. William and I leaned forward, examining the pictures.

They were all familiar snapshots of our lives, and I glanced up at our visitors. "These are all from my Instagram profile. I've posted all these. She must have printed them out."

William inhaled as he took in the large number of images.

"You said there were some photos of the two of us?" I prompted.

"Yes." He pulled a second set of images from the accordion file. This set, when placed on the table, caused a visual flinch from William.

Hack jobs of my favorite photos. One of William looking tenderly down at me, my face replaced with a cutout of Neena's face, beaming out. Another—one from our wedding, my dress topped with a too-large image of Neena, her grin angled toward William's handsome face. And worst of all—the photo of him and me and my baby niece. She'd replaced my entire body with hers, the three of them making a demented Frankenstein family.

"There are also these." The chief moved three more photos out of the stack, each one a demonic hack job of a group photo where Matt's and my heads were cut off.

"This is psychotic," William said quietly. "We need security on Cat. I'll pay for protection for Matt as well—at least until Neena is locked up permanently." He looked up at me. "You were right about her. I'm so sorry I didn't listen to you."

I studied his taut features, the guilt and emotion clogging his eyes. Did he mean it? Was he sorry? I thought he was, but would I ever be able to trust him again?

I cleared my throat. "What exactly happened inside the house? Someone tried to attack Matt? Did they break in?"

"The intruder either had a key, or a door was left unlocked. He seemed to be a professional. There are no fingerprints, no shoe prints, no hair. He came in around two forty-five in the morning, put a gun in Mr. Ryder's mouth while he was sleeping. Mr. Ryder woke up, then the intruder pulled the trigger."

William let out a low curse.

"The gun misfired, Matt tried to grab at the gun, and the man fled. We weren't able to track him down."

"But you think he was hired? This isn't someone who's going to come back and try to kill Matt again?"

"We're keeping two cars stationed at the Ryder house for the next few days, but our current thought is that Mrs. Ryder—or someone else—hired the hit. We're doing an audit of Mr. Ryder's bank and business accounts but haven't found any evidence of gambling, money owed, or suspicious contacts. He seemed to be well liked and honest, so the list of people interested in killing him is slim."

"He's a good guy," William said quietly, and I resented the look of guilt on his face. Matt was a good guy, but I had been a good wife. He had sworn to love, honor, and protect me, and that's where his guilt should have been focused.

I straightened in place. "Where's Neena now?"

"She's at the station being questioned. They're going through all the evidence with her. I'd like to say that we'll keep her there, but to be frank, we have a lot of speculative evidence but nothing hard. Though this has been a very scary incident for Matt, there hasn't been an actual crime, just an attempt at one. And we're going off Matt's testimony for that—nothing else."

William raised a brow at me, and I knew what he was thinking of—my trip to the emergency room. The poison in my system. Just yesterday we'd gotten the call from the hospital confirming the presence of antifreeze in my stomach. I shook my head at him, wanting him to stay quiet.

"Is William an official suspect?" Randall spoke up from his end of the table.

The detective and chief exchanged a glance. "At this moment, he's not even an unofficial suspect. We will let you know if that changes."

"In that case," William said, "I think we're done for now." He pushed on the arms of his chair and stood, running a hand roughly through his hair. "Please, take those photos. Looking at them makes me sick."

The chief was the first to rise, and she gave a curt nod. "We appreciate your time, Mr. Winthorpe. We'll be back in touch if we have any more questions."

"Call me William," he corrected, coming around the desk and extending his hand to her. "And thank you for your discretion."

"Well." She grimaced. "I can't promise it will last very long." She opened up her large leather bag and slid the file and photos inside it. "We may need you to come to the station at some point, but I'll try to contain everything, as best as I can, from this end."

I waited until she shook Randall's hand, then gave her another hug. "Thank you," I whispered in her ear. She squeezed me in response.

As they headed for the door, my phone buzzed with a response from Matt.

I'm at the White Horse. In a horrible mood, but misery loves company. I'll save you a barstool.

CHAPTER 47

Cat

The White Horse was the sort of place I used to find my dad at on Saturday nights during football season. The bartender had giant breasts, a pierced eyebrow, and an infinity sign tattooed on the inside of her wrist. I navigated past a family of five, a dozen empty tables, and an old man gnawing on a chicken wing, then spotted Matt almost hidden behind a poster-covered column. I set my purse on the counter and straddled the stool next to him. "Hey."

He turned his head and lifted his chin. "Hey, there."

I peered at the collection of empty glasses before him. "Wow. You've got a serious doom-and-gloom thing going on."

He chuckled and slid his drink toward me. "Want to join in?" He pointed to a card tent stuck along the back of the bar. "I'm moving down the drink list. Five more to go."

I eyed the list, a little concerned that he had already knocked back three stiff drinks. "I'm game to try a few. But I have a driver. Promise me you'll hitch a ride back with me."

"Fine." He slid his drink closer and peered at the contents. "I'll take a ride home on William Winthorpe's dime. He owes me that at least."

I didn't respond, catching the bartender's eye as she moved toward us. "I'll have what he's having."

"Sure thing." The brunette snapped her gum and collected two of his empty glasses. "Here you go." She set a bowl of Chex mix in front of me, and I vowed not to get drunk enough to eat from it.

"Who's the big guy in the corner? That your driver?" Matt nodded to my new shadow, a massive redheaded Irishman who could kill any threat just by sitting on them.

"He's actually private security, borrowed from Winthorpe Tech. The driver is out in the car. William is a little paranoid with everything that has happened." I gave an apologetic frown. "Sorry, if he bothers you—"

"No," Matt scoffed. "I should be the one apologizing. I'm the one married to the lunatic."

"Speaking of which . . . I saw them put Neena in a police car. Have you heard from her?"

"Not since . . ." He stabbed at the screen of his phone. "Two and a half hours ago." He turned the display so I could see the row of missed calls.

"They showed us the pictures they found in your bedroom. Scary stuff."

"They tell you about the cash? Bundles of it stacked underneath our floor." He belched, then apologized. "Around eighty grand. Who knows where she got that." He glanced at me. "Could William have given it to her?"

I shook my head. "I don't think so. I can check our safe and accounts, but I don't know why he would have."

"Well, she can find her own way home from the station." He took a long sip of his drink. "And she's not staying at home. I'm going to let her pack a bag, but then she'll have to find a hotel."

"Good. I hope she ends up at a Motel 6." Taking my drink from the bartender, I held it out in a toast. "Here's to misfires."

He winced, then nodded, clicking his drink against mine. "To misfires." Our eyes met; then I lifted the drink to my mouth and took a sip.

It was strong, the mixture almost pure liquor, and I swallowed it with a bit of a cough. "Jeez, that's strong."

He nodded at the brunette, who was drying off glasses by the sink. "Amber's the best. Hey, Amber!"

She looked over one shoulder, a glass still in hand.

"This is Cat." He gripped my shoulder. "She's the only person in the world right now who understands my pain."

"It's true," I agreed, smiling at him. "We're tortured twins."

"Tortured twins!" He cackled like it was the wittiest thing in the world. "Amber, Cat is married to the man who has been screwing my wife."

"Wow," she said slowly, setting the glass up on the shelf. "You guys are an unexpected pair. Where are the cheating scoundrels?"

"Well, my wife is in jail," he said grandly, and I let his exaggeration slide. "And her husband is . . ." He squinted at me. "Well, I don't know where William is. Somewhere expensive."

"My husband is talking to his attorney and figuring out the best way to fire your wife." I took another sip of the drink and shuddered.

"Ha." He slid the glass in a circle on the bar top. "You know . . . I've been thinking about what would have happened if the gun hadn't misfired."

I watched him carefully. "If the gun hadn't misfired . . . ," I said slowly. "You'd be hurt, or dead."

"Yeah." He nodded. "But"—he raised a finger in speculation— "*would* she have gotten away with it?"

I frowned. "They would have done the same investigation, right? Still discovered the photos and the money. And the photos were what really caused them to find the affair, right?" My voice broke a little, and he reached over and patted my arm in the helpless manner of a man who didn't know what to do.

"You know . . . ," he said carefully, "I don't know why he did anything with her when he had you. It doesn't make any sense."

I swallowed a burst of emotion that threatened to bring on tears. "Thanks," I said quietly. *Thanks, but so what?* It didn't matter if I was prettier or younger. Sweeter. Less psychotic. He still went for her. If I hadn't stepped in, how far would it have gone? What could have happened?

He withdrew his hand. "Have you talked to him about it? Found out how it started? Or why?"

"Yeah. He—" I took a deep breath. "He said it just happened. That it was a mistake. That he didn't know how it got to that point, but it had."

"Sounds like bull," he growled.

"Yeah."

He hunched toward me. "Did you suspect it? Anything between them?"

I made a face. "I haven't been a fan of your wife for a while now. I thought they were spending too much time together, but he brushed off my concerns."

The bartender paused by us. "Ready for the next on the list?"

Matt nodded, then glanced at me. "Are you staying with him?"

I had to lie. If I told him the truth, it might give him permission to follow suit. I hesitated, then slowly shook my head. "No." I met his eyes. "I can't forgive what he did. Do you think . . . that you would have forgiven her? If she hadn't—" I waved my hand in the air as if to indicate his situation in general. "You know. Tried to kill you."

He unexpectedly laughed, a contagious one that started as a chuckle and wheezed through his body, his chest racking, tears dotting the corners of his eyes. I joined in, and it was sad how much he needed my approval, his posture lightening when I began to giggle.

Then, as suddenly as he had started, he stopped. "I don't know what I would have done," he admitted. "But this wasn't the first time she's cheated on me." He looked down at his drink, then downed half of it in one continual sip. "Last time I didn't even confront her with it. I found out and never did a thing about it."

"Wow." My faux shock delivered well, but I wasn't surprised. I had pegged Neena for a cheater from the very beginning. And while Matt played the clueless husband to perfection, no one was that dense. We all had our instincts. He had to have known, at some point in his marriage, that he was playing the fool.

"I have all of the text messages between them," he confessed. "The detective is giving them to me. And the call logs. In case you want them."

"That's nice of you. And of the detective." I glanced at him. "Is that normal? Sharing all that?"

"I don't know. They—" He reached into the Chex mix and grabbed a handful, then offered me the bowl. I shook my head. "They are kind of putting this in my hands. They can't—at least not yet—find proof of a connection between the shooter and Neena, especially since they don't have any idea who the shooter is."

I frowned. "What do you mean, they're putting it in your hands?"

"The next steps. We have a meeting with the district attorney tomorrow to discuss my options."

"You and Neena?"

"No, me and Detective Cullen." He glanced at me. "I was wondering if you could come."

I hesitated. "Would that be appropriate? I'm not sure—"

"It'd be nice to have a friendly face there. Someone I trust. I . . ." He paused, as if he were trying to find the right words. "You've been through this. Right alongside me. Maybe not last night, but with you going to the hospital for poisoning, I think we're about even." He gave me a weak smile, and I returned the gesture.

I wanted to be there when they decided her fate. Desperately. Still, I feigned apprehension. "Honestly, I'm not sure Detective Cullen would even let me—"

"Cat," he chided, "if there's anyone in town they'd bend a rule for, it'd be you."

"Me or William," I said quietly, my gaze floating around the bar as I killed a dozen seconds of time. "Okay," I said as reluctantly as I could, "I'll come."

CHAPTER 48

Neena

Ten hours after a police car took me from my own home, I stepped outside the cab and stared at our house. The porch light was on, illuminating the bright-yellow tape that stretched between each column and to stakes in the yard. I stepped forward, my tennis shoes crunching across the gravel as I hefted my purse over my aching shoulder.

It should be a crime to be this exhausted, my emotions and body stretched beyond reasonable limits. Ten hours of waiting, of questions, of explaining my story over and over again. Constant accusations and photos and speculation and lies. Ten hours that had convinced me that someone was behind all this and out to get me. As I trudged up the steps, my purse slipped off one shoulder and knocked against my knee. I managed the final step and staggered to the front door. I tried the handle, which didn't give. I jabbed at the doorbell and considered finding my keys, buried somewhere in the bottom of my purse.

I peered in the door's glass cutouts, the interior dark. Matt *had* to be here. I opened the top of my purse and flinched when the heavy door moved, swinging inward, the porch light spotlighting a thin sliver that revealed my husband.

I flinched at the sight of Matt, his eyes bloodshot, his hair wild. He looked like he hadn't shaved today, his paunchy cheeks covered in a fine layer of stubble. His T-shirt, a baggy graphic tee that I could have sworn I'd thrown out, boasted the words *Don't Be A*, followed by a photo of a rooster and a lollipop. I hated that stupid shirt. He'd picked it up at a cheap tourist shop on Duval Street and insisted on wearing it on the cruise ship home, despite my staunch opposition to the garment.

So, this was the path he was taking. A childish T-shirt and making me get a taxi home. I pinned him with a look and went to step inside. He didn't budge, his body blocking the doorway.

I glared at him. "Are you going to *move?*"

"You have ten minutes to get anything you need out of the house." He spoke slowly, his words slurring. "Any longer and I'll have that officer escort you out." He pointed to one of the police cars parked on the edge of our drive, its parking lights dimmed.

I gawked at him. He was the one who had thrown me under the bus, he was the one who had given them the code to the safe, yet he was throwing me out? "Are you kidding me? Do you have any idea what I've *been* through in the last twenty-four hours? I had to take a *taxi* here. Why aren't you answering my calls?"

"I loved you." He wilted a little against the doorframe, but he would forgive me for the affair. He just needed some time. Some soothing. A reminder of how much he loved and needed me.

"Move out of the way." I pushed forward, using my shoulder to force him back. My purse strap caught on the door handle, and I yanked, almost tripping over Matt in an attempt to get fully inside the door. "What are you—" I shoved off him and made it to my feet. "What's *wrong* with you?"

"What's wrong with me?" He gripped the door with one hand and slung it closed with a ferocity that shook the entire wall. "You hired someone *to kill me.*"

"Oh my God." I threaded my arms across my chest, watching as he thudded past me and into the kitchen. I followed him, pulling on his arm. "Matt. You can't honestly believe that."

"I believe it," he sputtered. "You pathetic *whore*."

My mouth gaped, and there was a full moment where I couldn't even formulate a reaction. Matt didn't speak to *anyone* like that, much less me. I couldn't think of a time he'd ever said anything remotely rude to me. He knew better. Yet now, after everything I'd been through, had been accused of, he was making it worse. I swallowed. "You never called Mitchell, did you?"

It had been so embarrassing, expecting to see our attorney and then having a public defender walk in. The man had taken ages to appear and hadn't known anything about me or Matt or our history. Mitchell would have known I was innocent. Mitchell knew me. I could have told Mitchell everything and not sounded like a . . . a . . . *a pathetic whore*.

Matt's accusation echoed, the words fitting for how I had felt in front of that public defender. I'd been forced to tell him the intimate details of my relationship with William and had seen the judgment flicker across the man's craggy face. I'd hotly contested his questions about hiring someone to kill Matt and could tell he didn't believe me.

"Oh, I called Mitchell," Matt sneered. "I called Mitchell and made it very clear where his loyalties should lie."

My cheeks burned at the realization that Matt was the reason the public defender had been assigned to me. And I had believed in him the entire time in the station. Assumed, however naively, that he had been back at home, believing in me.

I let out an awkward laugh and tried to understand where all this had gone so wrong. "But . . . it's all crap, Matt. I didn't hire someone to kill you. You *know* I didn't do that."

"So, I'm unlucky?" He lifted his arms out to each side, and I couldn't believe I was being subjected to these accusations. I should be getting a hot shower right now. "I guess we just *happened* to be missing the screws on the railing I like to lean against every morning? I guess the liqueur you bought specifically for Cat just *happened* to contain antifreeze? I guess, out of all of the houses in this town, some random psychopath happened to come into ours, without breaking a single window or lock, and stick a gun in my mouth?"

"You can't be serious," I sputtered.

"Cat went to the *hospital*, Neena. I was one misfire away from death. Was it worth killing both of us for William?"

God, I hated that woman. Screw the shooter coming after my husband. He should have entered that diamond-encrusted mausoleum and shot her pretty little face right between the eyes. Then we'd be in our home, happy as pigs in crap, and it'd be *their* life being picked apart right now.

"You're lucky that Cat kept the police from investigating that limoncello. We *protected* you," he spat out.

"Were you protecting me when you told them to look in the safe? Did you enjoy stressing me out, holding that over my head?" I could feel tears burning at the corners of my eyes, my very thin thread of self-control frayed to breaking. "I fainted, Matt. I *fainted* when I thought that they were going to find my will. Why put me through that?"

"Oh, please." He shook his head at me. "You'd already removed it. Probably destroyed it. What was there for you to faint over?"

I froze at the implication of his words. "I didn't remove it, Matt. I—"

"I spoke to Cat this morning, and we decided—"

"We decided? Where did you talk to Cat? Did you see her? Was she here?" He knew the rules. I'd been very clear for the two decades of our relationship and drawn his lines in bloody red paint. Having a woman in our house, alone with my husband, was a football field outside those lines, *and he knew it.*

"You are not going jealous psycho on me right now." He held up his hand, and I wanted to grab it by the wrist, flip that switch by the sink, and shove it down the garbage disposal. "What matters is that she agreed not to mention the poisoning to the detective or share the broken railing with them."

"Oh, how *kind* of her," I sneered. "So generous. I should write her a freaking thank-you card. You believe that act? She probably poisoned herself."

"Sit down, Neena."

Had he ever said my name in such a cold way? He pointed to a stool. "I'm going to explain this to you one time, and I swear on my life, if you say one word before I finish, I'm going to slap the shit out of you."

I opened my mouth, then shut it, stunned at the stranger standing before me and the words he'd just growled at me. Stunned at how, if he had only shown this side of himself earlier, I might have actually respected him. *Stayed loyal* to him. I sat.

"I'm having Mitchell's office prepare divorce papers. I'll file on Monday."

"You're doing *what?*" The words exploded out of me as my panic flared.

The impact of his hand threw me backward, the stool tipping. I scrambled to grab the edge of the counter and failed, the expensive three-peg stool leaning to one side, the soles of my shoes sliding along the tile as stars dotted my vision.

He hit me. Matt had *hit* me.

If he had pulled up his shirt and produced a third nipple, I wouldn't have been more surprised.

I tugged at the edge of the counter and found my footing, my legs weak as I struggled to stand, my vision clearing. Matt stood across from me, still and silent, and stared at me as if I were a stranger. *Me.*

He pointed to the stool, which lay on its side, the wood knocking on the floor as it rocked a little in place. "Sit back down. Shut up. If you speak again, I'll hit you again."

It was pure torture to keep my mouth closed. *What was he thinking?* My cheekbone throbbed. I'd have a bruise. How would we explain *that* to the police?

I lifted the stool and righted it. I moved dully to sit atop it, my hands sweating as I gripped the counter and vowed to myself to stay silent. In my head, a slow-motion picture of Cat Winthorpe played. Laughing at my arrest. Feeding carbs and sugar to William in a sexy negligee and making him fall back in love with her. I was the one who was supposed to win this game. *Me.*

Matt continued as if all were fine, as if he hadn't just abused me. "You will not contest the divorce and will give me all the assets of our marriage, including my company." He looked at me, making sure that I was following his ridiculous monologue.

He might be saying this now, but he couldn't mean it. Through everything, Matt was my rock. The only one who loved me through my flaws. The only one who looked at me as if I had value. The one who had provided for me since the moment I'd lost my father. That emotional security had been the only constant in my life for the last two decades. It had been the foundation I had depended on when I had stepped out on him. His love for me . . . it wasn't going anywhere. It couldn't go anywhere. Him leaving me was never a piece of this plan.

"I will give you a thousand dollars a month in alimony for two years. That's all you'll get. Not one dollar of the bonus from Ned Plymouth. Not one dollar of our stocks or savings or the equity in this house."

I would never agree to that. He was crazy if he thought I would.

"You'll sign the settlement agreement and leave me alone, because if you don't, if you ever come *near* me—I'll tell them about your father. I'll tell them the story that you detailed in your will. And they'll believe it, especially if I have Cat beside me, sharing everything about the liqueur you gave her and the details of my fall. They'll believe your confession, and they'll dig up his body, and you'll go to prison."

I will kill Cat. I didn't know how or when, but I'd do it. I'd cut her brakes, or push her off a mountain, or get her drunk and drown her in her giant ridiculous pool.

I risked a glance at Matt's face and inhaled at the contempt and hatred that seeped from the look he was giving me.

Somewhere inside, there was still love. There had to be.

I pushed off the stool and bolted upstairs, needing to get away from that look before it broke me in half.

CHAPTER 49

CAT

I stood on our roof deck and gripped the thin spindles of the ladder. Built into the far end of the deck, it allowed someone to climb onto the roof, where they could walk along the pitched surfaces and see almost 360 degrees around. Around my neck the binoculars hung by a thick strap.

I made my way onto the peak and carefully walked down the opposite slope, settling in one of the elbows where the roof changed direction. Finding a comfortable position on the tile, I watched the front yard of Matt and Neena's house.

I'd missed her entrance, the taxi coming and going while I argued with William. I asked him again why he'd done it and was given a mountain of explanations that boiled down to one thing: because he could. She'd pursued him, and he'd been too weak to resist the ego boost.

I'd expected that this confrontation would unfold in a similar fashion to what had happened with the dowdy secretary. I'd scream about Neena, and he'd scoff and ridicule. I was prepared for that, but this was an entirely different William, one who looked at me with an almost rabid devotion, which contrasted completely with the fact that he'd screwed her in our company's boardroom.

William had apologized, over and over again, and I was already sick of hearing it. I didn't want his apologies. I wanted him to *hate* her, to grow nauseated at the sound of her name, to constantly associate this affair with pain and headaches and horror. I wanted him to bind himself to *us* and to vow to never so much as look at another woman.

I'd dismissed his apologies and told him I needed some time for myself. After two hours at the bar with Matt, I soaked in the tub, followed by a quiet dinner in the library, and now—fresh air on the roof.

I had needed the time to think and wanted this final moment for myself.

I thought of Matt's announcement that he would kick Neena out and wondered if he would actually stick to it. I'd had to tell him that I was leaving William, had to set that false trail to give him something to initially follow. I knew he'd need a push. I'd never seen a husband with such devotion and blind acceptance. I couldn't let Neena and William have an affair and her be forgiven and loved as if nothing had even happened.

Matt had proven it in our conversation at the White Horse. *Last time I didn't even confront her with it. I found out and never did a thing about it.* The confirmation of what I'd already known had warmed me, the tequila blurring the edges of my actions with a rose tint I'd already grown quite accustomed to.

He would have forgiven cheating, but murder? Could any spouse forgive that? Could any husband still love his wife knowing that she wanted him dead?

No.

No.

No.

Which was why I'd *had* to do this. I'd had to show him how terrible his life was with her. I'd had to *force* the break, or he'd never have done it on his own, and she would never have any repercussions for her horrible actions.

I cupped my knees to my chest and strained to hear anything from the Ryders' house. At this angle, I could see their bedroom windows, but the room was dark, their activity still restricted to the downstairs.

Neena had to be overwhelmed right now. Confused. She was probably turning hostile. Calling him crazy. I imagined them screaming, her face mottled in rage, surgically enhanced features twisting in ugly patterns as she denied crimes she knew nothing about.

She'd really made it all too easy for me. So focused on my husband. So rabid for time with him. She had been so concerned with destroying my marriage that she never paid attention to her own.

The lights flicked on in the big front window, and I tilted as far right as I could, watching the progression of their movements as the stairwell lit, then the second-floor hall. I gripped my knees in anticipation, praying that when the bedroom light came on, their curtains were open.

The four windows exploded into action, glowing bright yellow against the dark night. I lifted the binoculars and adjusted their focus, breathing a sigh of relief at the part in the curtain that was wide enough to give me a peek.

Neena stomped across the bedroom, her arms swinging, mouth moving. She stopped and spun, stabbing the air with her finger as she yelled something. I strained to see Matt, letting out a soft sigh when he appeared in the doorway, his own face red, his mouth jawing as he delivered something right back.

I wanted to cheer at the presence of his backbone. *I gave him that.* I watched as he pointed to the floor. He must be talking about the money.

The cash had come from our safe, the stacks of bills rewrapped with fresh bindings in case the originals held William's or my fingerprints on them. I'd worn gloves when I'd handled the money, though I'd been sure that fingerprints couldn't be lifted from dirty currency—and why would they try? Neena's fingerprints would be all over the other items in the hole.

I thought of the red box I'd placed in the hole and the moment she'd unwrapped her birthday gift and turned over the red container. *Shake it,* I'd said, and almost laughed at the thought of her following my instructions, her stupid play right into my hands. She'd opened the box and stared dumbly at the vibrator I'd grabbed off a discount rack at the local sex shop. She hadn't realized that she'd just given me the best thank-you gift possible—evidence. I'd gathered the box and the wrapping paper, stuffing them back in my bag and distracting her with chatter, the theft of the packaging unnoticed in the rest of the evening's festivities. After all, William had been there. I could have sliced myself from crotch to neck, danced naked amid the blood spurt, and I would have barely gotten a side glance from Neena.

It had been her eyes that had given me my first indicator of trouble. They'd watched him whenever he walked out of the room. Lit up whenever he spoke to her. Caressed his face when he smiled. I'd seen those eyes and known, from the beginning, that she would be trouble.

Now, I watched as she crouched before the bedroom dresser, yanking at drawers and slamming items onto the bed. She moved to the Bakers' old safe and worked her fingers over the dial, putting in the combination—that same combination that I'd found on the sticky note years before. She disappeared behind the door of it, and I imagined her looking through the scant items, searching desperately for the envelope that the cops had never found. I reached into the pocket of my robe and closed my fingers around the envelope I had taken from their safe. The one marked *Neena's Will and Testament.* I had almost skipped right over it in my exploration of the contents. After all, how interesting could a will be?

But, as it turned out, Neena's was a real showstopper.

I pictured her panic, the frantic flip through papers once, twice, a third time. She really should have used a safe-deposit box. This entire setup had been a cakewalk. The morning of Matt's fall, I'd had hours of alone time to move through their home and sift through her drawers, her closet, her life. While William and Neena had waited for Matt at the hospital, I'd tested my old key in the home's back door and verified it still worked. I'd checked the empty cubbyhole in the floor and envisioned how it could be used. I'd found the photo I'd taken of the safe's sticky note and tried the combination, smiling when it still opened the vault. I'd gone through the contents and read everything, including her will.

I remember my mouth falling open, my eyes darting around the empty bedroom, looking for someone to share the item with. I remember reading it a second time, then slowly folding it back into thirds and sliding it back into the envelope. I remember putting her house back in order and throwing away the trash from the railing, then returning to my home and lying down on the couch, the envelope warm in the back pocket of my pants.

I'd lain there and thought through everything. Remembered the conversation with William and Deputy Dan about the broken railing. The murder-attempt possibility that we had just scoffed over. I moved around puzzle pieces in my mind until they fit into place. Red flags to plant. Red herrings to deceive. The careful destruction of a life, one interaction at a time.

I made the plan and then sat on it for a long time. A time in which I watched her creep in. A time in which I monitored my husband's call activity and read his emails and text messages and placed a hidden camera in the one place in Winthorpe Tech where something might happen—the boardroom. I behaved until the afternoon that I watched the video of her sitting on the heavy mahogany table, her knees open, her hands clutching at William's shirt. Her, bent over, face contorted in pleasure.

I'd paused the video just after the act, when she was reaching for her underwear and he was buckling his pants. She was looking down and smiling. *Smiling.* I'd stumbled back from the video screen, my hands trembling, my stomach twisting, and barely made it to the bathroom before I vomited. I locked myself in the bathroom and turned on the shower jets, stripping down and drowning out my sobs under the spray.

I broke.

Broken women cannot be held accountable for their actions.

I needed my husband back. Needed to punish her. So I put my plan into action, and I did.

CHAPTER 50

CAT

William drove, the Maserati humming along the road. I pulled the neck of my jacket loose and turned up the air conditioner, opening my vents.

"I spoke to Chief McIntyre this morning," he announced, his eyes on the road. "She'll be present at your meeting."

I watched as we passed through the neighborhood's security gates, William's hand lifting to wave at the uniformed officers who framed the opening. After Matt's intruder, my confidence in them had waned, and I avoided eye contact with them. We wound through the curves of Atherton, heading to the police station, and I rested my head on the window, watching as the homes grew smaller and closer together as we neared the center of town.

"Neena called me this morning." William delivered the news somberly, and I lifted my head and turned to face him, feigning surprise. For months, I'd been monitoring his call activity through our carrier and had synced my laptop with his iCloud account, so all his text messages hit there as well.

"Is that the first time she's called since everything happened?" I waited to see if he'd pass the test. If he lied, what would I do? What would be the use of all this if he continued down a path of deceit?

"No." He sighed. "She called me a few times in the middle of the night, but I didn't answer. And once I heard about the intruder, I thought it would look suspicious if I called her back."

"It would," I agreed. "Plus, you aren't talking to her again." *Ever* again. I'd laid down several nonnegotiable rules, the primary being for him to be completely honest with me and cut all communication with her.

"Of course not." His hand closed over mine, and I struggled with my emotions on allowing a final talk between William and Neena. It felt as if there did need to be some closure. I wanted her to know that he had chosen me, and not because he had to, but because he wanted to.

But had he?

That was part of the problem with triggering the "attempts" on Matt's life. It stopped the affair before it died out on its own. As far as Neena knew, William could be pining over her and was only being kept at bay by me.

It was a problem I had yet to find a solution for. William's thumb ran over the back of my hand, and I pulled it away.

As we rounded the bend, Ravenswood Preserve came into view. The sun streamed over the colors of the marshland, the water glistening. He nodded to the view. "Remember what you said when we first moved here?"

"That it was magic?"

"That we'd create magic here." He leaned over, pressing a kiss to my forehead. "We have, Cat."

"And then you ruined it."

He moved over to the shoulder and stopped before a big **No Parking** sign. He turned to me, and I could see the ache in his eyes. "I'll fix it. I'll earn your trust back. I don't know how, but I'll spend every day of my life trying."

I shook my head and told him the truth. "I don't know if you can."

"Don't say that," he begged. "I—"

"You what? You *slept* with her. *Kissed* her. Gave up time and attention that you should have spent on me, on her. And you lied to me about everything." I started to cry, my words sticking, my breath sucking out wet little sobs I couldn't control.

I'd known for weeks, but the wound still felt raw, as if the pent-up emotions had been incubating in my chest and were just now bursting free.

He undid my seat belt and pulled me to him, lifting me over the armrest and against his chest, my legs too long for the position. Clutching me to him, he kissed my forehead, my cheeks, my nose, my lips. "Please," he begged, his voice ragged. "I can't live without you, Cat. I was weak and stupid. It meant nothing."

I was stiff under his touch, unswayed by his emotions. "She needs to be punished, William." I pulled away from his chest and looked up into his eyes. "She can't do what she did to you to anyone else."

He nodded, ready to agree to anything. It was the moment I'd waited for, the final nail primed and ready for her coffin.

"Call Nicole in PR. Leak the murder attempt and her firing to the local papers."

He hesitated. "Cat, I just want to be done with her. Forever."

"And I *need* you to do this. To show her that you're done. And to punish her for doing this to us."

He didn't like it. I could see it in his eyes, in the wary way that he nodded, then pressed his lips against my forehead. "Okay," he whispered. "I'll give her a call as soon as I drop you off at the police station."

"Have her do it today," I demanded. "It needs to be front page by tomorrow."

"I will."

I met his mouth and melted into his kiss, the connection fed by his emotion. In that moment, I didn't forgive him, but the scab over my wound grew a little bit thicker.

~

I found Matt at the police station, seated at the end of a long line of chairs. He stood and pulled me in for a hug that smelled of sweat and pizza. I squeezed him back and pressed a soft kiss against his cheek. He'd do well without her. He had money and was kind. He'd find a new young wife who laughed at his jokes, looked great on his arm, and could suck-start a Harley.

I smiled at Matt. "Looks like you made it through last night."

"Barely." He sat back down in the chair and glanced at his watch. "My head is killing me."

"What happened with Neena last night?"

"She came home for about a half hour. Packed her stuff and then left. I'm not sure where she spent the night."

Yes, I'd be curious to know where Neena had ended up. I'd spent the night in bed with William, still frosty and aloof, stretching out his punishment while I watched the fire flicker in our bedroom hearth and enjoyed the thought of a lonely Neena checking in to a cheap hotel room.

"Where's William?" Matt nodded out the front window of the station. "I saw him drop you off."

"He's going to the office for a few hours. I told him I'd call him when I was done."

He nodded, and I saw the tightening of his lips, the flash of anger in his eyes. I didn't blame him for being mad at William. The men had been friends, and not in the twisted and backstabbing way of Neena and me. I struggled to find something to say. "William was selfish, but he wasn't manipulative. He had a weak moment one day. He wasn't pursuing her, and I know he didn't intentionally mean to hurt you, just like he didn't mean to hurt me."

He shrugged. "I still hate him. He got her, and despite what you said last night, it looks like he's keeping you. It just doesn't seem fair."

I nodded, part of me struggling with the same emotions. But this event would change us for the better. If we emerged from this with a more loyal and open marriage, I didn't need to punish him out of spite. And I had this chip, this history, to use at any future point in our relationship if I needed it.

My stomach growled, and I instinctively put my hand on my belly to cover up the sound. Matt's eyes followed the movement. "Do you feel okay?"

I forced a smile. "Yeah. My stomach's still a little temperamental." I reached in my purse and pulled out the package of saltines. I had skipped breakfast, complaining of stomach pain, in an attempt to subtly remind William of Neena's poison. It had worked, his face darkening, manner shifting, and he'd brewed me some chicken broth and made me promise to come home and relax after this meeting. As a result, I was ravenous. Between my hospital visit and stress over Matt's "murder attempt," I was down four pounds in three days. I was starting to daydream about cheeseburgers and pound cake.

Matt sat back in his chair and crossed his arms. "You wouldn't believe Neena. She won't admit to anything. She's still denying there was anything in that limoncello."

Yeah, I bet she was. I would have paid a million dollars to see the look on her face when Matt accused her of poisoning me. I stuffed the saltine in my mouth to keep myself from smiling. Drinking a shot of antifreeze had been risky but well worth it. I'd known that William would rush me to the hospital. Putting a couple of drops in Matt's drink had been a spur-of-the-moment decision, an easy one once I convinced him to try the limoncello, also.

Matt glanced at his watch, then leaned forward in his seat, his knee bumping mine. He lowered his voice. "She accused you of poisoning yourself."

Of course she did. Neena wasn't stupid, despite her complete underestimation of me. I still flinched, as if surprised. "Why would I do *that?*" I pressed my lips together and growled, wondering if he had believed any part of the accusation.

He shouldn't. It was why I'd gone to such painful and life-threatening lengths.

"So, you faked your fall, also, right? And the gunman?" I choked out a bitter laugh. "All of us. A conspiracy against her."

He nodded. "Right. A conspiracy. I think she even used that word."

I considered hugging him but offered my sleeve of crackers instead. He took one, breaking the saltine in half before eating it.

"Mr. Ryder? Mrs. Winthorpe?" The uniform at the end of the hall smiled at us. "They're ready for you."

~

The evidence was stacked in three piles, the division quickly explained.

"This," Detective Cullen stated, her hand resting atop the smallest stack, "is what we can tie to Neena in a manner that would hold up in court. It includes the cash and photos found in her bedroom, phone records and affidavits that prove her sexual relationship with William Winthorpe, and the financial gain she would have secured by Mr. Ryder's death."

The district attorney sat to my left in a pinstripe suit that barely fit. His bald head nodded, as if blessing the designation.

She moved to the second stack. "This is circumstantial evidence. It's suspicious on its own but allows for more than one possibility. An intelligent person could look at all these facts and assume that Neena is responsible for all of them, but—"

"It allows for reasonable doubt," the district attorney rasped, leaning back in his chair and undoing the suit's top button. "And reasonable doubt is the death of all criminal cases."

I could feel—in the nervous tic of his hands, his avoidance of my eye contact—his concern about his record. For cases brought by the DA's office, he'd had fourteen wins and one mistrial. I'd been watching that record, which was why I was confident, no matter what opinion Matt voiced in this room, that there was only one possible outcome. They would drop this case and "await more evidence." Evidence that would never come, because it didn't exist.

Which was all fine by me. I wasn't a monster. I never wanted Neena to go to trial, or be sentenced, or have a record. All I wanted was for her life to be systematically destroyed.

Goodbye, reputation.

Goodbye, career.

Goodbye, husband.

It hadn't even been that hard. And completely unanticipated. Who would suspect the setup of an intentionally botched crime, designed for the purposes of sabotaging a marriage? I settled back in my seat and crossed my Manolo Blahniks at the ankle, listening as the DA justified to Matt why his "almost death" would go unpunished.

"What's the other pile?" Matt interrupted, lifting his chin in the direction of the third stack.

"Evidence we found that doesn't tie to Neena and might convince a jury of her innocence."

My eye twitched, my attention zeroing in on the short bunch of folders stacked at the end of the table. Outside, I kept my slightly bored expression, hiding a yawn behind one perfectly manicured hand.

"Evidence like what?" Matt asked.

It was a question I was both frantic for and terrified of. After all, I'd thought through everything. Worn gloves when handling anything important. Visited their home enough so that my DNA would be ignored. Put my own life in danger to mislead Matt.

Detective Cullen pulled the folders toward her and flipped open the top flap. "Let's see . . . there's the man who came into your home, obviously. We have little to nothing on him. No fingerprints, no DNA, no forced entry. He was either given a key or you left the doors unlocked, which . . ." She peered at Matt. "You said you didn't do."

"I didn't."

Of course he hadn't. I'd given the man a copy of my key to their back door. Easy entry had been part of the deal, along with four bags of the Bakers' cocaine. For my high school's old drug dealer, it'd been a hell of a deal. All he'd had to do was spend five minutes in a quiet house with an unloaded gun. It hadn't misfired in Matt's mouth. It had never had a bullet *to* fire. One trigger pull and he'd left, following my careful instructions to get out of the neighborhood and jog a quarter mile to the main road, where a car was parked in one of the only restaurant parking lots without security cameras.

"And no security system at your house," she finished with a sigh. "So we have next to nothing on him. We've gone over Dr. Ryder's business and personal accounts and can't find any large cash withdrawals or suspicious checks."

"But she was hiding cash," Matt protested. "Couldn't she have just used some of that?"

"Sure." Chief McIntyre took a moment to earn her paycheck. "And she probably did. But we can't prove that."

"My concern is that the shooter will try again." I spoke up. "Is Neena done?"

Everyone looked to Matt. "I think she's in crisis management right now. And she doesn't seem to *want* to kill me, though I'm apparently a terrible judge of that."

I leaned forward and gently touched his arm. "You should get a security system. Change the locks." Especially now that I was all done, with no need to go back in.

"I changed the locks this morning." He nodded adamantly. "And a security system will be installed this week."

"That's good," Detective Cullen added, returning to the folder. "Though in this scenario, with the spotlight on the victim, it's rare for a second attempt." She flipped through a few pages. "The rest of this is just junk. Though there was one interesting fact. Neena's fingerprints weren't on any of the photos of William in the box, including the one in the frame."

Inwardly, I winced. It was a detail I couldn't find a solution to, not without potentially raising Neena's suspicions later on, when she reviewed the evidence against her.

"She could have worn gloves when she handled them . . ." Detective Cullen glanced at Matt, and then at me. Was it my imagination, or did her gaze linger? "But that'd be odd."

Unsure of a proper reaction, I nodded in agreement. I wanted to point out that her fingerprints were all over the photos' box but wasn't sure if that was a fact I was supposed to be privy to. I had planted the cash and the photos on a day when I knew Neena and Matt were furniture shopping, my in-and-out errand done in less than five minutes.

"Again, this is evidence that could be used against us in court," the DA remarked. "You've always got one conspiracy theorist on the jury." He stood, and I could feel him warming to the crowd, a performer ready to deliver his opening statement. "Look, Mr. Ryder, we all know what happened here. But it's not a story of knowing events, it's one of proving them. And we don't have enough hard evidence to prove anything, especially when an actual crime hasn't been committed. Attempted? Sure. But that's a real hard tail to pin on the donkey, if you know what I mean." He paused and glanced from Matt to me.

"So we'll keep digging at this hole, and I'm confident we'll find more soon. But for now, if we go to the judge with this too early, we'll end up empty-handed and with egg on our face. That won't be good for your stress levels, it won't be good for the DA's office, and—even worse—after Neena gets off once, we can't go after her again." He clapped his hands together. "I appreciate you both coming down here. And I'll keep you both updated as to when we'll be ready to move forward to trial."

When they'd be ready to move forward to trial? *Never,* I thought as we stood, shaking hands around the table, the evidence folders screaming at me as I made my way to the door.

CHAPTER 51

NEENA

I woke on Saturday morning on a stiff hotel bed to the sound of a vacuum banging along the hall. Rolling onto my back, I stared up at the ceiling and stifled a wave of anxiety as the events of the last week came rushing back.

Cat's poisoning, paired with William's suspicious looks.

My text messages and calls to him, all unanswered.

The loud skirmish in the middle of the night. Matt chasing someone downstairs.

The hours and hours of questions.

Countless police officers, going through the most intimate details of our lives.

The hidden compartment. The money. The photos.

The safe—my missing will and written confession.

I had been certain that Matt would soften, would let me stay in the house last night, would accept my hollow apologies and welcome me into our bed. But he had acted like a complete stranger. I lifted my hand and lightly felt my cheekbone, the area tender from his slap. Twenty years together and he had never touched me, never touched anyone, save for that one night.

I could threaten him. Threaten to expose that night if he wouldn't take me back. But the police would have to believe my story over his. And a week ago, they probably would have. But now, after the cloud of suspicion floating around me . . . who would believe me? I let my hand fall back onto the bed and tried to search for a solution.

If Matt meant what he'd said . . . a divorce with no split assets, a thousand dollars a month in alimony . . . I'd have to get another job. I had a voice mail on my phone from the HR director at Winthorpe Tech, one I hadn't had the stomach to listen to. I knew what it would say. *Thank you for your time with us, but there is no need to return.* My items were probably already boxed up and sitting at the front desk for my pickup. Maybe I could sue them for wrongful termination. Sexual assault. I still had the recommendation letter from Ned. I could get another job at another firm that didn't run in William Winthorpe's circles.

I got out of bed and slowly stood, my back protesting. I needed to get to a gym, maybe the tiny one I'd spotted just off the lobby. I wasn't brave enough to face the filler-enhanced faces at the Atherton athletic center. Too many Atherton wives attended there, and word had probably spread to a few of them. But what version of the events? The masked intruder? My potential involvement?

It was all ridiculous. I was innocent! Maybe not completely innocent, but my crimes were focused on seduction—not murder. I didn't need to poison Cat Winthorpe—I could take her down in other ways. And why would I hire someone to kill Matt? I loved Matt. I did. Despite the gray tooth in his smile and his growing gut. Despite the fact that he once called caviar "jelly seeds" at a party. Despite all that—I *loved* him. Who else would desire me in such a complete and unwavering way? Even if I had entertained thoughts of leaving him—I would never have gone through with it. Not unless William Winthorpe had proposed, which he might have, if I'd had more time with him.

It had all been going perfectly until the hard right turn that had thrown me into hell. Hell and a queen-bed hotel room with a rattling air conditioner and questionable pay-per-view options.

I dressed in yoga pants and a sports bra, lacing up my Nikes while mentally moving through my daily affirmations. I opened the door to my room, my key card in hand, and came to a stop at the sight of the newspaper tossed in front of my door, an identical copy at each adjacent room.

LOCAL WIFE ATTEMPTS MURDER, AUTHORITIES ALLEGE

The headline could not have been in bigger font, a bold sans serif that competed with the photo of me—a horrible shot where my mouth was open, my attention sideways. I picked up the paper and studied the photo, which was from the July Fourth fireworks party. I looked terrible. Terrible and *old* and angry. *Local wife attempts murder?* How many people had seen this piece of trash? I pictured all my new friends, their features pinching in distaste, manicured hands reaching for their phones, frantic to share the news. *Oh my gawd . . . did you hear? Neena Ryder tried to kill her husband. Kill him.* It would hit social media, message groups, text threads. It would be everywhere within an hour.

Returning to my room, I engaged the dead bolt and sank onto the bed, reading the article in its entirety as my gut twisted into a tight knot.

When I finished, I read it again. I tried for a third but headed for the bathroom instead, my stomach heaving in protest. I vomited, then sank to my knees on the white floor mat and hugged the edge of the dirty toilet.

The article had included a quote from William, one in which he had called me "a deeply disturbed individual." How could he have said that? Had he not felt our connection? Had our kiss, our sex, meant nothing? Among all the sparks and subterfuge, I thought there had been a genuine connection between us.

I had eight thousand dollars in my bank account and no job. No assets that weren't controlled or being taken by Matt. This was supposed to have followed a simple path—a secret affair that led to William Winthorpe paying me off or falling in love with me. Two very clear outcomes, neither of which would have risked everything I had worked so hard for. Our house in the right neighborhood. *Now a crime scene.* My job at the right company. *I'd be fired.* My social standing in the right circles. *Destroyed by this article.* A husband who worshipped and loved me. *Who had kicked me out of my own home. Mentioned divorce.*

How did it all disappear in the course of a few days? Though if I really examined it . . . it was in the course of a few minutes and a misfired gun.

I almost wished the gun hadn't misfired. Matt would be dead, and I would have everything. The house. The life insurance. The money in the bank. His company. I might have been investigated, but at least I would have the money to hire attorneys, a crack team that could shine the light on this shoddy investigation and find the true killer. I warmed to the idea of being a rich widow, sympathetic looks all around. Finally, I'd be able to watch what I wanted on television. Get rid of his ugly leather furniture. Live without dirty towels on the floor or sports magazines on the coffee table or junk food filling our pantry.

If the gun hadn't misfired, there was the possibility that the gunman could have turned it on me. But honestly, death would be better than this. I checked the dramatic statement for accuracy and was horrified to see that it was true.

Death *would* be better than life as a divorced and penniless social pariah.

And yet . . . it could get even worse, because that envelope from our safe was still missing. Who could have it?

It had to be Cat who was behind all this. Cat, who had probably faked her poisoning. Cat, who had put lies in Matt's head about the railing. Cat, who had probably hired someone to kill Matt—all so she could hold on to her shaky marriage.

But how had she gotten into the safe? When had she planted the photos? How long had she been planning this?

And if she was the one with my will, what did she plan to do with it?

CHAPTER 52

NEENA

Two weeks later

My new life sucked. Somehow, I was climbing the steps to an apartment, my keys jingling from my hand like a janitor. When I opened the door, I'd be looking at a room of rented furniture, the additional fifty bucks tacked on to my monthly rent as part of a never-ended Christmas special.

I didn't belong here. Not in this cramped one-bedroom, not in this low-rent part of San Francisco, not on the losing end of divorce proceedings that seemed to hollow me out more and more with every meeting.

I didn't even recognize Matt. For one, it was his teeth. The man who never seemed to care about his appearance now had *veneers*. They sparkled from his mouth every time he opened it, and he was suddenly opening it a *lot*, filled with opinions on everything from alimony to what car I should be driving. He knew I had an issue with American cars, yet that ended up being my option—he'd buy me a cheap sedan, or I could buy my own.

I took the sedan with its cloth seats and clunky styling, my head ducked in shame whenever I entered and exited it. My old car, the

BMW that I had always taken for granted, now taunted me from a roadside spot at the used-car dealership, its windshield covered by a price tag I couldn't afford.

Couldn't afford. Two words I'd run from my entire life. Two words I'd buried in the dirt after I walked down the aisle with Matt. Two words I'd forgotten the second I'd gotten my degree. Two words that had come back to bite me.

I made it through the door and heaved my computer bag onto the round dining table, rubbing my shoulder with a sigh. Turning back to the door, I flipped the dead bolt and worked the security chain into the slide.

Trudging to the narrow couch, I sank into the cheap polyester, not bothering with removing my heels. I could feel my new job prospects wobbling loose. Maybe it was the desperation in my voice. Maybe it was the newspaper article, which was taking top spot when you did an internet search for my name. Or maybe it was the gossip. Word of my affair had spread, and I had a new appreciation for Ned Plymouth, a private and quiet individual who had kept his money (and his business) to himself. The secret termination agreement had been the only swell in the serene lake of our affair's existence.

Cat and William Winthorpe, on the other hand, were a tsunami. Volunteer committees I'd worked hard on had suddenly deleted my name from their rosters and sent polite *You are no longer needed* cards. My book club, which Cat wasn't even a part of, asked that I no longer attend. My personal shopper at Neiman's, across the country in New York City, left me a snippy voice mail that made her opinion clear. The judgment and loathing came from all directions, and whatever stone Cat found too heavy to turn over, William flipped with ease.

The worst were my past employers. I'd had to weed my résumé down to practically nothing, as the Winthorpes turned every past reference against me. Matt refused to give me a positive recommendation from Ryder Demolition, and Ned Plymouth wasn't returning my calls, so I'd crossed his name off my résumé for fear of the unknown.

I could feel myself sinking. Drowning. In college, I'd experienced this feeling, this helpless detachment as I had watched my world crumble. Of course, back then it was caused by a sorority rumor of an STD, a minor blip that could have been easily overcome by a catty retort and simple manipulation. But I wasn't Dr. Neena Ryder back then. I was young and insecure, with a too-big nose and too-small breasts. I wilted, withdrew from school, and fell in love with Xanax and Matt's constant reassurances.

I couldn't fall back in that hole. Wine was one thing. Pills were another.

I shifted until my head was on the armrest and tried not to think about the renters before me, their dirty arms resting on the same ledge. Spilled food, drops of beer, all soaking through the navy fabric. I was lucky it didn't squish against my ear.

I let out a sigh and tried to remember why I'd thought William Winthorpe was a good idea. Pulling myself upright, I stretched forward, looping my finger through the handle of my purse and tugging it toward me. Opening the neck of it, I grabbed the bottle of wine and placed it on the table, then looked around for a cup.

~

The floor hurt, but I couldn't seem to move my legs. It was the wine. Too much wine. Had I ever drunk so much? The last time I was like this, it was a decade ago. William—no, Matt—had carried me to bed. Brought a bucket to me and wiped off my face after I vomited. He'd been a good caretaker. So loving. So forgiving. That night, he'd sat beside me in bed and run soft fingers through my hair until I fell asleep.

Now, I had no one to play with my hair, or to carry me to bed, or to bring me a bucket when I threw up. The vomit was coming. I could feel it, churning the wrong way through my intestines.

I struggled to roll to one side and stared at my cell phone, the silver device close enough to my forehead to almost touch.

I'd have to file for bankruptcy. I'd have to find a new job. Doing what? Fitness? God, I'd be one of *those* women. In my late thirties and bouncing around in Lycra all day long, posting Instagram messages of carb control and inspiration, using hashtags like #fitover40 and #persistence.

I reached for the phone. I needed to call William. Surely he remembered how good we were together. Hadn't he seen that? Felt it?

I dialed his number, but like every other time, he didn't answer.

EPILOGUE

WILLIAM

One year later

The Ryders' house came down in thirds. First, the side with the master suite, with that porch where Matt had fallen off. Their bedroom and master bath all crumpled under the wrecking ball, sagging into the interior of the house like a rotten pumpkin.

Next, the front fell. The porch that Neena had so painstakingly decorated for the Fourth of July, all in a gaudy attempt to compete with my wife. The grand foyer, where police dusted for shoe prints. Matt's study, where Neena signed their divorce papers. Everything was destroyed, dismantled, and chucked into the dumpsters. Ten of them were filled and carted out of the neighborhood's service entrance, only to make the empty journey back.

The rest of the home followed. The kitchen where Neena and I whispered our agreement to stay away from each other. The living room where we all toasted our friendship. The pool, the cabana, the hot tub. Crews spent a week removing it all. Cat sat in our backyard gardens, a cup of hot chocolate in hand, and watched it occur, a small smile playing across her beautiful face.

My mother once said I had a weakness for crazy women. She voiced that opinion back in third grade, when I developed a crush on Sylvia Pinket, the girl who trotted around the perimeter of our recess area pretending to be a horse. On days when the wind was rough, she'd whinny and prance, then plant her hands in the dirt and kick up her back feet. I thought she was beautiful. Eight years later, after she peed in the punch bowl at the Rotary Club Christmas banquet, a psychiatrist confirmed all our suspicions and shipped her upstate to the loony bin, ending any fantasies I had of unbridled Sylvia passion.

My penchant for crazy women, it appeared, never ended. While I thought it had taken a hiatus with Cat, I was wrong.

My wife, like Sylvia, was crazy.

I'd always suspected it but finally confirmed it. Not that a little bit of crazy was a bad thing. Honestly, it turned me on to know how much work my dear wife put into our marriage, to see the smooth lies that came out of her mouth, the faux concern she painted for others' sakes, the orchestration of events she managed to effortlessly direct, all for the sake of our marriage.

If Cat were Sylvia, she'd have had everyone at that ball peeing in their own glasses, then pointing fingers at the other guests. And that, among other things, was why I loved her.

And I really did *love* her. Even more this week than last, and more this year than the one before. I think it's rare for couples to still be *in love* after a decade of marriage, but we are. Which is one of the reasons I still can't wrap my head around *why* I ever gave Neena Ryder a second glance.

Maybe because I like crazy women, and she fit that bill to a T.

Maybe because I'd grown comfortable in my love for Cat, and Neena posed a risk I needed to take.

Maybe because part of me wanted to see if I would get caught and what my sweet, perfect wife would do when she found out what I'd done.

Maybe because seeing Cat's response pacified the insecure part of me that was reassured by watching my wife fight for me.

I'd wanted to see that crazy. I'd yearned for it. I'd been sloppy and reckless and waited to see it flare.

But it hadn't. Mystifyingly, it hadn't, and I'd continued further over the line with Neena, a masochist eager for his beating, certain that surely, any day now, I'd come home to a royally pissed-off wife. I'd plodded forward and completely missed the bread crumbs that Cat scattered until I was sitting across from her and signing the paperwork to buy Neena and Matt's home.

I'd moved through the closing on autopilot, thinking through all the events that had brought us to this point, still struggling with my confidence that Neena Ryder could not have possibly attempted to kill Matt. And if not her . . . I'd met Cat's eyes across the conference table, our gazes connecting, and realized, before she'd even cracked a smile, that *she* was behind all of it.

It was brilliant of her, expertly played, a cat lying quietly in the bushes and watching all her mice dance to their deaths. Thank God she scooped me out of the fray. Had she wanted to, she could have burned me at the stake right alongside Neena.

But she didn't, and I loved her even more for her mercy.

I heard the office door open and turned to see her coming in the room, her eyes bright, smile big. "I just came from meeting with the architect," she said happily, dropping a roll of paper down on my desk and unfurling it across the surface. "Look."

I rolled forward in my desk chair and reviewed the plans. "Looks nice."

"Nice?" She arched a brow at me. "Come on. Give me your feedback."

I tried harder, pushing to my feet and coming around the desk to stand next to her. Bending over the architectural drawings, I tried to imagine the space. There would be a second guesthouse in the area where the Ryders' home once was. A spacious outdoor kitchen and day spa overlooking the valley. Gardens that stretched between both lots, fountains that rimmed the pool, and an outdoor pavilion for eating and parties.

We didn't need the space, but we also hadn't needed the constant reminder of our old neighbors, Cat's irritation and anxiety blooming with each new couple who toured the listing. I also think she enjoyed the act of literally destroying the home that Neena had never had a chance to really enjoy.

"The new firepit will be here." She pointed. "And they'll expand our pool and add an infinity edge. We'll keep the small hot tub on our lot, but this . . ." She dragged her finger over to where the Ryders' gazebo once was. "This will be the new hot tub, with a heated lap pool coming off it."

I smiled at her. "Do I want to know what all this will cost me?"

"No." She grinned back, hoisting herself up on the desk and looping her hands around my neck, pulling me between her open legs. "Do you like it?"

"I love it," I whispered. "And I love you."

"Forever?" she asked, tilting her head and waiting on my response.

"Forever," I promised, surging forward and pressing my lips to hers, frantic to prove it.

C AT

I stood at the edge of the electronics store parking lot and watched as Neena pushed in a row of carts. She wore a bright-blue collared top with cheap khaki pants that flapped around her ankles. As I watched, she paused, tightening the hair in her ponytail before resuming her task.

When she passed by me, I called her name. She glanced over and then froze. Jerking her head from side to side, she looked around for help, then cautiously regarded me. "Don't come closer," she called. "You can't come closer."

I stepped forward, holding up my hands as every part of her tensed. "I'm not here to get you in trouble. I'm approaching you at your job, and the parking-lot cameras will prove it. This isn't a violation of our protective order against you."

"What do you want?" Her jaw trembled, and I looked away from the weak action, focusing on her brilliant blue eyes.

A year ago, I'd have found joy in her fear, but now, with everything I knew, I felt only guilt. Guilt over torturing a woman who was clearly mentally unhinged. Guilt over ruining her marriage with the one man who could live with her faults. She had set out to destroy my marriage, but I had succeeded in destroying her life.

"I want to give you this." I held out the gold envelope, the paper limp with use, the document inside one I had read a hundred times. It hadn't been just a will—it had also been a murder confession, twenty years in the past. "I never shared this with anyone, and I never will."

The fight left her body, and she sagged against the closest shopping cart. Taking the envelope carefully, almost reverently, she held it against her heart.

"I found your childhood home and bought it. There is a deed in there that puts it in your name, along with the will. If you sign it and send it to my attorney, he'll complete the paperwork. I think you should have it."

"I don't want that house," she whispered. "You don't know the memories I have in it."

"Still . . ." I shook my head. "It's too risky, having someone else own it. All it takes is them deciding to put in a pool, and they might dig up his body."

She studied me, and it was the first time we'd had eye contact since the night the intruder came. "Have you seen Matt?"

I don't know what I expected. A thank-you for the generous gift. An acknowledgment of my covering up her crime. Something other than the hitch in her voice when she said his name. Was it possible that she loved him? Had ever? Still did?

"Matt moved to Foster City. I speak to him occasionally if he's in town."

The last time Matt had been in Palo Alto, we'd gotten drunk at a Mexican bar, and he'd confessed his undying love for Neena. He'd also told me the truth about her father, a truth that conflicted with the confession in her will.

They hadn't been high school sweethearts. Instead, Matt had been Neena's next-door neighbor—the chubby guy she'd never looked twice at, the social outcast who had listened to muffled sounds of her verbal and physical abuse, the guy who did nothing until the night he couldn't help himself. The night he'd rescued her. The night he heard her scream for help and beat and strangled her father to death after he found the man drunk and naked on top of her.

In that night, he became her hero, and by the time they dug a hole and buried her father in her backyard, fresh rosebushes planted over the grave, he was in love, and she was tripping over herself with gratitude. Grateful enough to go to prom with him. Grateful enough to ride to school with him. Grateful enough to publicly date the chubby boy with the goofy hair until the point where she fell in love with him. Married him. Took his ring and his name and then slowly and methodically turned into the woman who would try to steal my husband.

I swallowed the bitter taste that still lay on my tongue and reminded myself that a decade ago, Neena had done the right thing. She'd met with an attorney and penned a confession that gave intimate details of the crime, put the full weight of the killing on her, and exonerated Matt completely. She gave Matt a copy for their tenth wedding anniversary and filed backup copies with her attorney. With this exchange, Matt's copy was now back in her hands—probably the only thing she'd ended up with in the divorce.

"If you talk to Matt again, will you tell him that I love him?" She glanced down and flushed with embarrassment. "He changed his number. And when I call his business line, they won't put me through. I just want him to know that I do love him. That I'll—I'll always love him."

"Are you sure?" I gave an awkward laugh. "Neena, you never really seemed to like him, much less—" My voice fell off at the heartbreak on her face, and I think it was the most honest reaction I had ever seen from her. "Yeah," I said quietly. "I'll tell him."

"Okay. Thanks." She raised the envelope. "And, uh, thanks for this. Though you shouldn't have taken it to begin with."

I nodded and watched as she folded the envelope in two and pushed it into the back pocket of her khakis.

Leaning forward, she pushed at the handle of the cart, then paused. "It was you, right? All of it?"

I didn't respond. I had planned, upon driving here, to lie if confronted, but now, looking in her eyes, I couldn't.

She let out a low laugh, and her gaze darted away from me, back to the store. "I'd have done the same thing if I'd thought of it." She glanced back at me and stepped forward, pushing at the long line of carts. "Bye, Cat."

"Bye."

I waited until she was inside, the supercenter's doors swallowing her up, and then I walked back to the car and got inside. I shut the door and took a long moment to collect my thoughts. Inside, my emotions warred over what I had expected versus what I had seen. Finally, I let out a breath and turned to face Matt. "She asked about you."

"She did?" There was such painful hope in his voice. How did he still love her, a year later? A year full of blind dates, and one-night stands, and eating whatever he wanted, and pure freedom, and yet he wanted her back. Yearned for her. Called me in the middle of the night, drunk and heartbroken, aching for her.

"She said to tell you"—I sighed, terrified to open his emotional floodgates—"that she loves you."

He froze in the seat, his eyes pinned on a spot on my dash. I could sense his mind working, could feel the emotional war of decisions in his head. He looked at me helplessly, and maybe her dictatorial manner was what he needed in his life. "What do I do?"

I reached over and gave him a long, firm hug. "You go to her," I whispered in his ear. "And you let her win you back."

~

That night, I crawled into bed beside William and allowed him to pull me into his chest, his arms wrapping around me, his leg sliding in between mine. I rested my head on his shoulder and relaxed into his warm embrace, the huff of his breath against my neck, the beat of his heart, solid and sure, against my shoulder.

I thought of our adoption applications, pending in the system. The children whose photos we'd looked over, the interviews we'd had, the nursery three doors down that I hadn't yet placed a baby into.

I couldn't pull the trigger. Couldn't sign the paperwork. Couldn't adopt a life. My therapist says that I don't believe I'm worthy of a child, and I think she's right. I don't think either of us are. William was ready to throw us away over an ego boost. I was ready to destroy a woman's life out of protective spite. How can I raise a baby if I can't even control myself?

I expected, at this point in time, to feel happy. And I have, at times. Brief moments with William, when he told me he loved me, and I really felt it in his gaze. Brief moments when I looked out on our gardens and heard the silence in our life, the heartbeat of peace that seems to foreshadow another storm.

Brief moments. To be honest, I'm not sure I deserve anything more.

AUTHOR'S NOTE AND ACKNOWLEDGMENTS

I wrote this book for all those who have ever been cheated on. Those who have felt the rage against others and wanted to punish them in a hundred ways but felt helpless to do any of it.

Different women and men will read this book in different ways and associate with different characters. Some of you may hate it. Some of you will love it. If I made you feel something, then I've done my job. I will tell you this—I *love* every one of these characters. I've *known* every one of these characters. Built into their personalities and stories are a hundred minute moments of interactions, and I hope you enjoyed living in their world and experiencing their emotions.

This book changed a great deal in its many different drafts. I moved it from a small mountain town in North Carolina to Atherton, California. I changed Neena's job from that of a psychiatrist to a business/life coach. I added in Neena's father's storyline and tweaked her personality traits to be less anal and more relatable.

I owe a tremendous thanks to Megha Parekh with Thomas & Mercer and Maura Kye-Casella with Don Congdon & Associates for weathering countless discussions over these characters' journeys and their fates. Thank you, Charlotte Herscher, for fine-tuning the elements of the story and raising the bar it needed to jump over. In addition, thank you, Susan Barnes, Amy Vox Libris, Terezia Barna, and Tricia Crouch—all of you read and dissected early drafts and gave this book the love and attention it needed to reach one of the biggest publishing houses in the world.

An additional thank-you to the Thomas & Mercer team: Gracie Doyle, editorial director; Sarah Shaw, author relations manager; Laura Barrett, production editor; Oisin O'Malley, art director; and Erin Mooney, marketing manager.

I am indebted to many, but most of all to you, the reader. Thank you for picking up this novel and reading this story. Please consider leaving a review and recommending it to others. Your continued support is appreciated more than you will ever know.

If you would like to be in the loop on my novels, please subscribe to my email updates at nextnovel.com.

Until the next novel,

Alessandra

ABOUT THE AUTHOR

Photo © 2013 Eric Dean Photography

A. R. Torre is a pseudonym for *New York Times* bestselling author Alessandra Torre. Torre is an award-winning bestselling author of more than twenty novels. Torre has been featured in such publications as *Elle* and *Elle UK* and has guest-blogged for the *Huffington Post*. In addition to writing, Torre is the creator of Alessandra Torre Ink, a website, community, and online school for aspiring authors. Learn more at www.alessandratorre.com.